2-DIE-4

BY RANDY COCHRAN

OCT 2016

FR

This is a work of fiction. Names, characters, places and incidents are a product of the author's imagination or used fictitiously and are not to be construed as real. Any resemblance to actual events, places, organizations, or persons living or dead is entirely coincidental.

This book is dedicated to Larry Hoover, J-Prince, Gator Bradley, Crookville,

R.I.P

To all my homies who died young, you will always be in my heart, 2-Die-4.
Brad Thomas, Otis Thomas Jr., Edward Bell AKA Lil-Man, Keith Blunt, JuJu Blunt, Ralphy, Corratta Pratt, Leonard Thomas AKA Peanut, Mike Brown, Travon Martin, Mudd, Sandra Bland and to my outside brother, we love you. Toussaint-Burry- July 28, 1992, R.I.P Antwan Merrit.

Acknowledgements

First of all I would like to thank God for allowing me to be living today. I have been through so much in my short life, I have seen so many things, God is good...

Special thanks to my sister Tammy Cochran, I depend on her a lot. Also her son, Terrell Cochran, who does a lot too. Happy Birthday! 17 years old...

To my sister Tina Thomas, spoiled ass, you've been holding me down for years, thanks, love you...

Ok Net AKA Ollie Vail, you're a phone call away, thanks for always listening to me...

To my Queen!! Yes, my Mother, thank you for putting me up on game. These hoes aint loyal...

Special thanks to Eddie Lee Harp. For making my mom happy. Don't believe what the haters say, you have the best woman in the world and I got her back no matter what, 2-Die-4. Thanks to Standford Harp, and Christine Harp, when you make my Queen happy you make her son happy...

What's up to all my peoples, sorry if I missed your name last time. I love you all and thanks for buying "Heartbeat Don" Crookville, stand up!

Marc Berry, I want your son's to know they have a great father. What's up Marc Jr., Devin Berry, Elijah Isaiah. To my favorite lady, Shannon Berry. God bless you, the beauty will always be there, keep your head up.

Vessiel Mims, Sheveran Hardy, Wade tha Boss, Cathy Davis, Lenny Muhammad, Pop-eye, Ed Billie, Chuck-Morgan, Tuff-Toke, Raymond Bookman Hardy, Karud Brown, Jennifer Brown, Eric Douglas, Fred Mims, Meathead AKA Madd baber, Desiree Vega, Rose Adger, Christopher Gardner, Troy Gleep, Deborah Berry, Carina Slyles, Mooka, Missy, Maryann, Bernice Starks, Spoon, Bernice Lee, Woody, Steve Addison AKA BG, Duffy Starks, Buck, Bozack, Chad, Sam Dog, Love Mackey, Peggy Hardy, Meka Hardy, Lisa Harrison, Linda Harrison, my Godmother, love you, Tammy Harrison, Kevin Thomas, Sherri Holmes, Darnell Eight OEight, Chastity, Gina Edwards, Stephanie Thomas and Amber Cochran, you two stay close, your uncle loves you! Jennifer Asberry AKA Toy, Jerry, Lil-Rick-Boo-B, Tamara Roberts, Kelsha King, Ira Rick James Jr Williams, Levn Chandler, Pat, Cotina, June, Rodney, Pig Hardy, Desmond Applewhite, Daddy Yump, Cat-Man, Jent Foster, Bobby Foster, Tip-Lee, Jackie Thomas, my Pops, Edward Thomas, Sheldon Gaynor, Shanice Gaynor, Suh'Nyee, Ziiyah, Kussie Smith, Donte Brown Jr. AKA Dad, Candace Smith (Balley), Deseree Walford, Shaquana Cochran, Marta Villafane, Yvonne Harrison, Ernestine Hardy, Chain Gang, Mac Town 12 gang, GD-Nation, Double, RR, Pirv, What up? Blood, Rolling 30, Rolling 60, LA, Chi-G-Black Rob, Sandman.

To my man, Bobby Griffen AKA BG, keep holding it down. Last year we were wishing, this year we made our dream come true...I am a mastermind...

Heartbeatdon@yahoo.com
HeartbeatDon on Facebook

~ 3 ~

2 DIE 4

When the plane landed at Bradley International Airport David, Lisa, Linda and Justice stepped off the plane and got into an all-white limo. A white man dressed in a black suit with dark sunglasses shook David's hand and made small talk as David and his family stepped into the limo.

David picked up the phone and told the driver to take him to the big house. The big house was a mega mansion that David had built some years ago before all his troubles started.

After riding for about two hours the limo pulled up in front of a large house that looked like it belonged to a football or basketball player, it was nice.

The big house still looked the same to David. The grass could use a little work. He got out of the limo and went up to the door. After it was opened he waved for the crew to bring their bags. They were all looking around and smiling, there was no place like home.

David stepped into the kitchen and got on the phone. A lot had changed since he had been gone. He dialed his best friend's mom's number, if anyone knew where Juan was it was Mrs. Lopez. He waited for someone to pick up.

When Mrs. Lopez answered the phone David said, "Hello."

Mrs. Lopez said, "Hello David how are you doing?"

"How did you know it was me?" He asked.

Mrs. Lopez replied, "I don't forget voices."

David told Mrs. Lopez that he needed to see Juan and Mrs. Lopez told him that Juan had gotten a house out in East Hartford with his girlfriend Carmen. She gave David the number and he told Mrs. Lopez he would see her soon then he hung up.

He dialed Juan's phone number and let it ring about three times before a female answered the other line.

"Hello."

"Can I speak to Juan?" David asked.

The female on the other end asked, "May I ask who is speaking?"

David waited and then said, "It's his only brother, David a.k.a Lil-D."

The voice on the other end got excited and she said, "Hello David how are you doing? This is Carmen."

Juan jumped on the phone before David could respond back to Carmen.

"Nigga' where are you?" Juan asked.

"I'm at the big house." David replied.

Juan told David he was on his way over and hung up. David was left listening to the dial tone.

Chapter One

NEW YORK

Carlos and his men were getting together because someone had made contact with one of his people and told them David was back in Hartford Conn. Carlos was telling his men that they were heading out to Hartford to find David and his niece Lisa. He told his crew not to kill Lisa but take her and wait on orders, she had run off with the man who killed her brother and uncle. Carlos and his men got into their cars headed to Harford.

JUAN

"Bro I missed you! Shit is not the same," Juan said. He looked up and saw Linda and Lisa coming out of the house. Juan hugged both of them, then something caught his eye. A little boy came out and Juan was like, "Who is that?"

David said, "That is my son Justice, by Linda."

Juan picked Justice up and said, "Man he looks just like you!"

David started laughing. David and Juan walked off while Linda and Lisa went back into the house.

"What is the deal around town?" David asked Juan.

Juan explained that the money he had made was running low and that he was planning to sell his house. He told David that Jimmy was out of prison working at some fast food joint in downtown Hartford.

"Bro you will never have to sell nothing. I am back and I have plenty of money, but no connection. Now it's time to lay the law down." David told Juan.

They both started smiling because Juan knew that David did not play. David told Juan he was going to Linda's old house to get some heat. He told Juan that Carlos and his men would come after him soon and they would be ready for whatever.

"What's up with my first love and baby momma Tonya?" Asked David.

"Man Tonya is still the finest girl on the block, she is finer than ever. In addition, your son Justin is bad as hell. He stays on punishment," Juan said.

David just smiled and told Juan he would beep him later. They hugged each other and Juan walked to his car. David told him to get the old boys together, then Juan got in his car and pulled off. He felt good, his brother and best friend was back.

LISA

Lisa was telling Linda that she needed to call her sister in New York to see if she was okay. It had been a few years since they had heard from each other. Linda told Lisa to go ahead and call her sister, she had her back. Lisa and Linda had gotten real close over the years. They had that woman respect for each other.

Lisa picked up the phone and dialed her sister Katherine number. Katherine picked the phone up on the second ring.

"Hello Kate," Lisa said.

Katherine knew it had to be her big sister because no one else called her Kate. She told Lisa that Carlos was in a meeting with his boys and she overheard them talking about coming to Hartford.

"Hold tight I'm coming to get you," Lisa told Kate.

"There are two men here watching me, Albert and Charles."

Lisa knew them both, they were some of Carlos best guards. She told Kate she loved her and to be on the lookout, then she hung up the phone before Kate could say anything.

David went back into the house where Lisa and Linda were laying back, watching T.V. He picked up the phone and called his sister Betty. Betty answered and David said, "What up Sis?"

Betty was yelling, "Boy where have you been?"

David replied, "It's a long story. I need you to do something for me."

Betty said, "I would do whatever for you, but let me give you the run down on the family first." She told him that everyone was doing well. Gail and Jesse remodeled the house on Homestead Ave. Moreover, it looked good. All the girls were doing fine.

"That's good, now I need you to get me a rental car. An SUV. I'll be at Mom's house Sunday." David said.

"That's cool, see you then!" Replied Betty.

They each said love you and both hung up.

David got off the phone and told Lisa and Linda that Sunday they were going over to his mom's house to chill.

Lisa said, "Do not forget we are going to New York to get Kate."

"I have not forgotten. But first I want to ask you, do you know a good connection in New York?" Asked David.

Lisa replied, "Yes baby. I know two very good contacts. Everybody that is anybody knows me and my family in New York."

"Well I need your help, I am fixing to set up shop." David then told Linda that Justice would be staying at his mother's house for safety reasons.

SUNDAY

David pulled up in his mother's yard feeling good. Linda was in the front seat looking great while Lisa and Justice were in the back. It had been some years since he had driven his all-white Benz, however it was still an eye catcher. He parked in the back yard and greeted all kinds of faces as he got out. He was all smiles.

Gail, David's mother, along with his three sisters, ran over and hugged him.

Linda, Lisa and Justice also got out of the car. No one had ever seen David's other son, Justice.

When Gail saw him she said, "Oh My God!" She picked Justice up, who was a little on the chubby side. He never smiled like Justin did when he was young.

Then all the girls came and picked Justice up and were kissing all over him and his fat cheeks. Justice looked more like David's brother Brad but was quite like his brother Man.

David started telling Jesse and everyone what he had been doing over the last few years. He told Gail that he needed her to watch after Justice for a while until he got things in order.

Gail said, "I would love to keep him, it will give me something to do every day."

Betty came up and told David that his rental S.U.V was next to her car. It was an all-black Lexis with dark tinted windows.

"Good looking out," David told Betty.

Betty said, "I am going to bless you."

He told Lisa and Linda to get ready then David put his Benz in the garage and covered it up. He and the girls jumped into the Lexus SUV and took off. They were headed to Linda and David's old house until something came across his mind. It had been a long time, so David turned and headed down Albany Ave. and over next to Fox Middle School where Tonya's mom stayed.

He pulled in the back yard of Tonya's mom's house and waited to see if anyone came to the door. Mrs. Weaver's car was parked in the back yard, which meant that someone was home.

David got out of the truck and walked to the back door. He got ready to knock but the door came open and Mrs. Weaver said, "Hello David. How are you doing?"

She told David to come in and as he did he noticed Tonya was lying on the sofa sleeping. He walked over to her and kissed her hard on the mouth.

Tonya jumped and said, "Boy!" When she saw it was David her eyes lit up. She jumped up and hugged her baby daddy.

Tonya was still looking good and her body had come all the way out. Justin ran down stairs and hugged his daddy.

"Hello little man. You have gotten so big," David said and Justin started laughing. David told Tonya that he had another little boy name Justice and he was staying with Gail for now.

Tonya was looking crazy at first but David told her he was chilling in Hartford so they would have time to talk. He gave Tonya two thousand dollars and said, "You, Justin and your mom go shopping."

Tonya was all smiles when she said, "I want to see you and it had better be soon."

David said, "Cool," as he headed out the door.

He got back in the truck and he told Lisa and Linda it was time to make a move! The girls told him that they were ready.

David told them that they were going by the old house to get what they needed. When he pulled up in front of Pa-Pe's old house it didn't look the same. Now that David was back they would put a for sale sign in the yard.

He and the girls walked in the house and went to the basement. David grabbed 3 bulletproof vests and two Mac-11 semi-automatic sub machine guns, two 9mm taros and a 44 magnum. Then he pulled out an AK-47. He put all the guns in a bag except the one that he kept and the two he had for Lisa and Linda. He gave both of the girls a 9mm while he kept the 44 mag and put it in his waist band.

David looked at the girls and said, "Let's go!"

They walked out of the house, got back into the truck and headed to New York.

David asked Lisa, "Are there any phone calls you need to make?"

Lisa said, "Baby were just going to show up, so if something goes wrong it won't be on me."

"I can respect that, but I promised you that I would help you get your sister and if something does go wrong, I am willing to die with you," David said.

He jumped on the highway and headed for New York.

NEW YORK

David drove into Washington Heights where Carlos was holding Lisa's sister, Kate. It was an area populated with Hispanics and Dominicans. The project was ruff and the building Kate was in, was in the heart of Washington Heights.

David told the girls to get out with him. He told Lisa to walk alone until they got to the building, David waited very patiently.

When they got to building #66, Lisa said she was on the second floor. She didn't want David to know that Kate was being protected by two of Carlos' best men, so she said, "Let's play for two of them and be careful."

"We are going to let Linda knock on the door and we will stand to the side until it opens. Then we go in playing for two," David said.

Linda knocked on the door and someone yelled from the inside, "Who is it?" Linda could see someone looking out the peep hole, but when they saw Linda's fine body and pretty face, the door came open.

David had the gun to the man's face in a split second. He burst in and Lisa came right behind him as she headed to the back room.

David heard two shots and saw someone fall. Lisa had shot and killed one man and was still checking rooms for her sister Kate. She opened the last door and there was Kate laying on the bed crying. Lisa walked in and hugged her. Kate was just as glad to see her big sister.

David still had the gun to the guy's head when he asked, "What are you going to do with me? You got what you want."

David said, "You're right, I'm going to let you live in peace." Then he shot the man two times in the head.

Kate grabbed some clothes and they all headed out of the house. On the way down the steps two more of Carlos' men came out of nowhere with their guns pointed at Lisa. Kate saw them and started screaming. Everyone looked but David, he pulled his 44 out and blew the first man's head off. The other man was in shock while Linda grabbed her gun and shot him in the throat, he died in pain.

David and his crew had to run because people were coming from everywhere. They made it to the truck where everyone jumped in and David took off, driving fast. He couldn't go back to Hartford right away, so he got off on the first exit. A Howard Johnson hotel was on the corner and he told everyone, "Let's chill here for tonight until the heat dies down." He pulled up into Howard Johnson's and told Lisa to go rent a room with two beds.

Lisa jumped out and did what she was told.

JUAN

Juan headed to Stowe Village to meet Jimmy and Chad. When he pulled up in front of 65 Hampton St. he saw Jimmy and Chad outside smoking a blunt. He pulled the Vett up close to the sidewalk and jumped out.

"Yo what's up?" Asked Juan.

Jimmy said, "You!"

Juan told them that David was back in town and wanted to meet up with everyone. Chad's little brother Steven was there and they were hanging tight. David knew Steven very well and would love to have him on his team.

Juan had told David about the move.

CARLOS

Carlos was headed to Washington Heights to check on his niece and his money. He pulled up and jumped out of the car along with his two bodyguards, Tommy and Mandy. They had been with Carlos for over ten years and were willing to die for their boss without a second thought. Tommy was 6'6, 340 pounds and mean as a rattlesnake. Mandy was about 6'4, 220 pounds and loved to fight growing up.

When Carlos and his men walked upstairs Carlos could tell that something was not right because the door was wide open. He walked into the living room and saw Albert laid out in a lake of blood. Tommy and Mandy moved fast to the back while checking all the rooms.

Tommy yelled, "Carlos!"

Carlos went to the back and the first thing he saw was Charles laid out with a hole in his chest big enough to put a fist in. "Clean the house up," he said. Carlos knew it had to be some real killers to come in his place and kill two of his best men. Only two people came to mind, David and Lisa.

At that time David, Linda and Lisa along with Kate went into their room. It was a big room with two king size beds and a full bar. David told everyone they would pull out early in the morning to head for Hartford. He told the girls not to leave out of the room and not to answer or use the phone, because Carlos had people everywhere.

Everyone kicked back and was chilling. David and Linda were lying on the bed while Lisa and Kate were up talking.

Katherine, A.K.A Kate, was a dime piece. At 5'6 and 145 pounds, she had a body like Jackie O. Kate looked damn good at eighteen years old. She had not been touched by any man. Her Uncle Carlos made sure of that, he was very protective about her. Kate and Lisa's Mom, Joyce, died of an over dose of cocaine, that's when Miguel took them in along with their brother Luis. Luis was the weakest one out of the whole family. He was forced to kill himself by David some years ago when he killed his uncle in a big drug deal.

David looked over at Lisa while Linda was sleeping and pointed at the bathroom. Lisa headed to the bathroom. Kate was laying on the bed, faking sleep.

David walked into the bathroom and started kissing Lisa on the mouth and sucking around her neck. She was moaning and getting hotter. She dropped to her knees and put David's manhood in her mouth and went to work.

All the while her little sister Kate was watching under the covers.

David looked up and he could see that Kate was looking. He stood Lisa up and took all her clothes off. He bent her over the sink so that Kate could really see him enter Lisa's womanhood and Lisa was moaning loudly. David looked over and could see Kate's hand moving under the cover, she was playing with the moistness between her legs. David let his seeds go all over Lisa's cheeks and then they both got in the shower laughing.

GAIL

Gail was at home fixing breakfast when Tonya and Justin came in the back door. Justin had not met his little brother Justice.

"Come on in and have some breakfast," Gail told Tonya.

"Girl we just got finished eating," Tonya said.

As she was talking Justice came running out of the room. Justin looked at him and ran over to try and pick him up. That was the first time Gail had ever seen Justice smile.

Tonya told Gail that Justice and Justin looked like twins. The two brothers played together while Tonya and Gail talked.

"Gail I love David and I was so glad to see him the other day it made me cry," Tonya said.

Gail replied, "Girl let me tell you something, if its true love it will never die. One day you and David will be back together if it's God's will."

"I sure hope it's God's will," Tonya said and they both started laughing.

"Girl you are crazy, but I would love to see you and David together because you're the only girl I like that he done had!" Gail exclaimed.

Tonya hugged Gail and said, "Thank you mother-in-law."

DAVID

David told everyone to get dressed, it was time to hit the highway. Everyone got up and dressed quickly. They were ready to go within a few minutes and they all left together. Walking out of the hotel they jumped in the S.U.V. and headed for Hartford.

On the highway, David hit Conn. City limits and his beeper started buzzing. Soon as he got to Hartford he pulled over on Main St. and used the pay phone. He dialed the number and let it ring. When someone picked up David said, "Hello?"

The other person said, "What up bro? It's me Juan."

David started laughing.

Juan said, "Man we are ready to see you in the Village! The boys are at Chad's mother's house, same place they use to stay."

"Soon as I do something with the girls I will be over. Tell everyone to chill," David instructed.

Juan replied, "Cool," and they hung up.

David got back in the S.U.V. and headed to his house in Windsor. David pulled up outside his house and everyone got out. He told the girls not to let anyone in and not to use the phone for any reason.

All the girls said it was cool.

David said, "I will be back later, I have to take care of something," then he walked out, got into the truck and left.

KATE

Kate went in the bathroom and pulled out her cell phone, she wanted to make sure her uncle was safe. She was not going to tell him where she was, however she wanted to make sure that David did not kill him. She dialed Carlos' number and on the second ring Carlos picked up.

"Hello."

"Hello Uncle Carlos," Kate said, speaking softly.

Carlos was heated, he screamed through the phone, "Katherine are you okay?"

Kate said, "Yes Uncle Carlos."

Carlos said, "Tell me where you are."

"I don't know but it was a long ride and I am at a big house," Kate said.

The battery in the cell phone was starting to go dead and Carlos was yelling, "Tell me more," when the line went dead.

CARLOS

Carlos told his crew to get ready when they had the house all cleaned up. He called a friend at AT&T and asked her where the last phone call was made from that came to his number.

She put him on hold then after about two minutes she came back and said, "Windsor Conn, about ten minutes outside of Hartford Conn."

Carlos said, "Ma'am can you please pull up the address? I will make it worth your while."

The woman said, "Cool I will fax you the area where the phone call was made but I cannot give you an address."

Carlos said, "That is great."

Five minutes later a fax of the area where the phone call was made from came out of a printing machine. The pictures were in color and easy to see. Carlos sent three of his men to that area, they were going to hunt down David and whoever else got in the way. The men had something to prove to their boss.

KATE BREAKING THE RULE

Kate came out of the bathroom looking crazy.

Lisa said, "Damn girl you must have seen a ghost."

Kate didn't say anything, she just started crying. Then she said, "I called Uncle Carlos, I'm so sorry."

Lisa said, "What? You did what?"

Linda came out of the room and said, "What's going on in here?"

"Kate called Carlos," Lisa said.

"Damn, baby you shouldn't have done that. What if he finds us? We all will die," Linda said.

"I didn't tell him where I was," Kate replied.

Chapter Two

DAVID

David pulled up on Hampton St. and got out of the Lexus S.U.V. in front of where Chad's mother lived. He walked up the stairs and hit the door with the one, two knock. The boys knew it was a family member so Chad opened the door and hugged David. Then Juan and Jimmy came from behind and Juan gave David a blunt. Everyone was glad to see each other, David had shown them all so much love over the years.

Everyone knew that David being back meant more money. He sat at the table and told the boys that they were going to set up shop one more time with heroin and cocaine.

"First I got to find a good connection," David said, "but I'm going to take care of that. Lisa and I are going to New York to get a plug. Now all I want is for everyone to lay low and trust in me. Then watch the money pour back in."

All the boys were smiling because they knew David was the man.

CARLOS

Carlos was riding in Windsor, trying to find the house that the phone call was made from. But without the address, it was useless and this made Carlos mad. He ordered the other three men to stay in Windsor and watch who was coming and going.

DAVID

David pulled up at his house and heard all kinds of noise when he got to the door. He opened the door and walked in to see Lisa all up in Kate's face. She was screaming about something and Linda was standing between them.

David said, "Yo yo! What is going on?"

"Kate called Carlos and we do not know what he is going to do," Lisa said.

"We can't change what's been done," David said. He walked over to Kate and said, "2-DIE-4!" Kate was looking crazy and David said, "I put my life on the line for you. I was willing 2-DIE-4 you! Do not ever disobey my orders again, or I will personally kill you! Do you understand me?"

Kate looked in David's eyes and saw his cold soul. She said, "Yes."

"Lisa you and Linda need to go to New York and get a heroin and cocaine connection. I want you all to take the bus and a Nike bag with ten thousand a piece in them. Be careful and take those burners. If anything goes wrong lay low and call me," David said. He told the girls to get ready and after they were ready again they all got into the S.U.V. They headed to the bus station where David dropped Lisa and Linda off then he and Kate headed to his mom's house.

GAIL'S HOUSE

David and Kate were riding to Gail's house listening to some music. David looked over at Kate and said, "I didn't mean to be so hard on you. But the streets are cold and when you are in the streets you got to turn cold. If not the streets will eat you up."

Kate said, "My brother use to tell me about you. Luis was schooling me and I am not green." She knew Pa-Pe before he died and all about what went on back in the day. David started smiling and Kate said, "David can I ask you something?"

David said, "Ya cool, long as you can accept my answer."

"Did you kill my uncle?" Kate asked.

He looked Kate in her pretty eyes and lied to her. He said, "No." David learned years ago to never confess to nothing and never let a woman con you into letting your guard down.

David pulled into his mother's back yard. He and Kate got out and saw Gail out back hanging out clothes.

Gail said, "What's up Boy?"

He said nothing and Gail said, "Who's that?"

"This is Lisa's baby sister from New York. Her name is Katherine but everyone calls her Kate," He said.

Gail said hello to Kate and told David that she was cute.

David asked Gail, "Where is Justice?"

She replied, "Upstairs being bad." She told David that Justin had come over and played with Justice all day Friday.

David told Gail that he was taking his Benz so he could leave it at his house, then he and Kate went upstairs.

Gail came up and said, "David, Betty called about that truck."

Kate was in the living room playing with Justice. He was smiling and kissing Kate on the mouth. David told Kate that they were getting ready to go over to his baby sister Yolanda's house in Bloomfield.

Yolanda had just had a house built on Durbe St. last year and it was nice.

NEW YORK
LISA AND LINDA

Lisa and Linda got off the greyhound bus at 42-Second Port-Authority and waited on a cab. When they finally waived one down and got in, the driver was an old black man that talked real low.

Lisa said, "Sir, can you please take us to Spanish Harlem?"

The driver said, "No problem." He turned the meter on and took off slowly.

When they arrived at Spanish Harlem on 115th street, Lisa saw some Hispanics she knew. She told the cab driver to stop. She handed him fifty dollars and they got out. She told him to keep the change and the cab driver took off.

Lisa knew a few of the people on the block and all eyes were on her and Linda. Just two pretty girls that could be on King Magazine. Lisa said something to one of the men in Spanish, asking the young one where the heroin and cocaine was. The young Spanish kid told Lisa to walk down the alley.

She didn't trust anyone on the streets, so she told Linda to be ready. Linda put her hand in her pocket book on her 9mm, ready for whatever. They walked down the alley together. Suddenly they saw a shadow and stopped.

"It's an older man," Linda said.

"Let's keep walking," Lisa replied and they both walked until they got closer.

Linda saw the man and they both stopped. Lisa said something to the man and he told her that he was a runner. She told him what she and Linda wanted and the man was surprised that two women could want so much heroin and cocaine. He told them his name was Sam and he told them to follow him.

They all walked out of the ally and went up some stairs to the third floor. Sam knocked one time and a Spanish man came to the door. Sam told Lisa and Linda to go in where Lisa shook hands with the man that was there, while Linda stood at the front looking for ways to get out in case of trouble.

The man told them his name was Danny. Lisa told him how much money she had and they walked to the back. They stayed about 15 minutes then Lisa came out with a Nike bag full of drugs. She gave Danny her number and told him if he wanted more money to call her and she would tell him where to meet her.

Lisa and Linda left the building and headed for the New York City bus station. They were loaded down with drugs. They would stay over in a hotel and pull out early in the morning, after they rented a car.

DAVID
"DON'T CROSS THAT LINE"

David and Kate pulled up in Yolanda's yard in his Benz. David hit the horn and his little sister came to the door, Yolanda was smiling.

David said, "Girl who's here?"

Yolanda said, "Boy ain't anybody here but me! I have to go to work at Hampton."

"Well I'm going to chill here," David said.

He left Kate and Yolanda talking down stairs and went into the room and turned on the T.V. then put his 44 magnum under the stand. David had new clothes at all of his sisters' houses. He grabbed some clean clothes and went to the shower. He was really enjoying himself.

David stepped out the shower and went back to the room. When he walked in Kate was sitting at the end of the bed.

"Yolanda gave me some new clothes, so I'm going to take a shower," Kate said.

Kate and Yolanda were the same size. Kate went to the bathroom and got into the shower. While she was in the shower David had to make a few phone calls. He was half asleep when Kate got into the bed next to him with nothing on but her panties and bra. David could feel her soft, warm skin touching his body. He rolled over and so did Kate, they were facing each other.

Kate start smiling and David leaned in and gave her a sloppy French kiss then they started really kissing. David undid Kate's bra and eased his hand in her panties at the same time, then he eased them off of her. Now they both were in bed naked. David rolled over and laid on top of Kate kissing her from head to toe. She did not have a scared bone in her body and

David loved it, he started nibbling and licking on the inside of Kate thighs. He slid his fingers inside of her moistness.

Kate felt her body become so hot and her soft moaning bounced off the walls. She was going crazy, crying for David to enter her womanhood. David never moved when someone commanded him, Kate had him going. That body, those eyes, that hair. David decided that it was time to enter her body. He realized this was her first time and David loved it. It reminded him of Tonya, his first baby's mother.

Gently David penetrated Kate as she grabbed his body for dear life, she was now becoming a woman. Once the pain was over there was nothing but pleasure. Stars were bursting inside of her. A volcano was erupting, a war had started!

Kate wanted David to take it out, she screamed as David's body move to another place. The more Kate cried out the harder David stroked, he slowly established a rhythm. David was feeling Kate's walls as he kept a steady motion. He had to put in on Kate, that way she would always come back.

Kate had dreamed about this and she said to herself, "So this is sex. This is what I have been missing." She was definitely open from that day on. David and Kate were lovers and friends. They made hot passionate love on a regular bases. She was in love with David but his heart was sealed. He was an actor, love did not live there anymore and everything that had to do with love was a game.

LISA AND LINDA

Lisa and Linda were on their way to Hartford in a brand new Benz 500 rental. Linda was driving and she was very cool under the wheel, in fact her uncle had taught her how to drive safe. She was used to being with her uncle when he was trafficking over eleven hundred kilos a week. They made four to five runs to New York in five days. So she was a very safe driver.

Lisa was on the passenger side talking on the cell phone. She hung up and Linda did not ask her who she was talking too. Lisa said that it was an old friend of hers who was running shit over in Jamaica, Queens.

Linda asked, "What up with him?"

"He wants me to come back to New York and take over a hundred thousand dollar a week drug house." Lisa said.

"What about David?" Linda asked.

Lisa said, "I love David but him and Carlos are at war and it's not going to be easy for either one of them."

"I'm scared but I will not let David go down alone," Linda said.

She was in the driveway at that point and no one said a word as the two friends minds wondered. They got out of the car and went into the house.

YOU HAVE CHANGED DAVID

David and Kate were just pulling up to his house when David spotted the rental car. David asked Kate if she knew whose car it was and Kate said no. David pulled his 44 out and parked the car a block away, he told Kate to follow behind him.

They eased their way around to the back of his house and looked through the window. The two girls were sitting at the table eating. Lisa looked up and saw David so she went and opened the back door. David and Kate walked in and David still had the gun in his hand. Linda looked at Kate very hard and rolled her eyes.

Lisa pulled out the drugs and showed them to David who started smiling and said, "You have a connection?"

"I told you David, I got a lot of respect in New York," Lisa replied.

"That is why you are on my team, because we think somewhat alike. Nevertheless, you still cannot out think me so don't even try," David warned her.

Lisa said, "Dam baby where'd that come from?"

"Just popping that's what's in the air," He said.

Lisa said, "The person's name is Danny, we can get whatever and he will meet us halfway."

"Cool, but I want you all to chill here until I go handle something," He told them.

David walked out of the house on the phone as he called and told Juan he needed to see him. Juan told David he was at his mom's house so David jumped in the Benz headed for Juan's mom's house.

THE VILLAGE

When David pulled up in the Vill, he went over to Juan's mom's house. He got out of the car, went inside and went upstairs. He knocked and Mrs. Lopez came to the door.

"David, how are you?" She asked as she hugged him.

Out of nowhere, Juan's sister, Sonya came out and kissed David on the mouth. He had the Nike bag on his shoulder and he walked into the dining room as Juan came out.

"What's popping nigga'?" David asked, then he gave Juan the Nike bag and said, "Put this in the back, I'm on my way. Let me holler at your sister first though."

Sonya was mad. She was standing in front of David with her arms folded across her chest. David walked up on her and said, "What is it?"

"David how long are you going to be around?" She asked.

David replied, "Until the END OF TIME!"

Sonya started smiling and David pinned her on the wall. Mrs. Lopez knew Sonya was in love with David because Sonya use to come crying to her about their problems. However, Mrs. Lopez did not expect for Sonya to jump right back in David's arms after two long years.

David walked back into Juan's room and they started bagging up the cocaine and heroin.

At twelve in the morning David told Juan to fire up another blunt, he was getting ready to leave.

DAVID'S HOUSE

Airport Road was a very nice place in Windsor Connecticut. You could walk out of your house and leave the door wide open, it had a very low crime rate. Almost no crime at all happened in that area, unless someone was pulled over for throwing paper out their window.

It was about 12:30 in the morning and Linda, Lisa and Kate were up playing cards. A car had driven by at least four times.

"Lisa that car has been bye at least four times, I wonder what's up with that," Linda said.

"It has two men in the back and two in the front," Replied Lisa.

Linda said, "I believe they are up to something. Girl let's turn out the lights and act as if no one is in here."

"No!" Linda exclaimed. "They know someone is in here. Kate can you shoot a gun?"

Kate said, "Yeah I can shoot whatever."

"You and Lisa stay right here," Linda ordered.

Linda went down some steps and into the basement. She stayed down there about ten minutes and when she came back up she gave Lisa a 9mm and Kate a 38 special snub-nose. She had the AK-47 with a full clip.

"There are four of them and three of us. Therefore, we have to get a jump on them, come on!" Linda said.

They went out the back door with guns in hand and headed into the dark woods. The girls were waiting on the black car to come back around the block.

The driver of the black Ford Taurus was Frank, he had been around Carlos' family a long time and had seen a generation of bosses. Frank got on the phone and dialed his boss Carlos' number.

"Hello!" Carlos said in a very powerful voice. "What is going on Frank?" Carlos yelled into the phone. "Tell me some news."

"There's some girls in a big house, that might be them," Frank said.

Carlos told him, "Go in and see if it's them, then bring them to me." Then he hung up the phone.

Frank hated that but that was his boss and he always obeyed orders.

Linda saw the black Ford Taurus was fixing to stop in front of David house. Neither the driver nor anyone in the car saw the girls hiding.

The two men in the back opened the car door and got out looking around with the door still open.

Linda told the girls, "One step and we let loose."

The first man walked forward one-step and Linda let the AK-47 do all the talking! POW, POW Pa POW! The first two men did not have a chance in hell. The driver, Frank, got out and let some shots go and dragged the body of his friend back towards the car, he was not going to leave their remains. However, deep down he knew they were dead. If not he would put two shots in their head, no need in them suffering.

Lisa came up and let some shots go and then Kate, it was like the wild, wild, west. There were bullet holes all over the car when the driver hit the gas and spun away. He had no idea that it would be three women who would cause him to limp for the rest of his life.

Lisa, Kate and Linda ran in the back door of the house and called David.

David picked up replying, "What up?"

Linda told David about the men in the black Ford Taurus and the shootout. David asked if everyone was safe and Linda told him they were.

"Take a cab and get a room at the Courtyard hotel. Then call and tell me what room," David instructed.

"Ok, cool. One more thing, I'm ready to see my son," Linda said.

David said, "I promise I will take you by there tomorrow. Don't ever think he's not safe."

"Baby I know you love him just as I do. Nevertheless, he is all I got, you have your sister. In addition, you also have your mother. I have no one but you and Justice," Said Linda.

"You have the world, you just have to keep listening to me. Now go do what I said," He replied.

Linda said, "We all love you." Then they both hung up.

DAVID

David headed to his Benz. Leaving out of Juan's house, he was driving down Cleveland Ave when he got to the red light on Main St. A black jeep was speeding on the right side of him so David laid low. The jeep stopped and bullets riddled the Benz. David just laid there in the Benz motionless, he was scared but didn't panic. When the shots stopped he slowly eased out his 44 bulldog. The jeep stayed still to see if there was any life left and David came up letting the 44 loose. The men in the jeep were not expecting that and smashed on the gas, almost running head on into a truck. David was still putting holes in the side of the jeep, he was blessed to survive a hit like that. The Benz had holes all over it.

David's phone went off and he picked it up. Linda said they were in room 126 on the end. It didn't take David long before he pulled up in front of the Courtyard Hotel and got out. He looked at the bullet holes as all the girls came out the room.

"Some nigga's just tried to kill me. Linda call and get us a rental S.U.V., and have Main Street auto come get my Benz," David said as he walked into the room with Lisa and Kate.

Lisa could tell something had gone on between Kate and David because now Kate did not want to leave. David sat on the bed and called Kate over, she came running and sat on David's lap like a little kid. She was a doll and David was going to spoil her to death with all the better things in life, 2-DIE-4! She was now part of a team that did not stop for anything to get what they wanted. The father, the sons, the money and the power. David was planning to one day run the whole city with an "Iron Fist." He had struck fear in half the state and had much respect in the next state.

Lisa was looking at David very hard as David asked Kate if she wanted something to eat. Lisa walked over and stood next to David. He got up and said he needed to make a phone call, then went to call Juan to see how things were going.

Juan picked up and David asked, "What's going on over there in the Vill?"

Juan replied, "We have an apartment on 61 Hampton Street and the shit is doing its thing."

"I will be over to get that paper," David told him.

Juan said, "Cool," and they hung up.

A knock came at the door and David jumped up pulling out his gun. He looked out the window and saw that it was Linda and Justice.

David asked, "Where did you get him from?"

"I saw Gail at the store and Justice wanted to come with me," she said.

Linda had pulled up in an all-black rental Range Rover with tinted windows. She and Justice went into the room along with Lisa and Kate.

They were all playing with Justice when David said, "I need you all to sit still, I need to make a run."

They wanted to stay and play with Justice anyway so David went out, got into the Range Rover and headed to Stowe Village. While David was riding down Barber St, he saw an old friend named Roy Brown, they had went to school together. R. B. was what they called him in the hood. He was staying in Nelson Court, a project that use to beef with Stowe Village back in the days.

David pulled the Rover to the side of the road, let down the window and said, "What up R.B.?"

R.B. was shocked, he had not seen David in years, but word around town was that David was once 'The Heartbeat Don.'

David could see R.B. was not living to his fullest. He was wearing some old Adidas and a sweat suit that looked like it belonged to his baby brother. R.B. had just gotten out of prison and David sympathized with all the brothers coming home from prison with thirty-five dollars and no plans. Society made them have to hunt like animals to eat, but everyone wanted to live so you had to do you.

After day dreaming about the past David said to R.B., "It has been a long time but we are going to let the past die. Nevertheless, you broke a code years ago, a code that caused a person to breath for the last time. A code that would take you far away from your family. There would not be weekend visits or letters of forgiveness." David was hot he was letting out his hurts and giving R.B. some game 4-life. 2-DIE-4 was for real. He said, "Nigga' look in my eyes."

R.B. knew David had killed people back in the days. He looked David in the eyes and really saw a part of a person he had never seen. A mad man, a hurt human being that was so in love with the streets he was willing to kill an old friend because of the code. He would never understand the code of the street, 2-DIE-4.

David told R.B. from his soul and in a very low pitch voice, "Nigga' you are the first and last person I am going to ever forgive." He wanted to see where R.B.'s mind set was before he showed any love, he wanted understanding.

R.B. said, "Man I am hurting right now, my uncle gave me a half ounce of powder and I am trying to get my customers back."

David could tell R.B. was keeping it real. He knew what it was like to be hurt, he had been there and done that. Fucked up in the streets is one of the worst feelings in the world next to dying. After David listened to R.B. he decided to put him on one more time.

"You want to get some more real money?" David asked.

R.B. said, "Hell yeah nigga' what you think?"

"It's 2-DIE-4. No more games. I need my money when I give you my shit on your word. In addition, you lost your word with me years ago. I respect you because you got balls and that's all you got left so you better use them wisely. I will bring you what you need tomorrow in Nelson Court. R.B. don't let me down," David warned. He scribbled down his cell phone number and gave it to R.B.

"David I will not let you down, I promise you," R.B. said.

David pulled off and went into the Vill. When he got out on Hampton Street he saw Jimmy standing outside. Jimmy didn't know it was David.

David jumped out and said, "What up nigga?"

Jimmy said, "Yo! What up?" They hugged and walked up the stairs together to the apartment to see Juan and Chad. When they went in Juan was counting money all over the table with Chad.

Juan said, "The count is clear."

David said, "Cool." He then told his boys about someone trying to kill him last night. Then he called Lisa and told her to call the connection because they needed some more work.

"Okay baby, anything else you want?" Lisa asked.

David said, "Yeah! I want you to stay sweet."

David was back running 90% of Hartford on the drug tip. R.B. came back to David's mind. He had told David a friend wanted to buy a kilo and David gave R.B. one. He had not seen him since. It hurt David because he and R.B. went back to kids playing together. Now a code that was broke in the game would cost R.B. their friendship. David's heart had went cold. He said in his mind, 'I am going to kill that nigger no matter how long it takes, 2-DIE-4. Never tell on no one. Never cross your family. Never get caught with your hand in the cookie jar.' R.B broke the code.

KATE

Kate was enjoying herself, she had moved into her own condominium overlooking downtown Hartford. She and David had become very close, he had spoiled her from day one. There was nothing Kate wanted for, or waited for. If she wanted it, David got it right then. He took Kate to the B.M.W. dealership and got her a brand new, pearl white, 740 BMW. It was the talk of the town.

Kate was laying back in the Jacuzzi sipping on Dom when the phone rang. It was her big sister Lisa.

"What you doing girl?" Lisa asked. Kate said nothing and Lisa asked, "Have you seen David?"

Kate lied and said, "No I haven't seen him all week."

"Okay, I'll call you back later," Said Lisa.

Kate replied, "Okay girl, be good."

DAVID

It was a Friday afternoon and David was riding along Albany Ave headed to his baby momma Tonya's house. He was moving slow when he spotted a brand new, champagne color Benz with gold rims. It was fly and David was thinking, 'I got to see the nigga' who is pushing that there.'

When the driver's door opened David almost lost his mind. Roy Brown stepped out looking like he owned the world in a silk polo suit on point and matching gator shoes.

David said, "R.B. damn, damn!" He knew he could not step to R.B. sideways because he would kill some shit. Therefore, David said to himself, 'I have to be careful and not slip.'

David saw R.B. go inside the Jamaican Bakery and he got out of the Rover and went around to the back of the store where no one could see. He pulled out his 44 magnum and put his hand on the trigger. R.B. had his back to David as he walked back toward the front. The lady working the cash register looked up, saw what David had in his hand and started screaming. R.B. turned around and saw the 44 aimed at his face. David and R.B. looked each other in the eyes. R.B. knew he had to make a move, he refused to die like so many other young black males, without a fight.

"David, what up bro man I been," R.B. said and he made his move, but David was waiting and he let off. A shot hit R.B. in the left shoulder, but R.B. got his gun and let off a shot. Now it was a shootout, David fired some more shots at R.B. while the lady in the store was calling 911. R.B. was trying to get close to David but bullets was flying everywhere. David had made it outside the door and R.B. was right behind him.

David had to do something fast he had one more shot, the police were coming and R.B. was trying to get him. He spotted R.B. ducking behind a car and took a good aim at his head. When he came back up David pulled the trigger and saw R.B.'s head blow up like a tomato.

The police were everywhere now. David was surrounded so he dropped his gun and lay on the ground and said, "2-DIE-4."

The news of Roy Brown aka R.B.'s death had spread throughout Hartford. In every hood they were talking about the death of the legend R.B. and the arrest of David Thomas aka Lil-D.

David went to the county jail on Morgan St. He called Lisa and said, "Yo I cannot really talk so don't ask me nothing crazy just listen. I need you to get Linda, go to the Vill and see someone for me. Do you know who I am talking about? Do not say no name, tell him to give you everything he got for me, EVERYTHING!"

"Of course," Lisa said. She knew who David was talking about, his best friend Juan. Lisa made it her business to know David's business. She said, "Okay baby I will take care of that, anything else?"

David said, "Take half of that money to my mother's house and the other half get me the best lawyer a real nigga' can have."

Lisa replied, "Okay baby," and they hung up.

David lay back in the cell with not a worry on his mind

LISA AND LINDA

Lisa and Linda had collected over one million dollars of David's money in cash. Not bad for a guy who was running 90%

of Hartford. They were riding around snorting cocaine mixed with heroin, the streets called it a speedball. David was the last thing on the girls' minds. Lisa had been talking to Linda about pulling away from David.

"Girl David is up a shit creek, we might as well get this money and flip it," said Lisa.

"Girl you must be crazy! David would kill us," Linda replied.

Lisa said, "Only if we let him, I plan to fight back. So, are you in or out?"

Linda knew the price for crossing David was death but she loved Lisa and had a lot of respect for her handling the streets the way she did. Lisa was a gangster diva ready for whatever.

"I am in with you baby girl," she said.

They both laughed and hit a blunt with all the money in the back seat.

Kate didn't talk to Lisa or Linda, she was laying low and staying real to David, being there for whatever he needed or wanted done. She and David's baby sister Yolanda were very close and that was where Kate was staying, but she wasn't letting anyone know where she was. All anyone could do was wonder where she was and if it was David's order for Kate to stay low and not to be seen.

COUNTY JAIL

The fat, white officer called David's name and told him he had a visit. David took a shower and went to see his visit. When he got to the visiting room he was surprised to see his baby's mother Tonya and Justin sitting there waiting on him. Tonya jumped up and hugged David then kissed him on the mouth. David grabbed Justin and had a seat.

Tonya looked at David and said, "David, word on the street is that you killed R.B."

David replied, "I know, it's all good I will be out soon."

"I have a thousand dollar money order that I will leave on your books," she told him.

He said, "I don't need no more money."

"So." Tonya said.

While Tonya and David were talking he looked up and saw Kate and his baby sister Yolanda walking into the visiting room. They came over to the table where David got up and hugged them both.

Tonya was looking crazy while Yolanda and David talked on for about thirty minutes. Tonya told David she had to get back to work but to call her anytime. David said cool then he asked Kate what was up.

"Nothing, just missing you," Kate said.

David liked Kate because she was young and she never asked questions.

"That's fucked up how Lisa and Linda ran off with all that money. You trusted them with it," she said.

"Don't worry, they will have to pay for their own mistakes, 2-DIE-4," he replied.

David couldn't believe, out of all people that Linda was down with that shit. The money was a small thing to David, he had plenty of paper. It was the code, 2-DIE-4 that got him in the county jail on a murder charge. Now Linda and Lisa were on the other side, David was more heartbroken than anything.

Chapter Three

THE FUTURE

It was a hot summer day in Stowe Village. Lisa had gone back to New York and Linda had followed her but Linda was going back and forth. Carlos and Lisa were back in the good, she paid him all the money she had gotten from him. She had her own crew in New York and the word was they did not play.

Chad's little brother Steven was buying drugs from Lisa and Linda. He had the Vill on lock down while Steven had his own crew and they were doing damn good.

KATE

Kate had a job with Yolanda and was still staying in her condo. She and Tonya came to visit David every week. He was taking good care of both of the girls. David had a good lawyer paid for and made sure all Kate and Tonya's bills were also taken care of.

DAVID

This had to be the second happiest day of David's life. The first was when he was young and he got back with his mom, brothers and sisters. He was waiting on his appeal bond as he paced the holding cell back and forth, trying to waste time. He was dressed in an all-black Brooks Brothers suit with matching gators. He was thinking that it wouldn't be long now, he was nervous as hell and sweating hard through his suit.

David's lawyer Rob Smith, was a crooked Jewish man. He told David after he got convicted to hang tight, he would beat it on appeal and Rob did just that. He beat David's case on an appeal. It took a little longer than David expected, but Mr.

Smith did what he said he would do. He found a technicality in the case allowing David to slip through a crack in the system.

Now David was minutes from going home on an appeal bond. Rob Smith was on his job because David had given him a six figure salary under the table. They argued the case in a Connecticut Supreme court, successfully introducing new evidence. David knew he had to live with what happened to R.B., but that was all part of being a hood nigga'. Nightmares stay with you, it becomes part of your life so you always have to deal with it. David had no choice but to live with what happened because it might not be the last time he had to hurt someone he loved. It was killing David on the inside and if he could turn back the hands of time he would.

GAIL

David's mother Gail, his step daddy Jesse and Tonya were waiting outside the courthouse for David to get out. They were in an all-white, stretch limo with gold wheels.

David felt good to know his mother and step daddy were there along with Tonya, 2-DIE-4. David had a lot of plans and he was ready to move.

Lisa and Linda had no idea that David was being released from jail after the years he spent behind bars. He had so much to find out. He wanted to know where Lisa and Linda were at, then he wanted to find out where those nigga's were that owed him all that money. David had heard that Lisa and Linda were getting big money in Hartford.

The sound of keys brought David out of his day dream. The officer called his name and he said, "Yes sir."

"Okay Stowe Village bad boy, you have made bail. Someone posted a five hundred thousand dollar bail for you," the officer said.

David smiled and headed out the door. The sun was shining and he saw his son Justin first thing. Justin came running to his dad at 16 years old. Word was that he was hanging in the streets.

Tonya came behind him and hugged David, then his mother Gail got her hug and Jesse shook David's hand. They all got into the limo and headed to Gail's house where the rest of the family was waiting.

When the limo pulled into Gail's back yard David saw his sisters screaming and yelling. The door opened and David was covered with hugs and kisses. He got out and saw Kate. She had been faithful to David, being there for him every step of the way.

Meat was on the grill and music was playing. David started eating good and smoking the best weed in town. He was holding Kate's hand and telling her it was time for him to go hunt down Lisa and Linda.

Justice was staying in Dutch Point. He was running with a little crew call the D-Boys. They did not get along with the Ave boys or the Vill boys. Justin, taking after his daddy, was running with the Vill crew now for three years. Justin and Justice never spoke to each other and that hurt David.

JUSTICE

Justice was standing on the corner along with some friends when a Blazer stopped and asked the young boys who had the weed? Fat, Cornbread and Lil-Willie all looked at Justice.

Fat, whose real name was Tony Wood, was called Fat because he was just that at 14 years old. He was very street smart though, his mother was a hustler who turned dope head. Fat was on the streets trying to eat.

Cornbread came from a pretty nice family, but he was a bad kid. He got the name Cornbread from the kids in school, he loved cornbread. He was not that street smart, but he always carried a gun. Cornbread's name was Lester White.

Lil-Willie's real name was Willie Jones. He had a weed connection and he was slick for his age, but he was scary.

Justice Thomas came from a killer daddy, David Thomas and a Killer mom, Linda. He was very street smart and had a big heart but he never liked to smile.

The driver of the blazer asked, "Are any of you little punks going to sell me some weed?"

He got out and all the boys started running. The man went chasing them and Fat fell on the ground. The driver caught him and started kicking him in the face and everywhere. Justice was mad, he told Cornbread to give him the gun because the man was hurting Fat. Cornbread reached inside his pants and gave Justice the 9mm hand gun. Justice ran back over to where Fat was laying and said, "Hey get off my friend!"

The man said, "Where is my weed?" He jumped up and reached for Justice and that was the last thing the man remembered as Justice shot the man in the head. He died before he hit the ground.

Fat got up and he and Justice ran to an empty apartment. That would be Justice's first kill but not his last.

DAVID

David had gone with Tonya over to her house. She had gotten a nice three bedroom house with a big back yard on Blue Hills Ave. Justin was laying back watching T.V. while David and Tonya had been laid up in bed all day. David was telling Tonya that he wanted his boys to be close.

It was around 1:00am and David got out of bed, went to Justin's room and woke him up. Justin jumped and was looking at his daddy crazy.

David said, "Let's make a run, get up and get yourself together."

Justin was ready, he loved his daddy like no other.

David and Justin jumped in the rental Cadillac and headed to the Vill. Chad's little brother Steven owed David about ninety thousand dollars and now it was time to collect. The word on the street was that Steven had the money and Lisa and Linda were bringing him all the dope. He was selling out of an apartment in the back of 69 Hampton Street.

David and Justin were riding slow, they pulled up at Fred-D-Morris school yard and parked the car. David told Justin they would walk to the Vill. David had a Mac-11 semi-automatic and a sharp hunting knife. Justin had a 357 magnum and a tek-9, they headed to the Vill on foot.

When they got to the building David was the first one to walk in, then they went up to the second floor. David knocked on the door and it came open with Steven at the door. When he saw David he tried to close the door but Justin already had the gun to his head. David forced his way in and said, "Long time no see." Steven went to speak but David said, "Sit down you disloyal punk!"

Justin had the gun pointed at Steven's head waiting on the order to get his first kill.

David said, "I'm going to check the house."

When he walked through David saw a lot of money on the bed. He took the sheets and cut them into a few strips then went back in the living room where he tied Steven up real good. David left it where Steven could talk, David had a few questions for him.

"Okay Steven, where is the rest of the money?" Asked David.

Steven was acting hard but deep down he was shaking. He said, "There's some more under the bed."

Justin went and got the money, it was a nice amount.

"Where are Lisa and Linda? Give me the number." David demanded.

He replied, "Lisa and Linda stay in New York, Spanish Harlem."

"Call Linda and tell her to meet you at Howard Johnson's with two kilo of cocaine and a half-pound of heroin. Make this your biggest load," Said David.

"Lisa and Linda have drivers now, they hardly ever come out," said Steven.

David handed Steven the phone. He called Linda in New York and told her what he wanted, they had been dealing with each other for a long time and there was trust. Linda said it would be Friday at around 11:00 pm at the Howard Johnson Hotel. Steven said cool and hung up.

David told Steven, "Man, I had a lot of respect for your young ass, but you crossed me and now you got to pay, 2-DIE-4."

David grabbed Steven by the neck while Justin pulled his tongue out and cut if off. Justin put two shots in Steven's head and he died holding his own tongue.

David and Justin walked out of the house with over two hundred thousand dollars in cash. They walked back to the school yard, found the car, jumped in and headed back to Tonya's house on Blue Hill.

When they got to the house David and Justin went and took a shower, Justin down stairs and David upstairs. This was the start of a long pay back. The first time father and son committed a crime together, but not the last.

LISA AND LINDA

Lisa and Linda were on the phone when Linda told Lisa about the package Steven wanted. She told Lisa that Steven was rolling in the Vill.

"It's about time we pull something over his young eyes," said Lisa and they both started laughing. They were going to beat Steven out of all his money. "I will have Travis and Vick drive the drugs to Howard Johnson Hotel to do the deal and come back," She said.

Linda told Lisa, "I'm ready to see my son, Justice."

"Don't worry we will see him soon, but first we got to get more men and guns," Lisa told her.

DAVID

David and Justin were riding to Dutch Point because David had to go see about his baby boy and it was time Justice and Justin made up. As David was driving he saw some young boys at the corner store and pulled over real fast. Everyone was ready to run but Justice, then he saw his daddy and big brother and a smile came across his face. David got out of the car and hugged his son then Justin did the same.

David said to Justice, "Get in we all need to talk."

Justice told his friends he would see them later and got in the car. David pulled off and headed to Kate's house in Bloomfield Ct. When he pulled up at Kate's house all the lights came on, David and his two sons got out. He used his key to open the door and the three went inside. Kate was upstairs asleep so David rolled a blunt and told the boys to chill.

Justin and Justice looked just alike, you could mistake them for twins. Justin was a little bigger because of the two years in age difference. But they wore the same size in everything, clothes and shoes.

David sat down with his sons and said, "2-DIE-4 is a street code. It has a lot of meaning. One, you must stay real with family, never tell anyone anything even if it means going to prison for the rest of your life. Always have your Mom, Dad, sister's and brother's back no matter what. 140 means loyal forever, stay true to your friend even if he has full blown aids, be there and make him or her feel special.

"Now I don t want you two to think I am deaf, blind, or crazy. I was born one day, just not yesterday. I am gangster and been in the streets for years. Justin when you were a little boy and Justice was not born I had two brothers, Brad and Man, they died in the streets together. They died together because we were all close. I do not care about who lives where. Justin you and Justice will always stand by each other no matter what. Don't ever let a hood come between brotherly love. 2-DIE-4-140, do you two understand me?" Asked David.

They both shook their heads yes, meaning they understood where their daddy was coming from. The boys knew their daddy was not anything to play with, right along with their grandma Gail, who could put fear in everyone's heart. David was next, when he spoke you better listen.

"Don't ever go three years without speaking to each other again. Justice when was the last time you heard from your mom?" David asked.

"She called Pam, the lady who I'm staying with last week. But I have not talked to her in about a month," Justice replied.

"Don't worry, I want you and your brother to chill for a bit," David said.

He then went upstairs and got in the bed with Kate. She rolled over and hugged David because she had not seen him in about two weeks.

Justin and Justice stayed up smoking weed all night and talking on the phone with freaks. They also talked to each other about a lot that had taken place.

Justice said, "One day we will be rich."

Justin replied, "We are already rich, we just don't have control yet."

They both started smiling because they heard their daddy and Kate upstairs in the room.

LISA AND LINDA

The driver was headed out of the house when Lisa said, "I want you to be careful and if anything looks wrong come on back to New York, but kill whatever gets in your way. Don't risk all the drugs for nothing and keep a gun in hand." She stopped and looked at Travis, "I love you," she said.

Vick, the other driver, was smiling because he wanted to hurry back and sex Linda.

DAVID

David decided to call Juan for the first time in a long time.

"Hello," David said. "You ready?"

Juan replied, "I stay ready."

Juan had lost the big house, but he was still getting money it was just on a smaller scale now.

David told Juan that he and his two sons and would meet him in the Sportsman's parking lot. The Sportsman Club was on Main Street right across from the school bus company. Right in front of the hardware store in Hartford. David told Juan to bring some heat.

TONYA

Tonya was talking to her mother, Mrs. Weaver. She said, "Mom David and I are doing well. He's been staying at the house ever since he got out of prison."

Mrs. Weaver replied, "Tonya I told you love is something you have to wait out, true love will always hang around. David was your first love."

Tonya jumped in and said, "My first love and last love. The only other man that can get my heart like David is my son."

"It's going to work out. What god plans can't be unplanned. You and David are soul mates and one day you will get married," Mrs. Weaver said.

Tonya was smiling because that's all she wanted, to spend the rest of her life with David.

DAVID

David and his two sons were headed to the Sportsman Club parking lot to meet Juan. He told them, "Once this shit goes down tonight I want you two to tell me what kind of cars or trucks you want. I'm going to buy a condo in Avon, Conn. No one will know about it but us. Juan and Tonya can find out, but no one else. We will stay there when trouble is around. I want you two to save your money because in this game white folks will make sure you see rainy days, lawyers and bondsmen. You never know when you may have to kill a nigga' and don't ever trust a bitch, but you can trust a real woman."

As David was talking he spotted Juan and pulled in front of him. Juan opened the door and got in.

"What's popping yo?" Juan asked.

David said, "Them folks coming from New York to the Howard Johnson Hotel at 11:00 pm. We're going to get their ass along with Lisa and Linda's drugs."

Juan replied, "Whatever, now what's up with the boys? Justin done got big as hell. I am still you're God Father."

Justin and Juan were close. He had not seen Justin in some years but they knew each other well and it was 2-DIE-4-forever-140.

Chapter Four

FRIDAY 11:20PM

David and the crew were on the lookout, waiting on the car to come with the New York plates. After waiting for about two hours David was getting tired, but just when he was fixing to leave Justice said, "Yo Dad, there's a car driving bye."

David said, "Duck down, that's them."

The car pulled into the parking lot of the Hotel and David said, "Juan you and Justin circle around the hotel and me and Justice will come from the side. Try not to kill them because I want to send Lisa and Linda a message."

Everyone went to do their part. Justin and Juan were creeping up on the car and the two men inside never saw them coming. Juan put the gun to the driver's head and they didn't have a chance, they had been caught slipping in a dangerous game.

David and Justice came around and David said room 106. David made the driver walk to the room along with his buddy and they all went in. David cut the sheets and tied the men up, then patted them down like the police would. Both men had hand guns. The big man with the bald head was Travis and the slim man with the cut on his face was Vick.

David asked the big man where the drugs were while Justin, Juan and Justice were all standing around wondering how the once 'Heartbeat Don' was going to handle this.

David said to Travis, "Where are the drugs?"

Travis replied, "What Drugs?"

David smiled and walked over to Vick and said, "Where are the drugs?"

The slim man said, "Fuck You!"

David started laughing, he told Justin and Justice to pull the man's pants down and they pulled his pants down. David walked up to the slim man with some latex gloves and grabbed his dick. Vick was looking crazy when David pulled out his knife and cut one of his balls off. Blood went everywhere.

David looked over at Travis and said, "Where are the Fucking Drugs?" The big man was crying. He told David the drugs were in the car in a secret compartment.

Juan went to check the spot. He went to the truck and got the drugs then came back after putting everything up.

David told the big man, "I am not going to kill you this time because I want you to take your friend back to Lisa."

Then he pulled Vick's tongue out and cut it off. That was his trademark. Then he carved 2-DIE-4 across his forehead. When they all walked out the big man had shit all over himself and was crying like a baby.

David waited and watched Travis put Vick in the car then they got on the highway and headed back to New York.

David looked in the back seat at his two boys and said, "There is a price for all the good you do in life and there is a price for all the bad. Do what you think you can handle."

Justice was looking sick. David looked at him and said, "If you can't handle it get out of the car."

Justice said, "Dad I'm just thinking and looking out the window."

David went to the house and bagged up all the drugs then they all went to work. David gave everyone their share of money and in one month's time everyone was very happy. David got Justin a brand new, pearl black Lexus L.S.O. with the special kit. He got Justice a brand new H-2 Hummer with full chrome rims and T.V. in all the seats. Both rides were the talk of the town for the young brothers. He got Tonya a Mercedes Benz S-R. She was one of the most popular women in Hartford. Kate had gone on a two week shopping spree and David gave all of his sisters, Gail and Jesse money. Everyone was chilling, things were going good.

NEW YORK

When Travis pulled up in Spanish Harlem he was out of it. He wondered how he made it there. He parked the car in front of the building that Lisa stayed in and got out. He ran to Lisa door and started hitting the door hard.

Lisa came to the door fast and said, "What's wrong?"

Travis said, "Go to the car."

Lisa grabbed her gun and called Linda then they both ran to the car. When Lisa saw Vick's face she got so sick she could not move. Linda couldn't do anything but cry. Vick had died with his tongue in his hand, his skin was pale.

Lisa yelled out, "I will kill you David!"

She saw the letters '2-DIE-4' across Vick's forehead and she knew David was out of prison and ready for war. The news was on and Lisa saw where they had found Steven dead in his house with his tongue in his hand.

"Linda, David is a fucking monster. How the hell did he get out of prison?" Lisa asked.

Linda replied, "I don't know but we got to be very careful. David is going to come after us real soon."

"I have a plan," Lisa said.

"What is it?" Linda asked.

"We are not going to wait on David to come after us, let's go looking for his ass," she replied.

Linda said, "You crazy!"

"You, Travis and I are going after David. We are also going to bring Lenny. We're going to kill David before he gets us," said Lisa.

"I got to go with you but damn! Girl this is going to be the fight of our lives!" Replied Linda.

DAVID

David was kissing on Kate telling her how much he loved her. She had just told David that she was two months pregnant. He was happy as could be, he wanted a little girl so he could spoil her to death. He needed a girl so he could see a side of him that was not so cold blooded.

Kate was lying in bed with nothing on as David was kissing her. He laid on top of her and entered her slowly. She began to moan as she lost control of her body. They made love slowly while listening to R. Kelly's 12 play.

Afterwards David had Kate laid across his chest and he was telling her about some of the things he had to do to make it in life. He told Kate about some things he had done in prison just to live to see another day. David had opened up to Kate because he felt she understood him.

JUSTICE

Justice was coming from Avon Connecticut when his cell phone went off. He picked up and said, "Hello." He knew the voice, it was his mom, Linda.

She said, "Hello baby."

"What's up mom?" Justice said.

Linda said, "Baby we need to meet."

Justice replied, "Mom you need to stop hiding from dad."

"Now Justice don't you let David turn you against me," Linda said.

"Mom I promise I won't stand by and let no one hurt you," he assured her.

"I will be in Hartford soon, I'll call you and we can meet up just the two of us," she said.

"I love you Mom," Justice said as they hung up.

He had already made up his mind that he was not going to stand by and let no one hurt his mom.

LISA AND LINDA

There was four of them in a rental Range Rover. Lenny was driving while Lisa was on the passenger side and Travis and Linda were in the back. They all had guns and were ready to use them on who ever got in their way.

Lisa said, "I won't stop until I kill David for all the pain he caused me and my family."

Carlos had gone to prison for life. Lisa and David were at war and Lisa was ready to get it over with once and for all. They were almost in Hartford where the war would begin.

DAVID

David got out of bed and jumped in the shower. Kate was still in bed asleep when David got out of the shower. He got dressed and kissed her on the lips then headed out of the house and over to Tonya house.

David pulled up and got out, he could see Tonya had two of her friends over there. He saw her friend Nicky was there, she was a freak. David always wanted to get in them pants. Nicky was a brick house, one of the finest girls in town, but she was not shit. She would do two best friends and chase that money.

David got out his car and walked in the back door. Tonya, Nicky and Toy, the other girl, were in the kitchen chilling.

David said, "What's up baby?"

Tonya went off, "Mother fucker this is not a hotel, where the fuck have you been?"

David started laughing until a glass broke next to his head. He turned around and Tonya was coming at him. He grabbed Tonya's arms while Nicky and Toy held her back.

David said, "Don't start this bull shit Tonya!"

He grabbed Tonya by one arm and rushed her up the stairs. David told Tonya some good lies and she stopped bitching. He asked, "Have you seen our son Justin?"

Tonya said, "I can't keep up with him since he got that new car. He comes home when he gets ready."

"Tonya Justin is growing up and all you can do is show him all that is good because the streets are going to show him all that is bad." He looked in Tonya's eyes and said, "If you want a baby you got to have another one because your son has become a man."

~ 50 ~

"I don't want any more kids if this is how it turns out," she replied.

"A girl would be good," David responded.

Tonya said, "Not by you."

David looked real hard at her and Tonya started laughing.

"I am just joking," she said. She knew David did not play about those kind of matters. Tonya had only dated one other guy and they never had sex. David was her one and only and she was crazy about him. Tonya and David had done it all and it only got better.

JUAN

Juan had the streets on lock down, no more hoods. He worked his beeper along with Justin and Justice. They were all making money and Juan was laying low over at Sonya's house, watching a movie. Sonya told Juan to call David so they could all chill. Juan had another girl named La-La, whose real name was Pamela Holmes. She was black and Spanish and she was a heart breaker, a dime all day on whatever level.

Juan picked up his phone and called David.

"What's popping Juan," said David when he answered the phone.

Juan said, "I need you to come to Park and chill with me."

"Cool, I'm on my way," replied David.

"I have everything here, just come," Juan told him.

David jumped in his all-white Corvette and headed to Park Street. He was driving fast, with the Corvette laying low. He was reaching speeds of 100-120 miles per hour, the faster the car the more of a rush it gave David. He pulled up in front of Sonya's house and saw Juan's two door Benz. He parked next to it and jumped out. He was clean with his all-white Sean John sweat suit and shoes to match. He walked up to the door and Juan was standing there smiling.

David walked in and saw La-La, she was looking good from head to toe. He spotted Sonya and thought, boy what a battle, both girls were dimes. Sonya had trimmed down and cut her hair, she had a beautiful tan.

David said, "Hello ladies."

La-La and Sonya said, "What up?" At the same time, then they looked at each other and started laughing.

They were all watching a movie on a '64' inch flat screen with surround sound, it was just like the movies. David went over and sat next to Sonya and got comfortable. They smoked good weed and talked about the old days, just chilling, not worried about anything. Or so they thought.

LISA AND LINDA

Lisa and her crew had made it to Hartford. Soon as they hit the city limits they went and rented a room at the Hilton Hotel in down town Hartford.

Lisa told Travis, "Me and you will stay together."

She picked up her phone and the first number she dialed was Kate. Kate picked up the phone but didn't say anything. That was her mistake, all Lisa wanted was Kate's address so she could go to her house. Lisa looked at the phone and ran a wire to it, she opened up her lap top computer and went to work. She dialed Kate's phone number back into the phone and an address came up.

"Bingo! She stays in Bloomfield Connecticut, on Dorothy in a condo. Travis and I will go pay her a visit, Linda you and Lenny stay here. Don't let anyone in here and don't use the phone for any reason!" Lisa said.

Travis and Lisa headed to Bloomfield, trying to find her baby sister's Condo. When they hit Bloomfield it didn't take long to find Kate's Condo because they was one of the newest ones in town and the most expensive. When they spotted the address they pulled up outside.

Kate saw the car pull up outside and she ran to the room and grabbed a hand gun. She looked out her window and saw her sister Lisa. She felt bad and went down stairs to open the door.

Lisa said, "Hello girl, where is David?"

Kate said, "He's not here, I haven't seen him in a few days." Kate was lying but she was trying to protect the two people she loved most in this world.

Lisa said, "Pack your shit you're coming with me."

"I am not going no fucking where!" Kate replied.

"Bitch do what I said," Lisa said and slapped Kate in the face.

Kate went crazy, Lisa was the oldest but Kate went wild on her ass. Travis was trying to break them up.

"Lisa you're drawing heat, just chill," Travis said.

Kate got loose and grabbed her gun. She let two shots off, Boom! Boom! Lisa went down and she made sure she was not hit then she took out her 9mm. Kate ran for the back door when Lisa came up and let off about four shots. Kate never made it out the door, Lisa shot her baby sister one time in the back of the head and once in the back.

Lisa was hurt, she cried hard then walked over to Kate and said, "You were all I was living for."

Travis grabbed Lisa and they ran out and got in the car. Kate was not fully dead, she grabbed the phone and dialed David's number.

David was high as hell laying on Sonya's lap. When his phone rang he picked up and said, "Hello."

Kate said, "David Lisa shot me, help me, I love you."

David's heart dropped, he jumped up and told Juan to come on because Kate had been shot. David called 911 to go to Bloomfield over to Kate's address then he got in his Vett and headed out. Juan got in his Benz and followed along, they were pushing both cars to the limit. David got on his cell phone and called Justin and Justice and told them the deal.

When David pulled up at the house Kate was headed to the hospital on Blue Hills and he followed along, this was a sad day for David. When the ambulance pulled in they stopped and rushed Kate to the side door. They were calling for all the medical assistants STAT.

Everyone was sitting in the waiting room anticipating the news. David and Juan had seen this shit before. Yolanda and Justin were there too, along with Gail. Everyone was showing up because Kate and Yolanda were close and all of David's family loved her like family.

After about thirty minutes a doctor came out sweating, he took off his glasses and wiped his forehead.

David ran to him and asked, "How is she?"

The doctor said, "Sir she was a strong young lady but both she and the baby died from gunshot wounds to the head."

David could not believe what he had just heard, he cried for the first time in years. He let it all go when Juan came over and hugged him. Juan let him know it was going to be okay. He had never seen David cry before, but all of David's family was crying. Yolanda took it very hard and everyone was sad.

EVERYONE IS HURTING

A large pink wreath decorated the entry way of the funeral parlor as the proprietor showed their last respects to a very special young lady from New York. The funeral home began to fill with mourners, young people from the hood who knew Kate were there. She had made a lot of friends but no one really knew exactly what Kate was into, she never told anyone anything about her past.

Lisa came to the funeral dressed so that no one could notice her. Her conscience had been eating her up. She had killed her baby sister, her only sister. The person she loved the most in the world was lying in a casket with an all-white dress. She was not moving and her eyes were closed forever. Lisa started feeling ill, her stomach was in knots. While her eyes filled with tears her soul felt nothing but pain.

Lisa yelled out, "What have I done? Oh God help me! Forgive me please!"

Everyone was thinking that Lisa was just overcome by grief, but it was guilt that had overcome Lisa, she had killed her only sister. She never cried for Luis, her mother, Todd or Vick. She never really cried about anything or anyone. However she cried today, she cried for everyone and she cleaned her soul out. She was ready to face whatever was waiting on the other side.

Lisa watched as they took her sister to be buried. It was a day when everyone was hurting.

Chapter Five

DAVID

After Kate's funeral David stayed low key, he was not in the streets very much. Juan was handling things well, along with Justin and Justice. David had a lot on his mind and he was hurt. He would not call Tonya or Sonya back, he stayed in the house in Avon, Connecticut. He smoked weed all day and drank on E & J while watching TV.

Justice and Justin came by the house every day to see David and let him know what was going on. Juan usually came along with them.

David told Juan, "I want you to be careful around that bitch Lisa. She will get crazy and she has nothing to lose. She might do anything when it comes down to it."

"Man I will smoke that bitch without a second guess," Juan said. "Man word on the streets is you are the one who killed Chad's brother Steven"

David said, "Trust me, niggas' don't want that, if they did I would have gotten a message by now.

JUSTIN

Justin had pulled up at Tonya's house and was getting out of his car. Tonya came to the door raising hell.

She said, "Boy get in here now! Who do you think you are?"

Justin grew up spoiled but he would not talk back to his mother, he loved his mom and dad, but Tonya wanted to know where he had been staying. He hated to lie to his mother, but he was not going to tell anyone about David's house in Avon, Conn. They called it the hide out and the only ones who knew about it was David, Justin, Justice and Juan.

"Mom I have a girlfriend I be chilling with," Justin said.

Tonya said, "You need to find a job and chill with that." Justin started laughing and Tonya said, "Shit is not funny."

Soon as Tonya went to the back door she saw David pulling in. She was glad to see him because since Kate died he was on some more shit. She really was mad and that's why she started with Justin.

David got out of the car and walked to the back door as Tonya came out to greet him. She followed him all the way back to the house, hugging and kissing him.

Justin came out and shook his daddy's hand and said, "I am glad you came," then started laughing.

Tonya said, "Okay Justin don't make me kick your ass!"

David grabbed Tonya and said, "Why you giving my man a hard time?"

"That boy is just like you," said Tonya.

David and Tonya went upstairs to her room together where David laid Tonya down and they made love all day. She was laid out when Mrs. Weaver called. She picked up the phone and said, "Hello."

Her mom said, "Come over to the house."

"Later I can," Tonya replied.

"What are you doing now?" Mrs. Weaver asked.

"Nothing, David is over here asleep right now," Tonya told her.

"What you do in the dark will come to the light," Her mother said.

Tonya responded, "I hear you but I'm not doing anything."

Mrs. Weaver said, "You sound mighty happy. I will see you later Tonya." then she hung up the phone laughing.

LINDA

Linda called Justice and told him to meet her at the same spot they had been meeting each other for the last two weeks. Lisa was still hanging around with her two body guards Travis and Lenny. Justice went to the room, knocked on the door and Linda let him in. He hugged his mother as he came in the door.

"Have a seat big man," Linda said. Justice smiled but he was looking crazy. She told him, "Boy don't be looking at me fucking crazy like that! You are still my baby." Justice started laughing and Linda said, "Now come sit between my legs and let me braid your hair."

Justice went over and sat down then the first thing Linda said was, "How is your daddy doing?"

Justice said, "He got me that brand new H-2 Hummer, a brand new B.M.W. and a motor cycle. He also gave me fifty thousand dollars."

Linda said, "Damn! Be a good nigga' Justice, David don't play when it comes to loyalty. 2-DIE-4, David took that to heart. Whatever you do don't cross your dad because that's a cold hearted mother fucker and he will kill you without thinking about it."

"Mom I know how Dad is and I have a lot of love and respect for him but I am not going to stand by and let him hurt you. Now Lisa, I don't care," Justice said.

Linda said, "Baby don't say that, Lisa is like family."

"She killed Kate and that was like my sister," he replied. Linda couldn't say anything and Justice said, "I'm going to tell David that you and me been meeting and if he don't like it, that's too bad. But he better not ever try to hurt you, I will kill his ass."

Linda was now smiling on the inside because Justice was David's main blood line and he was dangerous.

LISA

Lisa was laid up in the room and had been snorting cocaine all day. She and Travis were watching TV when Linda walked in the hotel.

Lisa said, "What's up girl?"

"Nothing much just came from seeing Justice," Linda said.

~ 58 ~

"Did you tell him I said hello?" Lisa asked.

Linda lied and said, "Girl you know I did."

Lenny came out the bathroom looking crazy and asking Linda where she had been.

"Nigga' I can protect myself so don't question me!" Linda told him.

Lenny dropped his head and walked off, leaving Lisa on the bed laughing.

TONYA

Mrs. Weaver and Tonya were going to the doctor for a six month checkup. When they got inside Tonya told the lady at the desk her name and signed some papers. The lady at the desk said the first thing they needed was for her to pee in a cup. Tonya got the cup and went to the rest room. When she came back out she gave the lady the cup and the lady took the cup to the back. After about thirty minutes Tonya heard them calling her name. She got up went to the desk where the lady told her room-6, Dr. West. Tonya knew Dr. West, he was Justin's doctor too.

When Tonya walked in Dr. West was smiling, he said, "How have things been going?"

Tonya said, "I'm fine."

Dr. West asked, "Have you been a bad girl?"

"No," she replied.

Dr. West said, "You are two months pregnant."

Tonya was shocked.

Dr. West said, "Drink and eat healthy. I will see you in three months.

Tonya said to herself, David knew what he was doing, he didn't want to wear any protection and he lied about pulling out. Now she was having another baby. She was having it for sure, but she was going to raise hell with David.

Tonya walked out and told her mother she was two months pregnant and started crying.

Mrs. Weaver laughed all the way home.

Tonya had her head down like a baby. She said, "Maybe it will be a girl."

DAVID, JUSTIN AND JUSTICE

David and his two sons were coming from the hide out in Justice's H-2 Hummer. David was in the back seat behind bullet proof windows and his cell phone went off.

"Hello?" He said.

Tonya said, "David you need to get here fast," then she hung up.

David told Justice to get to Tonya's house fast and Justice gave it all it had while his brother Justin was ready to jump out with his gun in hand.

They pulled up in front of Tonya's house only to see Mrs. Weaver's car out front. David and Justice jumped out with their guns and got low as they ran to the back.

Tonya looked out the back door and said, "What the hell is wrong with you two? Justin put that gun away!"

"You called like there was trouble," David said.

Tonya replied, "There is trouble, but you don't need a gun."

David and Justin walked in the back door behind Tonya then spoke to Mrs. Weaver. Justin hugged his grandmother, she still treated Justin like a baby.

Tonya was looking at David with this mug on her face. David asked, "What's this all about?"

A knock came to the front door and it was Justice, he had his gun in his hand.

Tonya told him, "Boy put that thing up!"

Justice came in and spoke to everyone but he was looking crazy wondering what was up.

No one was talking until Tonya said, "David I'm two months pregnant."

David asked, "For real?"

Justice was happy and Justin jumped up and hugged his mom.

David walked over and said, "I hope it's a girl, that way you can chill."

Tonya and David walked to the car where Tonya leaned inside and said, "You lied all that time about taking it out." Then they both started laughing.

David and the boys got in his Benz and headed to Juan's house to chill. On their way to East Hartford David spotted a Range Rover. He couldn't see the driver's face but he spotted a female who he knew was a good looking lady, that lady was Lisa.

David asked Justin and Justice if they had their guns. They both told him they didn't leave home without them. David always carried his gun too so they were ready. The Range Rover didn't see David's Benz. He drove a little closer and saw Linda in the back seat with some guy sitting next to her.

"The only reason we aren't going to do them right here is because Linda is in the truck," David said. But he had an idea, he wanted to test the gangster inside Justice. David said, "I may still get their ass."

Justice said, "No not while my Mom is in there!"

David said, "Your mom was down with stealing my money."

Justice replied, "Dad if you hurt my Mom, you better hurt me first. It's 2-DIE-4, but never my mom."

David was feeling Justice because he felt the same way about Gail. He would kill the whole world over her. David said, "I'm going to talk to Linda but Lisa and them other clowns are going to pay in the worst way. Linda is going to have to leave town."

Justice said, "Dad let's talk to her because she may not really understand the code she broke."

"No one really understands until it's too late. Your mother and I have been through a lot and for her to do that, hurt me. She and Lisa took over a million dollars cash, they refused to get me a lawyer, they didn't do shit for me and they moved away. I will never forget that," He said.

David let the Range Rover go ahead but he followed it for about 3 miles without the driver ever seeing him. It then pulled inside the Court Yard Hotel and David started smiling because he knew it was just a matter of time before he caught them in their own trap. He watched the big man get out of the truck with Lisa walking next to him, then a slim man got out and Linda was walking next to him. David knew they were trained bodyguards.

They all walked to room 126 and went in. David pulled out of the parking lot feeling good, he was headed to see his boy Juan.

Juan had remodeled the old house, it was looking good and you could tell he was back to getting money. He had added on a few more rooms.

David and the boys got out and all shook hands. Justin and Justice went to the pool table and started playing while David and Juan walked to the bedroom and started talking.

David said, "I know where Lisa and Linda are staying."

"Let's go get them!" Juan said.

"No, you and I will surprise her body guards later on," He replied.

They talked about who would had been doing what and how the streets had changed over the years. Juan told David that Jimmy went back to jail for arm robbery and Chad was on heroin real bad and still gambling.

David said, "Guess what?"

"What?" Juan asked.

"Tonya is having another baby and I hope it's a girl," he replied.

Juan said, "Boy I'm proud of you and I hope it's a girl too, because one more boy and this shit will be crazy."

"Man we're fixing to go over to my Mom's house and eat. Gail cooked a big meal. I'll call you and let you know where to meet me," he told Juan, then he told Justin and Justice, "let's ride."

They hugged Juan and jumped in the Benz headed for Gail house.

GAIL'S HOUSE

When David pulled the Benz up in his mother's back yard all eyes were on his car. You couldn't see in the windows, they were extra dark with limo tint.

He saw all of his sisters, Betty, Jasmine and Yolanda. Yolanda had her boyfriend Mark with her, they always rolled together. He saw his cousins, aunts and everyone.

David and the boys were clean. David had on an all-white Versace suit with some white Gators. Justin had on a Sean John suit, gray with matching Gators. Justice had on a grey and white silk Polo suit, also with matching Gators. They were feeling good.

David saw one of his step cousins, Sharon. He always liked her because she was fine. All the girls were hanging on David and the boys. Jesse and two of his brothers were sitting around talking with two other men that David didn't know.

Jesse told the men, "This is my oldest son David."

The men reached out and shook David's hand. David walked over to where his mom and the girls were chilling. Justin was all up in one of Yolanda's friends face and Justice was trying to talk to a young Puerto Rican girl. She knew Justice because he was the only young kid in Hartford with an H-2 Hummer going to Weaver High School.

David walked up and said, "Hello ladies."

Sharon was the first one to speak. She said, "Dam you done got grown! Come give your cuz a hug."

David started smiling and Gail said, "He doesn't even hug me no more."

David walked over to Sharon and gave her a hug. No one saw David's hand as he let it slide down and touch her fast ass. Sharon was a nice looking girl. She acted innocent, but David knew she was a freak. When David was young, his mother use to let Sharon watch them because she was older. Then David knew she already had a little girl with a nigga' from Dutch-Point who was doing time for murder. David had run across him in the joint, he was a real nigga and David liked him. Bottom line was that David always wanted Sharon but never could corner her off.

He laughed as he walked off and went to where Justice was talking to a Puerto Rican girl name Rose. She stayed next door to David mom's house. Another girl walked up and David shook her hand.

He asked her, "What is your name?"

The lady said, "My name is Kim." Then she started smiling.

David said, "You're looking good."

"Thank you and you're looking great yourself," Kim said.

They made small talk while Justice was trying to get in Rose's pants.

David told everyone he would see them later with Kim and Rose was still standing next to him. He looked around to see his baby's mother Tonya's B.M.W. pulling up.

David said to himself, 'Dam!'

Tonya pulled up and got out. The first thing she did as she walked up was give David an ugly look then she walked over and hugged Gail. Yolanda ran over and touched her belly. Tonya was looking good and David walked up behind her to hug her from the back.

Tonya turned around and asked, "Who was that you were standing up here talking to?"

David said, "That was Justice's girlfriend's aunt."

"What did she want," Tonya asked.

David replied, "Damn you must be the police."

Tonya got mad as hell, she reached out and slapped David hard in the face and caught him off guard. Now David was mad. Tonya wanted to fight but she knew David wouldn't put his hands on her, she had put him to the test years ago. David was not a woman beater, maybe because of all the stuff he saw his mother go through with his step daddy.

David grabbed Tonya by the neck playfully and kissed her on the mouth. He loved the way she tasted and he had spoiled her. Justin ran down the step while Tonya and David were playfully fighting. He grabbed his mother Tonya and was holding her for David. Tonya called Justin a traitor then said, "That's why I'm having a little girl."

Justin said, "For real man?"

Tonya said, "Don't tell David." But she knew that was a waste of time because Justin told David everything.

David went upstairs to his old room, it looked the same. He had his gold and money in the safe along with brand new guns that had never been touched and four bullet proof vests. When he opened the safe he saw stacks and stacks of money, almost five hundred thousand dollars. David had a safe at each of his sisters' houses and one at Tonya's mom's house, it was all good.

It was getting late and Justin took his brother Justice to get his truck from Tonya's house. When they got there, Tonya was eating, talking and having fun.

DAVID

David called Juan and said, "Meet me at the Court Yard Hotel in Bloomfield. I will be in Jesse's old Ford Thunder Bird."

Juan said, "Cool, I'll be there."

David went down the stairs and asked Jesse if he could use the Thunder Bird.

Jesse said, "Man you can get anything you want from me."

David got the keys and headed to Bloomfield, Connecticut. The old Thunder Bird was clean and it road like a caddy. Jesse had done a lot of work to that car.

David pulled inside the Court Yard parking lot and parked but he didn't see Juan's car anywhere. David remembered Lisa and her crew had gone into room 126. He was sitting in the car with his 44 bull dog in his hand next to him and on the front seat was his P-89. He spotted Juan hiding behind a building and got out the car real fast then ran to the side of the building.

"What took so long?" Juan asked.

David said, "Nigga' I was waiting on you. Did you see anything?"

"Yeah I saw a big man come out of the room and a slim nigga' looking around," Juan said.

"That was Lisa and Linda's body guards so be careful. Here's what we're going to do. We are going to knock on the door and when someone answers we're going to rush in," He told Juan.

Juan said, "Hell no, nigga' you thinking crazy! Let's just wait on them to come out and ambush them."

David said, "Let's get in your car."

"I have a stolen car with the keys, it's covered for 48-hours," Juan replied.

"Go pull it around front," David told him.

When David saw the all-black 5.0 Mustang G.T. he got in with Juan and waited. They stayed in the parking lot for about an hour before the door of room 126 opened up. What David saw then almost made him choke.

It was Linda dressed to kill but she had on a long gold wig trying to change how she looked. When David saw her the anger came into his eyes, at one time he was deeply in love with Linda and for her to cross him made his heart bleed.

David told Juan, "That's Linda, let's follow her and see where she goes."

Linda was driving that same black Range Rover with David and Juan on her trail. She never saw Juan behind her at all.

Juan asked, "Do you want to kill her?"

David replied, "I promised Justice I wouldn't hurt his mother and I am a man of my word. But I am going to scare the shit out of her and sex her up real good."

Juan started laughing. Linda was headed to Bowls Park right next to Weaver High School, David and Juan knew the area. While Juan slowed down he saw Linda turn into the first set of apartments next to the gym. It was about 11pm and the streets were clear, all but the small time drug boys trying to get a dollar. Juan saw Linda turn in and he went right behind her.

She went into her pocket, took out a key, opened the door to an apartment and went inside. Juan and David were getting ready to get out when they heard some shots.

Boom! Boom!

David said, "Holly Shit!"

The door to apartment three came open and Linda rushed out and jumped in the cheap Blazer. She then went back to the Courtyard hotel and went into room 126 like nothing had happened.

"Juan that bitch is cold hearted. You saw all the shit she did when she was pregnant with Justice. I am the only one she won't try," David said.

He got them a room on the other side of the Courtyard and they were lying around looking at the news when it came across that three Cubans were found dead in Bowls Park apartments. The news lady said F.B.I. agents seemed to think the killings were a hit because each man was shot one time in the back of the head while on their knees. She said that there were no suspects at this time and no motive.

David said, "Damn man you saw that!"

He looked out the hotel window and was just day dreaming but as he kept looking around he spotted Linda going into another room upstairs. David said to himself, 'slick Linda went in room 212. He called Juan to the window and showed him.

David said, "Grab the gun we're going to surprise her."

David and Juan went up the steps but they couldn't hear anything. Juan was on the other side when David saw the lady who cleans the rooms. He rushed to her and said, "Miss I forgot my keys can you please come open my door, room 212?"

The lady looked at David crazy like, so David reached in his pocket and pulled out a hundred dollar bill. The lady went over and unlocked the door, she had no idea what David was up to.

Linda was in the shower, just letting the water run down her back. She was feeling good, she had talked to Justice earlier and things were fine. Justice meant everything to Linda because that was all the family she had left, only Justice.

LISA

Lisa had just got off the phone with Bobby, the man who she had running her operation back in New York. Bobby was an old gangster, he used to kill for a living but retired about two years ago. Now all he did was put hits on people who fucked up. He was the one that put the hit on the three Cubans in Bowls Park. Lisa was doing well, she said that she was going to stay in Hartford and give it to David however he wanted. Her money was right and she had sent for four more of her men to come to Hartford. She made up in her mind to hunt David down and she was not going to run, she was going to be the first person to chase and kill David on his own turf.

She said, "Today will be the last day at the Courtyard, never stay anywhere too long."

DAVID

David and Juan walked inside the hotel room, they had their guns out ready to let loose.

David said to Juan, "Wait here, I'm going in the bathroom where Linda is at."

Linda had the shower curtains closed with the hot steam on and her eyes were closed, she was enjoying the steam heating her body. She had her gun sitting on the sink. When David walked in and grabbed the shower curtains Linda opened her eyes and almost lost her breath. But she knew it was do or die so she jumped for her gun.

David moved fast and kicked her to the floor hard. Linda could not do anything, she looked up at David and said, "Do it go ahead and do it, just tell Justice I love him."

David knew that was game, he was not going to kill her. He grabbed her gun and said, "Get out of here."

Linda was buck naked and David made her go to the room. He said, "Now put your lotion and deodorant on and make your face up because we need to talk."

Linda said, "David let me explain, I'm not going to say it was not on me because you trained me for everything except what to do if you had to leave me."

David said, "Linda I gave you the world. We shared so much, we got rich together and went to war together. I was there for you and you were there for me, 2-DIE-4-4-ever 140. Time waits on no one. Baby you left me without food or water." He got in Linda's face and said, "What happens to a person if he don't have water or food for three days? A person dies! Water is life and you ran off with everything. If it was up to me I would kill you now, but I love our son." David started laughing he said, "Linda you and Lisa wanted me to die but I can't die, I won't die. I had a second plan for you girls. Fool, do you think I spent all that money I made? Think about the money I got from your uncle Pa-Pe! Do you think I would have sent you and Lisa to get my last?"

Linda said, "David I don't want to hear that bullshit, do what you came to do." She was lying on the bed naked with her legs spread wide open.

David looked at her and said, "You still don't think shit stinks."

Linda was smiling and looking up at the ceiling.

David walked over to the bed with his gun in his hand and he said. "Linda put your clothes on and move slow because I don't trust you no more."

Linda said, "Nigga' I am not putting on shit. I still love you and I am here naked, make me pay."

David called Juan and gave him both guns. He walked over to Linda and started sucking between her legs. He felt Linda getting wet and he put her legs over his shoulder and entered her like a man. Linda was screaming and calling David's name. He was trying to hurt her and she was too scared to tell him to stop. He flipped her over and did her doggy style. He was hitting Linda like a man on death row whose last request was pussy. David was getting turned on by all the noise Linda was making. He slipped up and entered into Linda's anus and she cried out in pain. But David wanted her to hurt for all she had done to him. She was trying to fight David but it didn't work.

Finally Linda passed out and when she woke up she wanted David again. She got up and was cleaning herself up. She wanted to kill David for how he treated her.

David and Juan were in the front room when Linda came out of the bedroom and said, "Let's go!" Then she shot a bullet over David's head. She let him know she could have killed him, she was trained to kill and trained to go.

Juan shot back at Linda but they were doing what she wanted and that was get out of her room. Juan and David ran out the door and Linda came out in her panties still shooting.

Lisa was down in her room and when she heard the shots she grabbed her gun and went to the back door where she saw Linda, then David. Lisa started shooting at David with her Mac-11.

As David looked back he and Lisa looked at each other right in the eyes. David let off four shots, then Juan came out shooting but the girls had too much heat. David ran and jumped in the Thunder Bird and headed out as Juan got in the 5.0 and went his way.

LINDA AND LISA

Lisa ran up to Linda and started hugging on her. "It's okay baby," she said.

Linda was crying and Lisa knew David had been in there. Linda told Lisa some of the things David had done to her and Lisa said, "Oh no he didn't!"

Linda said, "He could have killed me but I'm not what he wanted, he's a human hunter. He was letting me know he can catch me anytime. Lisa he knows everything, he told me shit we did two weeks ago."

"We got to get out of here. David is not around because of the shooting but he will be back. I have four more of my best men on the way, they should be here tonight," Lisa told her.

Chapter Six

DAVID

David pulled up at Tonya's house. He got out and opened the door with his key, then went upstairs and got in the shower. Tonya was sound asleep otherwise she would have been bitching about David coming in the house so late. He cleaned himself up then got in the bed next to Tonya. Her belly was real big now, she could have the baby anytime. David looked over at Tonya and was blessed to still be next to her at the end of the day, because that's what counts. David and Tonya had seen the storms together. He had to say that he had much love for her and her family.

JUSTICE

Justice was in Dutch Point shooting dice with some of his old friends when the game got kind of heated up and a big fight broke out. Justice and his boys were moving out of the way. But a nigga' came out of nowhere and grabbed Justice's gold chain. Justice and Cornbread took off after him. Cornbread was fixing to give up when Justice told him to move. Cornbread moved and Justice aimed the gun at the back of the man's head and pulled the trigger. The man's head exploded, killing him on the spot.

Cornbread was scared to death.

Justice said, "Man come on, fuck him. He tried to get my chain."

Cornbread was the only one who knew about the murder. The next day Justice was watching T.V. when the news came on. What he saw almost made him shit. His picture was on T.V. for the murder of a man in Dutch Point. The first thing that came to his mind was, 'Cornbread ratted me out.' He walked out of the house and got in his truck, headed to Avon, Connecticut to the hideout house.

He called David and David told Justice to turn himself in to the police.

Justice said, "Cool, I need to speak to Justin about something."

Justin and Justice had become very close, they shared a lot with each other and they even looked alike. Neither had to test the other one. Justice needed a big favor from his brother, 2-DIE-4.

LINDA

Linda was crying when she saw her son's picture on TV wanted for murder. Lisa was holding Linda because she was feeling her pain.

"It's going to be okay," Lisa said.

Linda said, "Justice is just like David."

"David will make sure he gets the best lawyer money can buy," Lisa assured her.

Linda said, "I hope he don't take out what I done to him on my baby."

DAVID

David had just got off the phone with one of the best lawyers in Hartford. He hired him on the spot. David had an all-white limousine waiting for Justice when he pulled up in front of Tonya's house. Justice got out with a suit and tie on, he hugged David and Tonya.

David told Tonya to call the Morgan Street Jail and tell them Justice was on his way to turn himself in. His lawyer Nelson Chambers was already there waiting for them and David, Tonya and Justice were on their way.

When the limo pulled up in front of Morgan St. Jail channel three news was there and a few more news teams. They waited then David got out and opened the door for his son Justice Thomas.

Justin was on the other side and all three of them looked alike. The lawyer and a jailer got Justice and walked him to the back. David stayed at the jail for three hours trying to get a bond hearing set up. At the hearing everything would come out, the witness and all.

Justice was given a cell but David promised him he wouldn't get any time. He was going to do whatever it took to get Justice off.

Tonya got real sick. She called her mother and told her she needed to go to the doctor. Mrs. Weaver called 911 and the ambulance showed up. Mrs. Weaver was already at the hospital waiting. She called Justin and told him to call David.

When David and Justin came to the hospital Tonya was in the room ready to have the baby. David put on his gloves and mask, along with the coat and walked into the room with Tonya. He walked to the side of the bed and started holding Tonya's hand as she lay there with her legs wide open. She was screaming and the doctor was saying, "Push!" Just then something came out and landed in the doctor's hands. It was a little girl who looked just like her daddy.

David and Tonya named the girl Daisy Leawanta Thomas. She was a pretty little girl, nine pounds and eight ounces. Tonya was happy and so was Mrs. Weaver and Gail, they were going to spoil that little girl rotten. Daisy was the talk of the family.

JUSTIN

Justin had gone to the county to visit his brother. When Justice came out they hugged each other and had small talk, then Justice said, "There's only one person who could have told on me, because there was no one else there." Cornbread was the state only witness, he had broken the code of the streets.

Justin said, "I got you little bro, 2-DIE-4. I will be there every step of the way."

Justice said, "I will do double what you will do for me. There's one more thing I want you to do."

Justin asked, "What's that.

Justice said, "Call my mother Linda and let her know I'm doing okay and tell her I love her."

"I will do that," Justin said.

Justice got ready to tell Justin something but Justin said, "You don't have to tell me, what we talk about is between us. I was trained by the best."

He got up and walked out of the visitation room.

LINDA

Linda's cell phone rang, it was Justin. He was calling to tell Linda that Justice was good.

He said, "Justice said to tell you he loved you and so do I."

Linda was so happy she didn't know what to say. She said, "I love you both, I love you two boys. When is he getting out?"

Justin said, "There is one witness that is going to tell on Justice. If he tells Justice will be gone for a long time. But if he doesn't come then Justice walks away."

Linda asked, "What did David say?"

Justin said, "Justice and I are brothers, we can handle each other. I won't let anything happen to my baby brother."

Linda said, "Be careful." Then they both hung up.

JUSTIN

Justin was riding late night in a stolen car, he was on the hunt for a kid name Cornbread. His brother's hearing was Monday at 10 am and Justin wanted everything to go well. When he got to Dutch Point he stopped by the corner store and let the car window down.

He asked, "Has anyone seen my cousin Cornbread?"

The fat kid said, "He just walked home why?"

Justin hit the gas and spotted a kid going down the alley. He rolled down the window and yelled, "Cornbread!"

Cornbread was thinking it was someone who wanted drugs so he said, "Wait man, I got you."

Justin jumped out of the car and walked to the alley where Cornbread was. He pulled out his 9mm and put it to Cornbread's head. He shot twice and Cornbread's body fell over. Justin walked and got back in the car, he said, "2-DIE-4."

He stopped on the Ave and lit the car he had just used on fire. He caught the bus and went to Blue Hill Ave, over to his mom's house.

David was there and he saw Justin coming in the back door. He could tell his son had been up to something but David didn't say nothing.

Justin took a shower and played with his little sister.

SUNDAY

Tonya had cooked a big breakfast for David Justin and herself. They were sitting at the table eating when the news came on and showed Dutch Point Projects. The news lady was saying a 16 year old boy was found shot in the head in the alley.

Tonya said, "Now that's some shit, who would want to shoot a 16 year old in the head for no reason?"

Justin could not say anything, he kept on eating and looking at his daddy out of the corner of his eye.

LINDA AND LISA

Linda said, "Did you see the news girl?"

Lisa replied, "No."

"They found a 16 year old boy shot in Dutch Point," Linda said.

"It might be the fool who was going to tell on Justice, you know David was not going to let that happen," Lisa said.

Linda said, "Justin is crazy as hell too, so he might be just like his damn daddy, a young monster.

MONDAY-THE HEARING

Justice was being held without bond and waiting for the person to tell his side of the story. He had seen the news and knew that it was Cornbread they found dead. He loved his brother even more for handling that for him.

Justice's lawyer told the judge a few big words then walked to the table and took a seat. After about thirty minutes, the clerk of court went to the judge's bench along with the D.A. The judge explained the case to the D.A. and said, "No witness, no case. The only witness was found dead Sunday night in the alley."

Justice was free to go, he hugged Gail and David and left. Justin was right behind them as they went out of the court house together. Cameras were everywhere and the news lady was asking Justice, "Did you have the witness killed? Do you belong to some big crime family in Hartford?"

Justice got in the limo and headed to his Grandma Gail's house. He was happy to be free and he told Justin, "Its nothing but love bro."

Justin said, "I got you young one." They both started laughing for the first time in his life.

Justice loved his brother like he loved his mother and that meant a lot.

JUAN

Juan was counting up all the money he had collected. He was hands on with the guys in Nelson Court since the death of R.B. He had Chappell Garden on lock and worked off his waist, meaning he used his beeper to make money. After Juan counted all the money he called one of his workers, John. He was better known as Big T and was from Nelson Court. Juan let him know that he was on the way and jumped in his B.M.W. and moved fast.

He hit the gas and made the car glide with the road. Juan could not see who was in the grey rental car coming up on him, but he could see fire coming out the windows. That meant someone was shooting at him. Juan did not panic he knew where to go for safety, Juan made a left up Westland St. and the car drove on by fire still coming out the windows. Juan went down and turned in Nelson Court, he seen Big T and told him what had just happened, Juan gave Big T the work and made a phone call to his sister Sonya. Juan told Big T he was leaving his car and to keep an eye on it. Sonya came, picked Juan up and they headed to her house on Park St.

SONYA

Sonya was driving fast headed to her condo. She was telling her brother how the game had changed so much.

She said, "Juan there is no more love in the streets."

Juan was hearing his sister but his mind was in another world. He had eighty thousand dollars that he owed to David. His girlfriend Carmen had not been home in two weeks and Juan had started using heroin little by little.

Sonya said, "What the fuck is wrong with you? Your dress code is falling off!"

Juan said, "I am feeling bad."

Sonya looked at him and shook her head.

Juan said, "Call David and tell him to come over."

Sonya pulled up in her yard and they both got out and went upstairs. Juan went to the guest room but Sonya wanted to chill. She called David and told him what Juan said.

Later Juan was down stairs trying to decide if he wanted to go out to a bar or not. He said out loud, "I am going to have some fun." He got dressed and walked over to a Spanish bar on Park St, where a lot of girls hung out. Juan was snorting and spending big money.

When Sonya came down stairs she saw that Juan was gone and she got mad as hell. She went back to her room.

DAVID

David was laid up in bed half sleep when his cell phone went off. He answered it and Sonya told him that Juan wanted him to come over. Then she hung up just like that. Sonya was mad with David because of Daisy. Sonya wanted to have David's next baby.

Tonya got up and asked David where he was going.

David said, "To my mom's house."

Tonya walked over and stood in David's face and said, "Stop lying, you know damn well you aren't going over your mom's house." David started laughing. Tonya pushed him in the chest playfully and David fell flat on the bed. Tonya got on top of him and started kissing him. She looked David in the eyes and said, "Nigga' I love you and I want to be with you forever. I don't care about them other hoes, just be good to me."

David said, "I will always come back to you because you understand a part of me the world doesn't know. You are everything to me."

Tonya said, "Now that I have Daisy I am complete."

David rolled on top and told Tonya, "We are going to be together for as long as God blesses me to wake up every day." He kissed her hard and was feeling on her, but Daisy started crying.

Tonya said, "See ya tonight."

David grabbed his gun and headed out to see Juan at Sonya's house.

JUSTIN AND JUSTICE

Justice was riding in his Hummer while Justin was on the other side playing the play station, they were headed to New Britain, Connecticut and coolin' smoking some weed. Justice was riding fast on the highway, he was going to meet his mother. He pulled up at the 3-Star hotel.

Justin asked, "What we doing here?"

Justice replied, "I came to meet my mother."

"What!" Justin said and they both started laughing.

Justice picked up the cell phone and called his mother. When Linda picked up Justice asked, "What room mom?"

Linda said, "201."

Justice said, "Me and Justin are on the way."

Justice parked the Hummer in the back. He and Justin checked their guns and headed to room 201. Justice knocked on the door and Linda peeked out, then opened the door.

She hugged Justice and Justin. Linda had to keep looking good, she kept herself up to date and she had a super model body. Linda told Justice he better stay out of trouble. She said, "Your daddy and me had a run in."

Justice was shocked, he asked, "Did he hit you?"

Linda started crying and told Justice, "Don't worry about it, David could have killed me but he didn't."

Justice was mad, he walked over to his mom and asked, "Did David touch you?"

Linda said, "We were in a shootout."

Justice said, "I told David not to touch you." He reached in his pocket and gave Linda two thousand dollars then he said, "Stay low I will be back tonight."

Justice and his brother were headed out the door when Linda said, "Baby be careful. If you ever try David he will kill you."

Justice looked his mother in the eyes and said. "That would be David's job to kill me because I would die for you mom."

The boys walked out of the hotel and Linda understood her son. Justice got in his truck and called David.

David picked up and said, "What's popping?"

Justice said, "I just saw mom"

David said, "Ya, so what?"

"We need to talk," Justice said.

David replied, "Meet me at the hide out at 9 pm. Where is Justin?"

Justice said, "He is right here next to me."

David said, "I will see you later," and hung up. He was thinking those two together are hell on wheels.

DAVID

On the way to Sonya's house David was coming down Cleveland Ave when he saw this fine ass girl from behind and he was like, 'dam!' David was in his white Corvette. He pulled up on the side of the girl and let his window down. When the girl turned around David was surprised to see it was fine ass Nicky.

He said, "What up girl?"

Nicky said, "I don't know." Then she looked at her body.

David started laughing and said, "You got a smart ass mouth." Nicky started smiling and David said, "Where the hell you going?"

Nicky said, "Over to my mom's house."

He asked, "You want a ride?"

She replied, "Now David don't start no shit because you know Tonya is crazy about your black ass."

David said, "You must be going to tell her."

Nicky said, "Hell no!"

David said, "Well get your ass in then."

So Nicky got in the other side while David rolled up the window and then they took off. You couldn't see in any of David's cars because of the tint. He made a left and headed out to Windsor. He was headed to the Super-8 motel and Nicky was sitting on the other side smiling.

Nicky asked, "David you always wanted to get in my pants, why?"

David said, "Because you walk like you the baddest bitch on earth."

Nicky said, "In bed I am a pro, you can bet on that."

David pulled up at the hotel and rented a room. He came back to the car and told Nicky they were in room 115. He gave her the key and told her he would be back. He went in his pocket and pulled out a fifty dollar bill, he gave it to Nicky and told her to get something to drink. David jumped in the Vett and headed to Park Street.

When David pulled up at Sonya's house she was sweeping off her front porch. David got out of the car and went to the door.

Sonya said, "You can come on in."

David stepped in and took a seat then asked, "Where is Juan?"

Sonya said, "He is in the guest room."

David opened the door and found Juan nodding off from the heroin. David said, "What the fuck is wrong with you?"

Juan said, "Nothing I just been up all night." Then he handed David a brown K-Mart bag with money in it and said, "It's about five thousand dollars short."

David said, "What's up with that?"

Juan said, "Niggas' coming at me short."

David said, "Nigga' you got to put your foot back down."

Juan said, "I will make up the loss."

David said, "Cool. I'll talk to you after you rest, because right now you're talking out of the side of your neck." David walked out of the room.

He saw Sonya on the phone and said, "Yo I need to ask you something."

Sonya put her hand up telling David to hold on. She hung up the phone and said, "What's up?"

David said, "What's popping with Juan?"

Sonya said, "He's acting like he is on something."

David said, "I'll be back later." Then he walked out the front door with a lot on his heart and mind.

David got in his car headed for Windsor to knock off Nicky. He had two blunts rolled up and ready. When he pulled up he could see Nicky peeking out the window. He knocked one time and Nicky opened the door, she had let her hair down.

David fired up the blunt and took off everything but his silk boxers. Nicky was drinking E & J and smoking that good weed. David sat on the bed and Nicky got in front of him and fell to her knees. She took David's manhood in her mouth. When David pulled out Nicky said to herself, 'no wonder Tonya's crazy about this nigga', he's nine men strong.' Nicky was excited because she had not had nothing that big. She took all her clothes off and straddled David. She let out a loud noise and she began to ride David like a wild bronco, up and down, around and around. Nicky was moving her hips rapidly, whipping that hot stuff on David. David rolled Nicky over and hit her from the back as Nicky was biting on the pillow. She was throwing it back at David when he let go inside Nicky and had on no protection.

David said, "Damn it!"

Nicky was the best he ever had. He made love to her the rest of the night. Nicky put David to sleep around 10 pm then she woke David up and said, "Boy take me home!" She was smiling and she said, "I won't do that no more with you."

David gave Nicky a thousand dollars and Nicky said, "Damn! For this kind of money we might be able to go again." Then she started laughing.

David went and took a shower and he made sure things were on point. He dropped Nicky off at her mom's house and headed to Avon where he was going to meet his two sons.

David pulled up and saw his boy's chilling. He got out of the truck and said, "What's up?"

They all went inside the house where Justice asked, "What did you do to my mom?"

David said, "Nigga' I don't answer to no one."

Justice warned, "Don't touch my mom no more."

David turned around and threw Justice into the wall and said, "What the fuck is wrong with you? Don't think I won't give you a one way ticket to hell."

Justice said, "Do what you got to do, but don't put your hands on my mom anymore!"

David saw a part of himself in his own son's eyes and he was not going to push him so he calmed down. He said, "I didn't mean to go off on you like that, we are family. You are my son and I want you to always stand up for your mom. I respect you more for that. I won't touch your mom no more, you got my word. I'm not worried about her, everything is cool. But Justice don't ever bow up at me again."

Justice said, "Yes sir."

David said, "I'm going home. I want you and Justin to bring Juan that work and meet me at my house at 6 pm."

TONYA

Tonya was on the phone talking to her friend Peaches about some bull-shit that was going around. Peaches told Tonya word was that David was going with this girl name Pam who moved down to Hartford from New York.

Tonya was going off on the phone when David walked in. He walked up behind Tonya and she turned around and said, "David don't put your fucking hands on me! Who is this bitch Pam?"

She was all in David's face. He knew the girl Pam, but he played the man roll, crazy. David went upstairs while Tonya was still raising hell. He was laughing when he picked Daisy up and started playing with her.

Tonya came up stairs and told David to get out. She called Justin's cell phone and told him to come home.

Justin pulled up in front of his mom's house. He got out and went in the house where he heard all the loud talking. Justin knew David would not hit Tonya, she was just mad.

David walked down stairs laughing and Justin said, "What is up?"

David said, "Your mom, out listening to her so called friends."

Tonya came down the steps and David turned real fast and grabbed her arm, he scared the shit out of her and she fell back. David got on top of her and started kissing her. She was trying to bite him as she was yelling telling him to stop. Justin was just standing there laughing.

David got up and Tonya told Justin, "You going to stop standing around letting someone jump on your mom?"

Justin said, "If that was not Dad he would have been dead for touching you."

That made Tonya feel good. Tonya said, "What if your dad is trying to hurt me?"

Justin said. "He is not going to hurt you because he loves you."

Tonya said, "Damn! He done brain washed you."

David said, "I am fixing to go."

Tonya said, "Don't come back."

David said, "Okay."

Justin shook his head, he said, "Mom you say that all the time."

Tonya said, "You shut up and go with him!"

Justin went upstairs to play with his little sister.

JUSTIN AND JUSTICE

Justin was riding in the rental car, he and his brother had been collecting money all day for David. Justice had been over at Rose's house all night. Rose turned out to be a gangster girl and Justin loved that about her. Justin was going to the hide out and count some of the money.

A blue car came into view and Justin turned in the parking lot and hid behind the house. The car turned behind Justin and two men jumped out with their guns pointed at Justin and Justice's heads. They had been caught slipping.

There was about three men altogether. Two of the men had on ski-masks and one was showing his fat face and looked Cuban. The men made Justin and Justice go in the house. The house had a basement that you could get out from. The man without the ski-mask made a phone call. He had called Lisa?

He said, "I have two brothers."

Lisa said, "Well do they have money?"

The man said, "Yes, lots of money."

Lisa said, "Get it all and make them tell you where the rest of it is."

The man told Lisa, We are in Avon at a hide out. The house sat off in the woods, it's a big house."

David had the house specially built. There was a lake out back of it and the basement was underground. You could go through the lake and get into the basement where it would lead you to the inside of the house.

DAVID

David was on his way to Sonya's house to see what was up with his best friend Juan. He made it there, pulled up and got out. When he walked in Juan was in the guest room on the phone. David went up the stairs where Sonya was laying on the bed watching TV. David lay on top of her and Sonya said, "Nigga' get off me."

David said "Damn it's like that?"

Sonya got up and said, "David I don't have time for games. I have someone who I am really into." She was lying but she had to because David had her head fucked up and she could not show it.

David grabbed Sonya and said, "who is the nigga'?"

Sonya started play fighting David off of her. David started kissing his way down her body, Sonya was going crazy. David went into her woman hood and Sonya started moaning loud. David went to work. Sonya had some long legs and he had her spread out like she was having a baby. Sonya started moving fast and made David move faster, they lost control and lay with their bodies joined together like Siamese twins.

Sonya said, "Damn that was great."

David lay back and looked at the sky. Sonya went to the bathroom when Juan walked upstairs and said, "What up?"

David said, "You."

Juan said, "I made up for that loss." He told David he gave Justin and Justice everything.

David said, "Well, now pass the blunt nigga."

Sonya came from the bathroom with nothing on but her bra and a thong. She saw her brother and said, "What the hell you doing in here?"

Juan was laughing and David said, "He with me."

Sonya put on her robe and went over and sat on David's lap.

Juan said, "Looks like you're in a good mood."

Sonya said, "Yeah because if I was not you would have been out of here."

David was rubbing on Sonya's legs, Juan said, "Damn man, at least wait until I leave."

David started laughing until his cell phone went off. He waited then said, "Hello."

A voice on the other end said, "David if you follow orders your two sons may live to see another day. If not I will enjoy killing them."

David picked up on the voice, it was Lisa.

Lisa said, "I have three men at your hide out house and I have three hundred thousand dollars, but I want the rest. So you tell your boys to obey and they might live." Lisa hung the phone up.

David was in a state of shock until Juan said, "Man what's wrong?"

David said, "Man Lisa has Justin and Justice at the hide out. They must have been caught slipping and somebody got the jump on them. Lisa wants more money."

Sonya was looking at David because she knew he was a fool when you took him there. David pulled out his cell phone and copied the number. He said, "Sonya call one of your friends at AT&T and get the address to this number, then call me and let me know what it's going to cost." David looked at Juan and said, "What's up?"

Juan said, "Let's go get my God son and his brother."

David called Rose, Justice's girlfriend and told her to chill and not let no one in the house, she said she wouldn't.

Juan and David were headed to a place he had not been in years. He was going to sell it but changed his mind. He just

~ 87 ~

made sure everything was kept up. It was Pa-Pe's old house, Linda had signed all the papers over to David after Sandy got killed. He pulled up at the house, got out and hit the code, then he and Juan went in the house.

It smelled fresh and David walked over to open the basement. Juan followed David down the stairs. He had never seen so many guns and bullets.

David said, "Get what you need in the time of war." David grabbed a Mac-11 and two 9 mm and a bullet proof vest.

Juan looked over at David and said, "Yo, who the other vests for?"

David said, "Tonya."

Juan replied, "Man you crazy."

David said, "When she finds out Justin is there, she's coming anyway. Don't worry she can handle herself better than 90% of the street niggas' you know."

When they got everything David pulled his car under the garage and jumped into an all blue Jimmy G.M.C. with dark tinted windows. No one knew this was David's Jeep.

When Juan and David were riding along Juan said, "I can't see Tonya handling this shit."

David said, "I know her well, I trained her."

David pulled up in front of Tonya's house, he and Juan got out and David said, "Come on in."

Tonya stopped David at the door. She said, "Can I help you?"

David said, "There is something going on."

Tonya knew David was not joking, Tonya said, "Boy come on in."

David said, "Lisa done had Justin and Justice kidnapped. They are at my house in Avon."

Tonya started crying and David got mad, he said, "We don't have time for that, let's move. I trained you better than that Tonya."

Tonya asked, "Are they still alive?"

David said, "They want money."

Juan's cell phone went off and he picked up and started talking Spanish real fast. David was mad because he couldn't understand what they were saying. Juan hung the phone up and told David the call came from Bloomfield, a house on Chestnut Road.

"Let's ride out to my house," said David.

Tonya said, "I'm going."

"Where is Daisy," David asked.

"Your mother has her so it's all good," she replied.

David said, "Let's go."

Tonya went upstairs and came back with a long wig over her head. She had on jeans and Timberland boots with her black gloves.

David led the way, he gave Tonya a vest and they headed to Avon. When David got there he started riding slow and Tonya said, "There goes the house there."

David said, "I see it, I bought this house for a reason. It's set off in the woods and has a lake behind it."

Juan said, "We use to come out here and steal bikes."

Tonya started laughing and David told them, "We're going to park the truck and walk through the woods."

David parked and they all got out with guns in hands and the bullet proof vest on. They had to climb over a pretty high fence and David said out loud, "Damn!"

Tonya said, "Boy I'm in good shape, don't worry about me. Let's not slow down the plan or change anything because of me."

When they all hit the fence Tonya was the first one on her feet and again David said, "Damn."

They walked through the woods which took longer because of the water but kept them under cover.

JUSTIN AND JUSTICE

Justin was not saying much, he and his brother were tied to a chair facing each other. The man with the mask told Justice he was going to kill him first because of his big mouth.

He turned to Justin and asked, "Where is the rest of the money?"

Justin said, "I don't know about any money."

The man hit Justin with the gun and when Justice saw the man's head next to his brother he reached out and kicked him in the face. The man with the mask was ready to shoot Justice but the man without the mask said that they would be no good dead then started speaking Spanish. Justice did not like anyone hurting his brother and he could see that Justin had a little blood running down his head.

LISA

Lisa had not told Linda about having Justin and Justice kidnapped. She needed more money bad. Buddy had been gambling in New York and had lost over a hundred thousand dollars in cash and drugs. Lisa was hot, she left Travis at his mother's house along with Bo-Bo, another one of her men that came down last night. Travis' mother stayed in Hartford and she would be gone to work. Lisa and Linda, along with Lenny, were riding around looking for David. They even drove by his mother's house on Homestead Ave but didn't see him anywhere.

DAVID'S CREW

The water was cold because the sun had gone down. It was about 8 pm and David was the first one to get in the water. He, Tonya and Juan had to swim across the lake like navy seals but they were just a team off the streets who loved each other. They made it to the other side where David told Tonya to wait in the water for a second until he opened the gate. He opened the gate and told Tonya to swim his way. She did and the water went the other way. David told Tonya to come on and she got out and walked up the hill. David opened the door to the basement of his house, it was so big you wouldn't know if someone came through the basement. They all got inside with their guns in hand.

David told everyone to move slowly. He heard a voice so he looked out the door and saw Justin lying on the floor bleeding from the head. David didn't want Tonya to see it, but it was too late, she was leaning over his shoulder. Tonya started crying in a low muffle and David said, "He's not dead."

Juan said, "There's three of them. Let's ambush their ass, just don't hit the chairs or the floor."

David said, "Tonya let's go." Tonya couldn't move. David said, "Look baby we have come too far for you to freeze up on me now."

Tonya replied, "Let me rest a minute."

They all chilled for about five minutes and Tonya said, "I'm ready. I'm behind you David."

David looked out the door with his gun pointed and Tonya on his side. The first man they saw was about asleep. David threw a spoon that hit the kitchen window and all the men ran into the kitchen. David shot the first man in the head before he knew what hit him. Tonya shot the other man dead center in the chest and Juan had about five holes in the other man.

Tonya ran to check on the boys. She untied them and they were ready, Justice went to the back and grabbed the P-89, while Justin had the street sweeper ready to go. The three men were dead and the money was all over the floor.

David hugged both of his sons and said, "2-DIE-4-140-4-ever. Lisa did this and I don't understand why Linda is still following her."

The crew took care of the bodies. They had another part of the lake with self raised gators and they were hungry. They cleaned everything up and were headed out the front door when a car pulled up. David told everyone to stop because he saw that it was Lisa in there. David and the crew laid low.

"Let her go only because Linda is in that car. We don't want to risk hurting Linda," David instructed.

Justice felt good because he loved his mother no matter what.

Lisa, Linda and Lenny pulled up at David's house in Avon but they sensed something was not right. She told Lenny, "David has been here or my men would have come out when I pulled up. She called the cell number and no one answered. Lisa slowly backed out of the drive way. She told Linda that David had done something to her men and she was not going to stop until she got her hands on him. She went to Farmington Ave and rented a room at the Hilton Hotel where she, Linda and Lenny were going to chill until they could find out what was going on.

Linda went in and ordered two rooms that connect to each other. She came back and told Lisa room 331 and 332 so they all went upstairs to chill. When they got in the room Lisa pulled out an ounce of cocaine and they started snorting and smoking some good weed.

Lisa's mind was on David. She was wondering what move he would make next. David use to always beat Lisa in Chess, now she had to think of a move that would save her life.

JUAN

Juan was telling David to chill and they would catch Lisa because her crew was falling off and she really had nowhere to hide in Hartford.

David said, "Lisa is smart and she knows some powerful people. We all got to be extra careful.

STOWE VILLAGE

David jumped in his all-white Benz and headed to the Vill. He went the back way and came in the Vill almost unseen. He parked his car up under Sherry's window on Hampton Street. He got out, covered his car up, then he grabbed two bottles of E&J and headed upstairs. He knocked on the door and after two knocks it came wide open.

The girls were deep in that bitch, Sherry, Missy, Love, Nicky, Tasha, Betty Boo and Mary Ann were all chillin. There was about ten girls in there, some David didn't know.

David walked up and said, "What's popping?"

All the girls said, "You!"

David started laughing, he saw Nicky and knew she had told her friends how he had hit that ass. Missy was looking between David's legs smiling. He sat down next to Sherry on the couch. Sherry said that David was real cool. He had knocked Sherry off one time and she fell in love, but she had to back up because Tonya was about to kill her. Nicky had to step in and cool things off because she was friends with Tonya and Sherry. Sherry still had deep feelings for David but she refused to let him see it.

David sked Sherry, "How's my baby doing?" As he put his hand on her leg.

She said, "I am cool, now get your hand off my leg."

David said, "Don't start that shit."

All the girls started laughing. David saw Nicky looking his way so he said, "What's up Nicky?"

Nicky said, "Don't make me tell you again!"

The girls started laughing even harder, they were fucking with David hard. He put some E & J in his cup and told Mary Ann to light up a blunt. Sherry put a movie on and they laid back, got high and watched King of New York.

David was all over Sherry and Missy, he was joking and making everyone laugh. All the girls liked David because he loved to have fun and plus when David was with the girls they didn't spend any money.

Sherry got up and was headed to her room when David grabbed her on the butt. Sherry looked back and said, "You know what it is, you done had it before."

Missy told David that Chad had a small crew and they were doing good getting money in a major way.

David said, "I'm glad to hear that, Chad won't talk to me for some reason and plus I don't see him much."

Missy said, "They are having a big party at the Main Tower, everyone that's somebody is going to be there."

David said, "I'm going to be there with my folks."

Sherry came out the room and flopped on David's lap. She started kissing David for real and Nicky was looking crazy. Sherry jumped up and started dancing and all the girls started showing what they got. David got on the floor and they all had a good time for old time sake.

Chapter Seven

MAIN AND TOWER

David and the boys were at Tonya's house, everyone was clean from head to toe. Tonya looked like she belonged on the cover of King Magazine. She had on a full body leather Polo suit, with matching pumps where you could see every curve and she had a perfect body. Tonya had not shown her body off for years and tonight David was going to let her show it off.

David had on an all-white silk Brooks Brother suit with white and gold Gators. Juan had on a Versace suit with white snake skins, while Justin and Justice had on army fatigues and they had big gold chains around their necks.

David told Justice to drive his Hummer and David would be driving his new champagne colored, 600 Benz, with the M.G.M. kit and 22" rims with gold dip. No one had seen the car yet, it was David's first time bringing it out. The Benz had bullet proof windows and tires.

It was 10:30 pm and David had a big V.I.P. table waiting on them with five chairs. They all had guns but were not looking for trouble. David led the way, pushing the Benz coming down Blue Hills Ave, headed to the Main Tower. When David pulled in the parking lot it was full of people from all over New York, D.C., Hartford and Boston. Everyone was laughing, drinking and checking out who had the baddest ride and baddest bitch. The cars were lined up like on soul train, moving slow down one lane trying to park.

The Benz cost David a hundred grand, so that spoke for itself, plus he had it cleaned. When the crowd saw the car every mouth came open and the noise stopped. You couldn't see in the Benz but David could see you. People were pointing and hoes were yelling because a sign flashed across the window that said, 'bullet proof.' The black Hummer was right behind the Benz and everyone knew it was Justice.

David and Tonya got out of the Benz and nigga's were going crazy. Tonya was at David's side and hoes were looking hard with hate in their eyes. David and his crew walked in to the Main & Tower, the club was packed but it was big, everyone could see David and his crew. They all went to the V.I.P. section and sat at the table that they had waiting on them. Drinks started coming from everywhere but Justin and Justice couldn't drink but Tonya was drinking a little.

David was looking around when he spotted Sherry, Mary Ann, Love, Black girl and Nicky. He told Tonya, "I will be back, let me get the girls a drink on you. Justin, you and Justice come with me."

Juan was chilling, talking to a fine ass red bone.

Tonya said, "I'm cool."

David walked over to the table with his two boys at his side. When he got to the table Sherry said, "What's up David?"

David said, "My girl, Tonya told me to buy all of you a drink on her."

All the girls looked over at Tonya's table and waved."

Justin and Justice were smiling and looking at Missy and Love. Justin was always hot on Love but she was fast and plus she was a sack chaser. David told the girls to be cool and walked off. Justin and Justice were checking out some twins, they were from New Haven, but they hung out in Hartford. Brandy and Candy, two fine ass twins. Justin was trying to talk to Brandy and Justice was hitting on Candy.

David walked back to the table and hugged Tonya, he was sitting in her lap facing her and kissing her on the mouth. Everyone was looking at David because he was a well-known dealer in Hartford. He was once the Heartbeat Don and now he was living the good life.

Tonya and David went to the dance floor. Tonya was dancing all over David and she was moving her body like a stripper. Tonya was the baddest girl in the club, hands down. As for the ladies, there were a lot of fine hoes but they didn't count. The music slowed down and David danced with Tonya a little more and then Tonya was ready to go home, the drinks had her horny. She was sucking on David's neck and kissing him hard on the mouth.

When the song stopped David had to make Tonya sit down, she was off the chain. David was chilling when he looked around and saw the girl Pam from New York. He was hoping Tonya did not see her.

Justin and Justice were back at the table when Chad walked over and said what's up. He was clean and looking good. David shook his hand, Chad still had it in his head that David had killed his little brother about that money.

David was talking to Justin then he looked up to see Tonya and Pam face to face and a crowd was standing around. He jumped up and ran over to Tonya.

That wild bitch Pam was talking shit so David told her to chill. Tonya was telling Pam she would beat her ass then two girls grabbed Pam while David was holding Tonya. Justin was standing next to his mom and when the girl let Pam go, she ran to jump Tonya from the back but Justin turned around and knocked her out. The other girl started talking shit to Justin but Justice came over and slapped about three of them. He grabbed his brother and they headed out of the club.

David and Tonya jumped in the car and headed home with Justin and the boys right behind them. When they got home everyone was laughing.

Tonya went upstairs and Juan went and found a room. Justice and Justin woke Juan up because David was not letting them back out. David went upstairs with Tonya and got in bed. Tonya was already asleep so David just hugged her and went to sleep with all his clothes on.

Tonya was his baby and one day he was going to marry her sexy ass.

LINDA

Linda called Justice on his cell phone and told him where to meet her. Justice told his mother he was bringing David. Linda said she didn't care as long as she got to see him.

Linda told Justice to meet her at the Hilton Hotel in downtown Hartford, room 221 Friday. Justice said okay and hung up.

He called and told David the news. David said cool and that they would both go just in case Linda had done flipped for that bitch Lisa.

DAVID AND JUSTICE

David was driving his Corvette and he was driving fast. Justice was in the passenger seat looking crazy.

David asked, "You can't drive like that?"

Justice said, "No, not yet but soon! Justin and I got to practice on my turns and spin a rounds."

They pulled up at the Hilton and David said, "Watch everyone and we will meet up at her room."

Justice made it to the room and hadn't seen anything to make him change the plan so he knocked on the door.

Linda opened the door, she saw her son and hugged him with a big smile.

David waited about ten minutes before he knocked on the door. Justice opened it and David said, "It's cool."

Linda came to the door and told David, "I love my son, so you don't have to do all that shit, I would never hurt him."

David said, "Well Lisa had him kidnapped the other week, did you know that?"

Linda said, "What? No that bitch did not!"

Justice explained to his mom what had happened. Linda had tears in her eyes, she could not believe Lisa would do her child like that.

David walked over and looked out the window. Linda was talking to Justice and watching David at the same time. David walked up on Linda and kissed her on the mouth. She kissed David back then he went back and stood at the window. David was still in love with Linda, even after she had crossed him and that was rare. David had no hate for Linda, he was just hurt because she was his better half before Tonya and all the other girls. But David had a child by Linda, a son. Not a weak ass son but a gangster boy who was not going to let anything happen to his mother and David loved that. Growing up he was the same way about his mother Gail.

Linda laughed and talked to Justice for over an hour. She and David had small talk and she kept trying to show David her ass.

When Justice went to the bathroom Linda said, "David you tried to hurt me last time, but I liked it. Next time I'm going to be ready. I still love you.

David started laughing just as Justice came out of the bathroom. David told Linda to stay low key and stay one step ahead of Lisa. Then David and Justice left the hotel to go chill.

TONYA

Tonya was at home raising hell with Justin. She was telling him that he needed to get a job before he ended up in prison. Justin was her first love and everyone had spoiled him growing up. He was lying on the floor playing his play station and Tonya walked over and stood above him.

She said, "Boy do you hear me?"

Justin said, "Yes mom chill!"

Tonya replied, "Chill my foot! Monday I want you out looking for a job."

Tonya was hot. Justin didn't talk back because she would pick up anything and hit him with it. In David's family, respect was part of growing up. You had to respect your Mom. Justin was mad and Tonya knew it.

He went to his room and closed the door.

DAVID

David had dropped Justice off at his girlfriend Rose's house. He went to his Mom's house and chilled out in his old room for about an hour. He got up, took a shower and headed to Tonya's house. When he pulled up Justin was out back washing his car.

David got out of his car and said, "What's up man?"

Justin walked over to his dad and said, "Mom is tripping about me not having a job!"

Justin and his dad were like brothers. David walked in the house and went off on Tonya. He said, "You need to chill the fuck out!"

Tonya said, "Who the fuck you talking too?"

David was up in her face. Tonya was tough, but to have her way all she had to do was start crying. She started crying but David still told her that she had been acting crazy lately.

Tonya walked off and went to her room. She turned the music up loud and closed the door.

Justin was loving that because he was fixing to go see his girlfriend Tiffany. David told Justin to be careful over on Albany Ave. Justin had his gun in his waist and had the Lexus looking good. He headed to his girl's house riding high.

David went into the other room and went to sleep. He said to himself, 'To hell with making up to Tonya.'

CHAD

Chad was building a big crew in Stowe Village. Lisa and Linda were still bringing him drugs and he was rolling well. Chad was telling one of his workers, Ta-Ta, that Juan was still his boy but he had to stop working on the block.

Ta-Ta said, "Man Juan been around a long time, how you going to stop him?"

"Nothing last forever!" Chad said.

He had been in touch with Red-Man and had the big head now. He was trapping out of 69 Hampton Street on the 1st floor. He was making good money, but that was where Juan was born and raised. All Juan ever knew was the Vill.

JUAN

Juan had just left his Mom's house and was walking down the breeze way headed to get a sack of weed when he saw two nigga's come out of the hallway. He reached for his gun but it was too late, a nigga' already had a 357 to his face.

Juan put his hands up and said, "What's up?"

He knew Slim and Red-Man. He stayed on Garden Street and was known for robbing.

Ta-Ta spoke first, he said, "Yo Juan, no more selling dope in the Vill. We are not going to hurt you this time but nigga' we catch you again we're going to kill you."

Red-Man took Juan's gun and pushed him out of the way. Juan still had his hands up when the two men went into the building. He was so hurt he had tears in his eyes.

The first building Juan went into was Sherry's. He knocked on her door and she let him in and said, "What the fuck wrong with you knocking that hard!"

Juan said, "Nothing I need to use your phone."

Sherry said, "Go ahead, I'm going back to bed. Let me know when you leave so I can get up and lock the door."

Juan got on the phone and called David, who was his best friend and brother.

David was half asleep when Juan said, "Bro I need to see you. I'm over at Sherry's house, come low key," and he hung up.

David knew something was wrong when Juan said come low key. That meant don't be seen. David jumped up, put on some jeans and a shirt, grabbed his 9 mm and helmet. He reached over to the dresser and got the motorcycle keys, he was going to ride the 1100 Kawasaki today.

David headed out of the house and got on the bike headed for Stowe Village the back way. He made it to the projects without being noticed and parked close to Sherry's building. He got off the bike with his helmet still on. When he got inside the building he took it off and went to Sherry's door. David knocked twice and Juan knew it was him. He got up and opened the door.

David walked in looking crazy. He asked Juan, "What's up?"

Juan told David about Red-Man and Ta-Ta pulling a gun on him and telling him he can't sell any more drugs in the Vill.

David was mad, he said, "That punk Red-Man ain't from the Vill! Ta-Ta ain't no Vill nigga' either. We will see about this. They both work for Chad so he called the shots."

Juan said, "Man I can't believe Chad is letting money change him."

David said, "Man it's a dirty game. Who is here in the house?"

Juan said, "Sherry opened the door for me, then she went back to bed."

David told Juan to hold his 9 mm. David opened the door and saw Sherry laying on the bed asleep. David went into the room and laid on top of Sherry. She rolled over fast and told David to stop. When she rolled over her and David were face to face. Good thing when she got up and opened the door for Juan she brushed her teeth before she laid back down because David was putting his tongue down her throat. Sherry was starting to get hot so David went to reaching for his pants. Sherry was moving.

David got his manhood out and eased Sherry's panties to the side. She was so wet when the head of his manhood touched her, it slid right in. Sherry was now holding David for dear life as he was pumping her hard and fast. She was moaning loud and telling David to slow down. He picked her legs up and went to work. He knew Juan could hear them in the other room, but he didn't care. Sherry had some good sex, it had been over a year since David had some of that. He was about to let loose and he started moving fast as Sherry locked her legs around his back. He let a load off inside Sherry's womanhood.

David looked down at Sherry, she was smiling because it felt good to have a thug give you love. He said, "I got to go."

Sherry said, "I know."

She got up and went to the bathroom while David went back in the front room with Juan.

Juan said, "Boy you beat that pussy down!"

David started laughing then Sherry came out of the bathroom and said, "I heard you Juan."

Juan said, "Girl I ain't said shit."

David told Juan the plan about Red-Man and Ta-Ta, then he told Sherry to give him a key to her house. She was glad to do that because she wanted some more of David.

David and Juan left the house and locked the door. David jumped on the motorcycle with Juan on back and headed to the Vill the back way. When they got on Main Street David let the 1100 roll. He pulled up on Enfield Street over at Pam's house. She had two of David's cars and some guns at her crib. She also had a safe with some of David's money.

Pam was a good woman, with no kids. She had never married and had a good job as a doctor's assistant in downtown Hartford. She had two hundred and fifty thousand dollars in the house, a brand new Escalade truck and a brand new big girl Lexus. Pam was 5', about one hundred fifty pounds, red-bone, long black hair, nice tits that stood up on their own and a fat round ass. On top of it all, Pam was a gangster girl. David had put her to the test and trained her very well.

When David pulled up, Pam came to the door. He and Juan got off of the motorcycle and went in the house. It was a big French made home with thick grey carpet all over. It had black handmade leather furniture in the living room and a fire place in all the bedrooms. All the furniture had polo covers and the Jacuzzi in the living room was shaped like a heart. Pam had on a pink baby phat pajama suit, with a pink thong.

David walked up and kissed her. She was another one who was in love with David. Juan saw how fine Pam really was. They had met about two years ago when Juan was dating Pam's sister Belinda, but Belinda had gone back to New York to take care of their mother back home.

Pam told David that she was getting ready for work.

David said, "Cool." Then he and Juan went to the basement where David gave Juan a 9 mm and said, "Tonight we will pay Red-Man a visit at his house on Garden Street. We're going to see what the beef is!"

He pulled out a blunt and he and Juan got high while drinking on some E & J. It was getting late, David said, "We are riding in the Chevy Impala because it's low key. Juan, this is going to either stop the problem or start some more shit."

Enfield Street was right next to Garden Street so the ride was short. David parked the car then he and Juan walked to Red-Man's house. When they got close David looked in the window and saw Red-Man. He was laid up with some girl. David saw a crack head on the street and called her over.

He said, "You want to make fifty dollars?"

The crack head said, "Hell yeah, what you want, head or ass?"

David said, "No! No! All I want is for you to knock on a door and when someone answers you can go."

The crack head knocked on Red-Man's door and it took about ten minutes before Red-Man came to the door talking shit. "Bitch what do you want this time of the night?"

He looked up and saw two men with ski masks on. David had the 44 to his head as Juan busted in, Red-Man was scared to death.

He was acting like a bitch when David said, "What's up bad boy?"

Red-Man said, "Yo I'm just chilling with my girl, I ain't got no problem."

Juan came out of the room with the girl, she was naked. David told Red-Man to sit down on the couch, Red-Man was looking crazy and David said, "Go head and try something. Make a country break so I can kill your ass before God gets the news."

Red-Man was shaking but the girl was calm like she had been through this shit before.

David walked up and slapped the shit out of Red-Man with the gun. The girl started crying and David told Juan take her and put some clothes on her.

David said, "By the way what's your name?"

The girl said, "Jessica Shaw."

"Where do you live?" He asked.

She said, "Westland Street."

David said, "Damn you stay right near my boy Todd. I might pay you a visit sometime. Jessica what do you see in this coward Red-Man?"

She didn't say anything and Juan let her go get dressed.

David told her, "We are going to let you go, but Red-Man, I'm going to show you something." Then David shot him in both knees.

His knees popped out like a baby's do at birth. Blood was everywhere and David told Red-Man, "We are Vill niggas, don't forget that."

He and Juan walked out of the house. They laid low in the car before they moved. They saw the girl running out of the house crying. David started the car and he and Juan went to see what Ta-Ta was about.

TA-TA

Ta-Ta was at the Trap working. He was laughing and telling Chad how Red-Man and him punked out Juan and told him he couldn't sell no more drugs in the Vill. Chad was smiling on the outside, but deep down he knew Ta-Ta had fucked up by pulling a gun on David's best friend Juan and not using it. Ta-Ta was getting off in about thirty minutes, he said he was going to get laid and chill.

David and Juan were across the breeze way waiting on Ta-Ta to come out of the dope house. After about forty-five minutes of waiting they saw Ta-Ta walking out of the house counting money and headed their way. They both put their ski masks on and were waiting. When Ta-Ta got close David jumped from the hallway and grabbed him with the gun to his head.

Ta-Ta had a gun on him but it was no good, David had the jump on him. Juan reached over and took the gun off Ta-Ta then made him walk up the hill in back of the Vill where the school was.

It was dark and Ta-Ta was scared. Juan had went and got the car while David was walking with Ta-Ta. He asked David what was going on and David said, "Shut the fuck up bitch boy!"

Juan pulled up and David told Ta-Ta to get in, he still had the gun pointed at Ta-Ta's chest. They drove to Kenny Park where David got out of the car and told Ta-Ta to follow orders.

David asked, "Who sent you at Juan?"

Ta-Ta said, "Man it was Chad."

David tied Ta-Ta to a pine tree and cut his tongue out then put two shots in his head. David and Juan jumped in the car and headed out of town to chill. They went to New Haven and rented a room at the Courtyard Hotel where they were going to chill for a day or two. When they got to the room they smoked and drank, talking about what was next for them.

The next day David was asleep when Juan woke him up and showed him the channel 3 news. A city worker was cleaning up and found the body of a young man in Kenny Park. He was naked and tied to a tree with his tongue cut out. He also had two shots to his head. In Hartford they found a young man in his home with both his knees blown off. They believed the crimes were connected somehow.

CHAD

Chad was lying on the bed with his girl Melissa when he saw the news.

Melissa said, "Baby that's Ta-Ta!"

Chad yelled, "He just left me last night!"

Melissa said, "Do they know who did it?"

"I don't know but they're the police, we may never know. The streets always know what time it is though. I'm going to go to Red-Man's Mom's house to see what's up."

Red-Man was now in a wheelchair until they could order him some special legs to walk on. Chad went to Red-Man's house feeling bad. He knew David had done that shit and now Chad was forced to respond. He pulled up at Red-Man's house and got out. He walked in and Red-Man was lying down on the couch.

"What's up?" Chad asked.

Red-Man smiled and said, "Nothing man, time caught up with me."

Chad said, "How did you slip?"

Red-Man told Chad, "Those nigga's had ski masks on and they meant what they said."

Chad replied, "Man they found Ta-Ta in Kenny Park with his tongue cut out and two shots in the head."

Red-Man said, "Who could be that cold hearted?"

"It ain't but one nigga' cold hearted like that. His name is David Thomas, AKA Lil-D," Chad said. He told Red-Man that he and David grew up together as best friends. He told Red-Man that David was a killer and had no mercy on those who went against him.

DAVID AND JUAN

David and Juan were riding on the highway headed back to Hartford, David had a lot on his mind. He and Juan were talking about the old days in the Vill. David pulled into his mom's back yard blocking Justice's Hummer in. He and Juan got out and went inside the house where Gail was playing cards with some of her female friends.

David said hello to everyone, the women was checking David and Juan out. Justice was in David's old bed room asleep and David walked in and jumped on his back.

Justice jumped up ready to play, he said, "Daddy where you been?"

David said, "Damn boss I been out of town."

They all started laughing. David fired up a blunt and closed the door. Justice was telling David that Tonya called and she was mad. She was asking Justice if David had been over at Pam's house. Someone had seen David and called Tonya.

David told Justice, "Fuck that, Tonya is getting a little too damn bossy. I'm going to stay here at Mom's or at Pam's house and that he could stay with him."

Juan said, "Man you and Tonya always start this shit."

"Man Tonya is spoiled and wants me to stay at home all day. If she isn't fucking with me it's Justin," David replied. He told Justice to chill with Juan that he was going over to Tonya's house to see what was up. He did not have time for this shit.

TONYA'S HOUSE

Tonya's two aunts were visiting her from Yonker's, NY. They were loving Tonya's house and all the nice cars she and David had along with the 64" TV, the play station and all the good food.

Tonya's Aunt Debbie was fine as hell, but she had twin daughters that were twenty-two years of age. Sandy and Candy could give Tonya a run for her money. David had known them for years, Debbie's husband was cool. His name was Fred and he and David use to smoke weed together.

David pulled up in the yard, parked the Chevy Impala and got out. Everyone was looking at him and Tonya was rolling her eyes. David's 600 Benz was covered up in the back yard, and that's what he was going to leave in. Mrs. Weaver and Tonya's sister were looking crazy when David walked over and said hello to everyone.

They all started smiling and spoke back.

Tonya said, "Go back where you been nigga'!"

David said, "Girl I've been over at my mother's house!"

Tonya walked over and got in David's face and said, "Nigga' before that you was over at that bitch Pam's house! Now Lie!"

David said, "Chill!"

Tonya slapped David in the face and he started laughing.

Mrs. Weaver said, "Tonya that was wrong."

David walked off and went in the house. He went upstairs, took a shower and changed clothes. He put on an all-white polo suit with some Jordan's and a Jordan cap. He grabbed his 44 and went out the back door. He was mad because his eye was red from Tonya's finger nails hitting it.

David uncovered the Champagne color Benz and walked around it. Everyone's mouth dropped open, the car was clean and expensive.

Tonya said, "David come here." David open the door to get in the car and Tonya said, "David I'm not playing come here."

David got out and met Tonya halfway. She said, "Don't touch me no more and you should get all your shit out of my house because the locks will be changed."

David said, "Okay," then jumped in the Benz burning rubber.

Tonya had tears in her eyes. Her Aunt Debbie said, "Tonya you need to stop listening to your so called friends."

Tonya said, "They don't lie on David all the time."

Debbie said, "I bet none of them live or ride like you, every day for over ten years."

Tonya could not say anything, Debbie said, "Be smart Tonya, David is in the streets but he is good to you and if he's doing something and you have never caught him that means he has respect for you."

Mrs. Weaver said, "I done told that girl the same thing over and over. I use to hate David but now I love him like the son I never had. He is the only man I let stay in my house and lay up with Tonya."

Tonya's cousin said, "That nigga' got it going on. He could have whatever girl he wants."

Tonya said, "But he doesn't know what comes with them girls. I'm real and I got that fire!"

Her cousin rolled her eyes and could not say a word.

JUSTICE AND JUAN

Justice and Juan were riding down Barber Street headed to get something to eat. David was on their ass in his Benz. They turned in the plaza and David was right behind them. They were getting Chinese food and Justice and Juan jumped out waiting on David. When he got out they all started laughing and went into the Chinese place where they ordered some food.

They were sitting down eating when Chad and about three of his boys walked in the place looking hard. David had his 44 in his waist, so he was not worried. He knew Justice was strapped.

Chad wanted to pick on Juan for some reason. He said, "Yo! Juan why don't I see you anymore? Is the Vill too rough for you Boy?" Chad and his boys started laughing.

David didn't saying anything, he was calm and still eating. Juan was just chilling, he didn't get off on no bullshit.

Chad looked at Justice and Justice looked back at him hard. One of Chad boys said, "Yo! What's up with that nigga'?"

Justice said, "No nigga' what's up with you?"

The man was heading over to the table when David jumped up and put the 44 in his mouth. Chad was watching as David looked at him and said, "Nigga' if you want war with Juan look for me. We will be at Fred D. Morris School yard hill at 8 pm. Bring whatever, I'll show you war. No rules Chad, I will kill your whole family and shoot up their graves."

Chad was shocked. David slapped the man in the mouth with the gun and blood got all over Chad's white suit. David and his boys walked out with blood in their eyes, it was a civil war.

CHAD

Chad told the two men on his side, "That was David and he's a cold blooded nigga', but don't worry we are going to take him to war on his own land."

Chad got on the phone and called Bobby in New York. He told him David wanted war and that's what it was going to be.

Lisa got on the phone and said, "Chad please don't fuck with David!"

Chad said, "I grew up with that nigga' fuck him! He wants war that's what it is."

Lisa said, "It's all about the money and you got to have your money and game right."

Chad said, "I got both on point, so it is what it is!"

DAVID

David was telling Justice and Juan that Chad wanted war and they were going to get his ass. Justice had put his Hummer up at his Grandmother Gail's house. While they were riding in David's Benz, David saw Lisa in a rental car with New York plates, she was alone. David told the boys they were going to follow her.

They followed Lisa to Water Berry where she went to a little hotel down in the woods. David knew the hotel, back in the days it was called the Honey Corn Hide Out. Lisa got out and went to room 8. David was waiting on her, he got out of the car and told Justice and Juan to come behind him but move slow.

They had the room blocked, all they needed now was to get up in there. This was David's first time in some years getting this close to killing Lisa. He looked in the window of room 8 and saw Lisa lying in the Jacuzzi like a queen. He picked the lock on the back door and they all walked in. Lisa was still laid back in the Jacuzzi and David was moving like a cat. He made his way to Lisa and was right behind her.

He said, "Hello bitch!"

Lisa turned around and tried to jump out of the Jacuzzi but David and Juan grabbed her. She tried to scream but David had his hand over her mouth. David told Justice to get a towel and David put the towel around Lisa's mouth and tied her up. Lisa didn't have any clothes on.

David said, "I told you it was just a matter of time." He started laughing.

Lisa was looking at David hard but she was not crying. She still had a nice body and a pretty face.

David looked Lisa in her eye and asked, "Why? Why did you cross me?"

Lisa couldn't talk all she could do was listen.

David said, "It was 2-DIE-4 bitch. You broke a code."

He slapped Lisa in the face real hard but Lisa didn't cry. David told Juan to go turn the stove on and get him a knife. That was when Lisa started crying because she knew David would kill her without thinking about it. Justice came up and David told him to go chill in the back room. Juan came back with the knife and gave it to David. He told Juan to hold Lisa. David wrote 2-DIE-4 across Lisa's chest. She was screaming and crying as her flesh started to burn. David took his gun out and beat Lisa in the head. Blood was everywhere and David was losing it until Justice ran up and grabbed him.

Lisa's nose was broken and she was out of it.

David kicked her in the face and said, "You are going to suffer."

David told the boys, "Let's go and leave this bitch to die.

LISA

Lisa could hear the knocks on the door but she was fading in and out of consciousness. She made it to the door and opened it. Lenny grabbed her and she fell out.

Lenny called the other two men in and they put Lisa in the car and took her to the hospital. Lisa had lost a lot of blood, the doctor said she would have died in ten more minutes if it was not for Lenny finding her.

Lisa couldn't talk for a week, she was in a light coma and when she came out the only person she wanted to see was Linda. Linda went by to see her best friend, she was hurt. The hospital staff was nice and they had private guards watching Lisa. When Linda walked in the room Lisa had tears in her eyes.

They hugged and Linda said, "Baby I am sorry about what happened. That nigga' David is a monster and I mean he's a cold hearted man."

Lisa said, "Linda tell Chad don't do what he is thinking about doing to David because if he slips David will make him suffer. Girl I told Chad and all he said was, its war!

DAVID

David, Justice, Justin and Juan were in a blue minivan which was loaded with weapons, Ak-47, two Mac-11 and a submachine gun. They were waiting on Chad and his crew, if anyone showed up that was a sign that war had started.

David heard some shots and saw some nigga's running their way. David and his crew lit the fire up. They fired the AK-47 and P-89. They had too many weapons for the little crew Chad had. They ran down the hill into the Vill and shot Chad's dope house up, his cars and whatever else got in their way. Bullet holes were everywhere. People were running for cover, crying and yelling.

Chapter Eight

AFTER-MATH

The next day both the shooting in the school yard and in Stowe Village were all over the news. The F.B.I. were riding around because of the bullet holes they found that had knocked bricks out of the side of the building.

The people in Stowe Village were crying out because no one had ever come inside of the Vill and put them on the defense. The guys in the Vill were running scared because they knew David had grown up there and he knew all the hiding spots.

CHAD

Chad was scared as hell, Linda had told him what David had done to Lisa. He told Linda to chill with the dope for now because the block was hot and money was going to be slow.

DAVID

Rose had called Lisa and told her that Justice was with David. No one knew Rose was Miguel's daughter but Lisa. They sent Rose to Hartford to get up under David by messing with his baby son Justice. Rose was a killer and she was waiting on the say so to kill David. She and Lisa use to meet at the most expensive hotels where no one would notice them together, they put on wigs to change their looks.

JUSTICE

Justice had got a call from Linda so he broke off from the boys and got in his Hummer, headed for the Super 8 Motel to meet his mother. Rose had told Justice she was going to be out of town. When Justice got to the Super 8, Linda was standing on the second floor looking down at her son and smiling.

Justice got out of the Hummer and went upstairs. He hugged his mom and they went in the room and chilled out. Linda was telling Justice to be careful. She was telling her son some real street game, David had trained her very well years ago.

"Baby street wars have no rules, don't trust no one. Money will make a poor nigga' change," Linda told him.

Justice said, "Mom I'm in this game and I don't trust. I won't put trust in any niggas'." Then he fixed up a blunt and they smoked.

"Lisa done lost her mind, she told Justice what David did to her," said Linda.

Justice wasn't going tell his mother that he had been there. He was lying back and his cell phone started ringing. He picked up and it was his daddy checking on him. Justice told David where he was and who he was with then David told Justice he was on his way over and hung up.

DAVID

David was turning off Main Street headed over the bridge to the Super 8 where he could meet Justice and maybe get with Linda on the side. He pulled up and Justice was looking out the window. He hadn't told his mother that David was coming over.

David was headed up the stairs when Justice opened the door to let David know where he was. David walked in the room and sat down on the couch. Linda was in the back room and when she came out she was surprised.

~ 115 ~

"Damn!" She said and began to smile.

She had on a pair of hot pink shorts with a silk shirt. Her hair was done and looking good. Justice started laughing and Linda said, "Okay Demon!"

Then David was laughing too.

Justice jumped up and said, "I'll be right back, I need to check on something." Then he walked out the door.

David lit up a blunt and was watching TV when Linda walked to the back room and came back with her shoes off. She sat next to David on the couch and they watched New Jack City together and chilled.

David moved close to Linda and she started laughing. He leaned over and started kissing her and she responded to him.

Linda started licking on David's neck and pulling his shirt up, sucking on his chest. She undid his pants and pulled out his manhood. She was sucking and licking on David like a porn star while David laid on the couch enjoying himself with the blunt in his mouth. Linda got up and pulled down her shorts then she got on top of David and rode him like a cowgirl. She was moving fast, moaning and telling David how much she loved him.

David got up, bent her over and entered her from the back. Linda was wet as a river. He couldn't last long and he started moving fast. He let a load off in Linda and started sucking on the back of her neck. Linda looked back at David and smiled.

They went to the bedroom and made love for about two hours then went to sleep in each other's arms.

CHAD

Chad had gone to his friends and told them that he and David were at war.

Justice was riding down the street and spotted a car with about three heads in it. The car turned and started following him but the Hummer-H-2 took off fast and Justice was a damn good driver. He was doing speeds of up to a 100-MPH but the car was close and he could see Chad was the driver. They looked right at each other and at that moment Chad knew he had to catch David's son. Justice picked up his cell phone and called David.

David answered, "What's popping?"

"Dad Chad is chasing me, him and two other nigga's that are in the car with him," Justice told him.

"Come to the Super 8, Linda and I will be waiting," said David.

David woke Linda up and told her that Chad was chasing Justice. He jumped up and grabbed his 357 magnum. Linda got her 9 mm off the table then she and David headed down stairs to the parking lot where they waited to surprise Chad.

Justice was fixing to turn into the Super 8. He made a sharp turn and went off into the grass, he lost control but stayed on point and got things back under control.

Chad was thinking that they had Justice but when he turned into the parking lot, David came out shooting. Chad saw him and slammed on brakes. He saw that Linda was also shooting so Chad took off then stopped and his two men got out. They let several shots off as they got out.

Justice pulled the AK-47 out and sprayed towards Chad and his crew. They jumped back and took cover fast.

David told Justice to follow him as he went to the car. Linda cleared the room out and jumped in the car with them and they headed to Enfield, Connecticut to rent another room. Justice was right behind David when they got to Enfield and turned into the Courtyard Hotel. David told Linda to go get a double room so Linda got out and went to the front office while David and Justice sat in the parking lot talking.

Linda came back and said, "We are in room 424 on the 4th floor."

After they all got into the room David said to Linda, "It's a long road but one day it's going to end."

Linda said, "Lisa's got some men on the way. I just want to get out of all this shit."

Justice was listening to his mother tell David how much she really loved him but that she knew things wouldn't ever be the same.

David said, "Linda just lay low. I'm going to run Lisa out of town, but first I need to make some phone calls to New York and get a back ground check on Rose. There's just something about her I don't trust.

JUSTIN

Justin was riding late chilling, coming from his girlfriend's house on Albany Ave. He had smoked a blunt and was drinking so he was driving slowly when he noticed someone in a black Blazer was on his tail. He hit the Lexus and sped up but the blazer was fast. It hit Justin's bumper and the Lexus spun out of control.

He ended up in a ditch when four men got out of the Blazer and fired about twenty rounds into his car. He couldn't do anything but ball up and pray, he was hit but he refused to die. He started fading in and out of conscious and thought about all the things he had done in life. He thought about Cornbread, his first murder and all the money he had seen. His baby sister came to mind, his brother Justice, his daddy, his mother and his two grandmothers. Justin let out a few tears, he was fighting to stay alive. He could hear some noise outside the car, it was the men making sure he didn't came out of the car. Justin stayed still until he passed out.

Two ladies were on their way to work and saw the car in the ditch. One of the ladies grabbed her phone and called 911 for some help. The police came, along with the ambulance.

Justin had lost a lot of blood and when he got to the hospital they took him right to surgery to remove the bullets that were in him. No one knew who Justin was because his ID was in the car.

LISA

Lisa and Rose were at the hotel when Lisa's main man Lenny called her.

She said, "What's up?"

Lenny told her, "They shot one of David sons and they think he's dead."

"You are crazy! Are you sure it's one of David sons?" Lisa asked.

"Yes we followed him in his Lexus. He never saw us, we were in the special built Blazer, its super-fast," Lenny said and started laughing.

Lisa said, "Lenny listen to me, you and the other three men need to lay low. Go to a hotel in Bloomfield and I will come talk to you." She hung up.

Lisa told Rose the news, "Rose, David is fixing to go crazy when he find out about his son. You should lay low because David is not going to stop until he gets his man or men.

DAVID

David made a phone call to New York to an old gangster friend name Joe Taylor aka Big J. Joe, had pull everywhere. He knew how to find out dirt on anyone.

David said, "Joe I need you to find something out for me."

"What is it young gangsta?" Joe asked.

He said, "I need to know all about Rose Freedo. She's Puerto Rican or Cuban."

Joe replied, "That isn't a problem where did she move here from?"

"She came down to Hartford from New York," David told him.

"Call me back in about two hours," he said.

TONYA

Tonya was watching late night love stories around one am when the phone started ringing. She said, "Damn! Who is this," and answered the phone.

On the other end she heard a white male voice. The man said, "Ma'am is this Tonya Weaver?"

Tonya said, "This is she."

"Ma'am you need to come down to the hospital, your son has been in an accident," the man said.

Tonya's first question was, "Is he alive?"

The man said, "Ma'am you need to get here soon."

"Where is he?" She asked.

He said, "On Blue Hill Ave, Saint Francis Hospital."

Tonya was crying and out of control when she called her mother and told her the news about Justin. Mrs. Weaver told Tonya she would meet her there then Tonya hung up and called Gail and told her. Gail and Jesse jumped up and headed to the hospital, Gail was crying. Tonya grabbed Daisy and a gun and headed to the hospital herself.

When she got there Betty was crying, Tonya hugged her and told her it was going to be okay, trust in God. She told Tonya to call Yolanda to pick up Daisy so Tonya called and told her the news and asked if she could come get the baby."

Yolanda asked, "Does David know?"

Tonya said, "No we can't get ahold of him anywhere."

"I will get in touch with David," Yolanda said.

Jasmine was also there and crying badly.

DAVID

David was lying next to Linda and Justice was asleep when his beeper went off. He jumped up fast to see the number and he saw that it was his baby sister, Yolanda's number with 911 next to it. He woke Justice up and called Yolanda. She answered on the first ring and told her brother that Justin had been shot real bad and might not make it. David was yelling asking Yolanda where he was. Justice was standing by listening with tears in his eyes for his brother as David told Linda to chill there.

David and Justice were getting dressed when the phone started ringing. David knew it was Joe from New York because no one else had that number.

He picked up the phone and said, "What's popping?"

Joe said, "Rose Freedo is from New York. She's 18 years old and she's Miguel's daughter. She was a part of his crime family."

David couldn't believe what he was hearing, he told Joe, "Thank you. I'll put you two stacks on the wire."

Joe replied, "Thanks," then hung up.

David's mind was gone. He and his son jumped in Justice's Hummer H-2 and headed to Saint Francis hospital on Blue Hill Ave to check on his other son Justin. While they were riding David told Justice the news about Rose being sent to Hartford to kill him.

"Lucky she didn't kill you," David said.

"That bitch! I'll take care of her," Justice responded.

David said, "Don't let her know, but take care of her. She broke the code 2-DIE-4."

Justice had other important matters on his mind right now, he was thinking about his big brother.

They pulled into the hospital parking lot and jumped out. David saw all his family there, the people he really had love for.

Tonya's family was also in the emergency room waiting on the doctor to come out with the news. Tonya was still crying so David went over and hugged her.

David said, "Justin is strong, he isn't going anywhere, there is too much out here waiting on him."

LISA

Rose and Lisa called Lenny then headed to Bloomfield to meet with the crew and talk about the next plan. Lisa had some more stuff she wanted to do like find out why she had not heard from Linda in three days. Something was just not right with that. She said to herself, 'either she's dead or she's back with David.' That would mean she would have to change everything.

Rose was rolling with Lisa, she was a cold blooded killer. Rose had killed six people before she turned 16 years old.

They pulled up at the Howard Johnson Hotel on Bloomfield where Lenny came out and met them. He told Lisa face to face, word for word what happened.

Lenny said, "if he's alive he is a lucky nigga'."

Rose and Lisa went to the room where the other three men were sitting down. Lisa knew them well, they were some killers. Lisa and Rose were standing there when Lisa told them to catch David.

"Hold him until I get there or kill him on the spot and bring his head back so I can make sure it's him," she said.

She gave all the men up to date photos of David then explained to them that if they slipped David would make them pay.

"You can't ask the one's before you because all of them are dead and they died horrible deaths," Lisa said.

Rose said. "I'm going to trick David to come to a place where I can meet him. Then I'm going to call Lenny and you all can move in on him."

THE FAMILY

Everyone was sitting in the waiting room when Dr. Kim Chang came out with sweat on his forehead. He was taking off his gloves and looking crazy.

He told the family, "That's a strong young man, he's going to make it."

Everyone hugged each other and cried tears of joy. David even hugged the doctor.

Dr. Chang said, "Justin Thomas will be put in a private room but only family can come to visit him."

David replied, "Yes sir, that's what I requested."

Justice was sitting alone when the news came to him that his big brother was going to make it. He hugged Tonya and said, "I love my brother, someone got to pay."

JUSTIN

Justin was wheeled to a private room on the second floor of Saint Francis Hospital with guards posted around the clock to protect him. David and Gail were the first two people Justin saw when he came out of the light coma. Gail hugged him and then started crying. Justin was talking but very little.

David hugged him and said, "You can't leave me."

Tonya walked in and hugged her baby long and hard.

Justice was feeling like a little boy all over again with a big smile on his face.

David told Justin he would be back and Justin said cool but that he wanted to see his sister Daisy.

Tonya filled Justin in on his sister, she was already being bad at the age of six. She was already talking back and running around.

JUSTICE AND DAVID

Justice and David got in the Hummer and headed to Juan's sister's house on Park-Street to let Juan know what was up. David told Justice to put the Hummer up and ride in the Chevy because no one knew it was theirs. They changed rides and headed to Park-Street to see his best friend Juan.

When they got to Sonya's house it was four in the morning. David used his key to let them in like he owned the place, Sonya was upstairs in her room sleep. Justice sat on the couch while David looked in the guest room and saw Juan asleep. He told Justice to come with him upstairs and they went to Sonya's room.

She was in bed half naked, nothing on but a long T-shirt that David had left there. Justice was looking at Sonya's body, she had always said Justice was a fine ass nigga'.

David said, "What's up to Sonya?"

Sonya said, "Nothing just lying back."

David told Sonya about what happened to Justin, but told her he was doing better. He told Justice to fire up a blunt, so he put one in the air. Sonya, David and Justice got high together there in Sonya's room, she didn't care and she always got real freaky.

David ended up getting Sonya so hot that she took off her shirt and didn't have anything on underneath.

Justice jumped up to leave and David asked, "What's up? Where are you going?"

Justice said, "I was going to give you some time alone."

"Nigga' chill," David told him.

Justice started laughing and sat back down. David started licking and sucking all over Sonya body. When he started rubbing between her legs Justice started getting a rush, he got up and David told him to feel between Sonya's legs, she was wet. Justice put two fingers in her and Sonya smiled. Justice started feeling on her ass.

Sonya was a dime, long pretty black hair and a sun tan out of this world. She had a perfect body and some fat lips.

Justice wanted some head so David made Sonya get on the bed doggy style. Justice took his manhood out and Sonya said, "Damn!" David and his son were both packing. David went up into Sonya from the back and she let out a light noise. Justice put his manhood in her mouth and Sonya began working her ass and sucking Justice at the same time. She was enjoying herself, moaning as she swallowed both men.

David got ready to cum and he waved for Justice to come to the back. David put his manhood in Sonya's mouth and let off a load in her warmness. Justice was hitting Sonya from the back and Sonya was moaning louder now. Justice made

~ 124 ~

Sonya roll over and lay on her back. He got on top of her and put both her legs on his shoulders. He hit Sonya for about thirty minutes, just like that.

David got hot again watching his son, so when Justice got up David jumped back on Sonya and put her to sleep.

Juan was down stairs and didn't hear anything.

Sonya got up and told David that it was her dream to have two men at once. She said, "I love you daddy."

David smiled at her then went down stairs and woke Juan up. He told Juan about Justin and Juan was ready because Justin was his god son. Juan had spoiled him when he was a baby and was the only one that could keep him for the weekend.

CHAD

Chad got the news that David's son Justin had been shot about nine times. He told his boys to be careful because David was going to make someone pay for that. He told everyone that David and Juan were still best friends and that David was the one who shot Red-Man. He also told them that David killed Ta-Ta, but no one on the streets would talk.

JUSTICE AND JUAN

The crew got in Juan's rental car and headed to David's mother's house. Juan was driving the Caddy fast, it had tinted windows so no one knew who they were.

They pulled into Gail's back yard where they all got out and went upstairs. They were talking shit to each other as they were walking in the door and Justice's beeper went off. He got inside the house and used the phone.

It was Rose.

ROSE

Rose asked Justice to meet her at the bowling alley in the meadows so they could talk. She told him that she had not heard from Linda in over a week and that it wasn't like Linda. Rose asked Justice if he had he seen her. Justice lied and said no, but Rose kind of believed him.

JUSTICE

Justice hung up the phone and told David that Rose wanted to meet him at the bowling alley in the meadows.

David said, "Be careful and don't trust that bitch."

Justice replied, "Dad I got her." Then he headed out of the house to meet Rose at the bowling alley. He was riding in the Chevy impala low key.

JUSTIN

Tonya and Gail were still at the hospital with Justin, he was doing fine. The police talked to him but he told them he could not remember anything. A witness had told the police that they saw a black Chevy Blazer speeding away from the crime. Justin remembered seeing the black Blazer then everything flashed back to him. Four Cuban men, the gun shots, Justin jumped.

Tonya ran over and hugged him, she started crying. Justin had been hit nine times. Three in the chest, two in the arm and four shots in his side. God was with him because one of the hits had been life threatening.

Gail told Justin that the doctor said he would be out real soon.

Justin loved the nurse who was taking care of him, she was mixed, 5'6, with long hair and a nice round ass. She had green eyes. She and Justin had been sitting up and playing cards at night while everyone else was asleep. Justin called her Miss Muhammad, but her first name was Ieasha. Other people called her China doll because she looked so good, but Ieasha was Muslim. She kept her hair wrapped up and was always wearing big cloths. She told Justin that she moved to the U.S. from Iran. Her daddy was a black man and her mother was from Iran. She told Justin that no one cared when young black man and Latino's killed each other, it was less work for the police. Ieasha told Justin that she was 28 years old and that she had no kids. Ieasha and Justin had become very good friends.

Tonya liked Ieasha because she was a very respectful young woman. Gail liked her also for the same reasons, but they didn't understand why she kept her self wrapped up.

Chapter Nine

DAVID

David had been telling Juan that they needed to go see Justin, it had been a week and Juan had not seen his god son. They all got in Juan's rental car and headed to Blue Hill Ave to the hospital.

When they got there they checked in and David told the lady at the counter he was there to see his son Justin Thomas. She asked for I.D. and asked a few questions, David passed the test so she told him second floor room 201.

David and Juan got up to the second floor and there was a police officer standing outside the door of Justin's room. David just walked in and Juan went right behind him.

Justin was sitting up playing cards with a pretty nurse and said, "What's up Dad!"

Juan ran over and hugged him then the young nurse stood up.

Justin said, "Ms. Muhammad this is my dad, David and this is my god father, Juan."

She shook both of their hands and headed out the door without saying a word.

David said, "Boy she good looking, but what's with all the stuff on her head?"

Justin replied, "She's Muslim."

"So what's been going on?" David asked.

Justin told David about the police talking to him and he told them he couldn't remember anything. But Justin told David that he saw the Black Chevy Blazer and four Cuban men.

David told him, "I will find that Black Blazer."

Juan asked Justin, "Did you see the men's faces?"

He replied, "A little, but not much because they were trying to kill me. They just walked over to the car and shot it up real bad. I feel good the doctor said I should be home in two weeks."

BOWLING ALLEY

Justice was pulling up in the bowling alley slow, making sure he was not being trapped. He parked in the back and walked to the front. When he walked in the front door he saw Rose sitting on a bar stool waiting on him.

He walked over and said, "What's up pretty girl?"

Rose got up and kissed Justice, then sat back down and started telling Justice they had not heard from Linda.

Justice started acting like he was worried, he knew where his mother was but didn't trust Rose since she came to Hartford to kill his daddy, David.

Justice changed the subject, he asked Rose, "Where is Lisa?"

Rose lied and told Justice she had not seen Lisa. He told her what had happened to Justin and Rose played crazy. Justice told her to come take a walk with him so he and Rose went out the back door of the bowling alley.

There were some rail road tracks in the back so they walked back to there. They were a good ways from the building and no one could see them because of the woods. Justice stopped walking, grabbed Rose and started kissing all over her. He was feeling on Rose and felt the gun she was carrying. She always carried a 9 mm and she was good with it. Justice kept kissing and touching Rose until she got hot.

They both laid down and Rose took the gun off her and laid back. Justice was kissing down her neck and went in her pants playing with her wetness. Rose was ready, she had her eyes closed and her back arched. Justice reached behind him and pulled out his hunting knife when Rose opened her eyes she was seeing the last days of her life.

Justice cut her throat as she tried to scream but nothing came out but blood. He reached in her mouth and cut her tongue out. He felt bad but Rose had broken the code 2-DIE-4.

He walked to the Chevy Impala and headed to the Super 8 Hotel. It was right down the street from the bowling alley.

Justice pulled in and rented a room. He walked in the room and lay across the bed while he fixed up a blunt.

He had tears in his eyes. 2-DIE-4 was all he knew and lived by. From his father to whomever, you break the code you die!

LISA

Lisa was still at the hotel with Lenny and the rest of her men. She told Lenny that Rose was going to trick Justice into a trap and they were going to kill him and David.

She was waiting on Rose to make the call. It had been over two hours and Lisa had started to worry, she should have called by now.

She got up and called Rose's cell phone.

DAVID AND JUAN

David and Juan were driving to Stowe Village, going to Sherry's house to chill. But when they turned down Main Street David saw a bunch of police cars headed over the bridge.

David said, "Man the bowling Alley! We need to check on Justice!"

Juan said, "We can beep him when we get to Sherry's house and put the code in."

Juan rushed to Sherry's place and they ran upstairs. Sherry had already seen them and she had the door open as they got to it.

David and Juan went in and Juan grabbed the phone and hit Justice on his beeper then he put the code in. Juan was looking at the TV when they showed the Bowling Alley parking lot the news lady said an 18 year old girl was found dead on the rail road tracks in back of the building. She was found with her throat cut and her tongue cut out about an hour ago. They didn't yet know the 18 year old girl's name.

David said, "Damn!" The phone started ringing and David picked up, "Everything okay?"

Justice was clam, he said, "Everything's cool."

David told Justice to go to Enfield and chill with his mother Linda. He told him that he would be alone in the morning. Justice asked David how his big brother Justin was doing. David told him that he was fine and that he remembered seeing a black blazer.

David said, "Be careful because Lisa is out there looking."

Justice said, "I'm looking also."

They hung up and Sherry said, "Did you all see that shit on the news? Someone killed a girl on the rail road tracks behind the bowling alley."

"That's why the police are everywhere," David said, "damn!"

Juan said to David, "2-DIE-4, 4-ever."

David replied, "It's all part of this life we live. Honor, respect, money and power."

LISA

Lisa was lying in the bed with Lenny when one of the men came in and turned on the TV. As it flashed on they showed a picture of Rose Freedo. Lisa's mouth flew open and she started crying because her and Rose were close.

She said, "Justice killed her. He's just like his daddy David, they will all pay!"

Lenny was mad because he had told Lisa to let two of the men go with Rose just in case something happened but she didn't.

Lisa got out of the bed and got dressed. She told everyone to get their guns ready then they all left the hotel. Lenny and Lisa were in a rental car and the other three men were in the black Chevy Blazer. They were headed for the bowling alley in the meadows.

DAVID

David and Juan were leaving out of Sherry's house when they bumped into Chad and one of his boys named Mike-D. David reached, but Chad and Mike-D already had their guns out.

Juan said, "What's it going to be?" His gun was pointed at Chad's head.

Chad looked David in the eyes and said, "I had love for you when we grew up together Lil-D, but you killed my brother and one day, you going to pay."

David didn't move, he was still looking Chad in the eyes with his hand on his gun.

Juan said, "Mike-D, you shoot David, I shoot Chad. I really don't give a fuck."

Chad put his gun down and so did Mike-D. Juan kept his gun pointed at Chad and now they really had the ups on them.

Chad and Mike-D walked away without saying a word.

Juan jumped in the rental and he and David headed for Enfield. But when they got on Main Street they saw a black Chevy Blazer trailing a rental car and a blue Grand Am.

David looked close then said, "That's Lisa and her men!"

Juan asked, "You want to follow them?"

David replied, "No, but let's get a good look at the Blazer because they will pay for what they did to my first born."

Juan got on the highway headed to the Courtyard hotel to see Linda and Justice.

TONYA

Tonya was on the phone telling Gail that Justin would be home in a few days and she didn't want him back in the streets.

Gail told Tonya that one day Justin would see that the streets don't love anyone. She said, "Tonya I love David but I told him a long time ago that he's in God's hands."

Tonya replied, "I love David too, but sometimes I think he's crazy."

"Girl, you and David will make it, just hold on," Gail told her.

Tonya said, "That's real."

JUSTIN

Ieasha came to Justin's room and woke him up with his breakfast in her hand. He ate, then got up, brushed his teeth and washed his face.

Ieasha was smiling when Justin said, "Good morning."

Ieasha said, "I respect when men are talking, a woman should leave the room. I know you were going to ask me why I left the room when your dad and his friend came. I respect you Justin."

Justin walked up on Ieasha and she moved back real fast.

Justin said, "I wasn't going to touch you."

Ieasha said, "Respect, I just got out of your way."

They both started smiling.

LINDA

Linda and Justice were at the hotel in Enfield. They were chilling, laughing and talking. Linda was telling Justice about the girl Rose who was found dead on the rail road tracks in back of the bowling alley.

A knock came on the door and Justice jumped up to grab his gun. He told his mother to go to the back and she moved fast because she knew her only son was a young man now and he would do whatever it took to protect his mother.

Justice looked out the door and saw his father standing there. He opened the door and David along with Juan, walked in.

David said, "What's popping?"

Juan said, "Your mom is back there."

When David walked in the room Linda was counting money. He said, "What's up lady?"

Linda said, "What did I tell you about that lady shit? It's woman to you."

They both started smiling and David gave her a bear hug.

Linda backed up and said, "Lisa will be looking for me, but I can handle her."

Linda was still looking good David could see. He said, "Justin gets out of the hospital Monday."

David told her that he and the crew were going to get him big. Tony and Cheese were going to drive the limo.

Linda told David that she was alright, she had a condo in New Haven and that's where she was going. No one knew about it. She gave David her cell number and said, "Hit me on the hip anytime."

David said cool and walked back to the living room where he told the boys they were going to get Justin and take him to Gail's house.

Justice went over and hugged his mother and told her that he would be in New Haven soon.

They all walked out of the hotel together.

LINDA

Soon as David and his crew walked out Linda got on the phone and called Chad, she told him where she was. Chad was in love with Linda. They never had sex, but Linda was feeling Chad and plus she had a plan. Chad told Linda that he was on his way, so she hung up the phone and started smiling.

JUSTIN

Justin was feeling good, all his clothes were packed and he was looking good too. He had on an all-white silk polo sweat suit, with the brand new all-white throwback Jordan's.

Ieasha came in the room and told Justin, "You can't leave until 9 am and its only 8 am." Justin started smiling then Ieasha said, "I have three questions for you Mr. Justin Thomas."

Justin responded, "Go ahead let me hear them."

Ieasha walked up to Justin and looked him in his eyes. She said, "The first question is, what do you plan to do with your life from this point on, after Allah blessed you to live after being shot nine times?"

Justin was fixing to answer but Ieasha said, "Number two, do you ever plan on getting married or having a family? And the last one, are you going to always run from what's real?"

Justin was listening then he said, "I like those questions. They caught me off guard but I'm going to give it to you like it's on my heart. At this point I want the people who tried to kill me. Number two, I don't have a plan for my life and who is Allah?"

Ieasha said, "Allah is another word for God, the one who saved your life."

Justin said, "Do I ever plan on getting married and having a family, yes I always wanted my own family. What's real is, the streets have my heart and sometimes I want to get it back, but right now I can't, there's too much going on."

"I don't have time for you to go there but here is my number and address," she said, "if you ever need me just call and I'll be there."

Justin walked up to Ieasha and this time she didn't move. He gave her a big hug and told her that he look forward to seeing her again. Ieasha was smiling a great big smile for Justin.

Someone knocked on the door and they both jumped. Ieasha said, "One day," then she opened the door and the room keeper said, "Can Mr. Thomas wait in the lobby?"

Ieasha said, "Sure." She grabbed one of Justin's bags and some of the balloons as they both went to the lobby to wait on his ride.

Dr. Chang came up to Justin and shook his hand. He said, "Mr. Thomas you are very blessed to be here."

Nurse Mohammad was looking Justin up and down because the boy was looking good. She just wished he was a single Muslim man.

Mr. Chang walked off then stop in his tracks. He saw a long white and gold Mercedes Benz Limo pulling up in front of the hospital door. Everyone was looking at the car and the driver of the limo was Jimmy. He stood about 6' 9, 260 pounds and his partner Cheese stood 6', 320 pounds. They were dressed in all black silk suits.

Jimmy opened the back door to the Limo and David, Justice and Juan got out. They walked into the lobby and hugged Justin as they put all kinds of money in his pockets. Everyone was happy as they could be.

David said, "Nigga' you act like you don't want to leave that pretty young woman."

Ieasha started laughing and Justin said, "I don't' want to leave her."

He hugged Ieasha and touched his pocket to let her know he had her information safe.

Justin and his family walked out and got into the limo as Ieasha stood at the exit doors with tears in her eyes. She had fallen in love with Justin Thomas and never had she done that before. There was something about this young man that made her want him.

GAIL

Gail and all the girls were home with Jesse. Tonya had on her summer dress, she had Daisy, Yolanda and Betty playing with her. Jasmine was cooking on the grill laughing and talking as a white limo pulled up in the back yard. Gail told the girls that's got to be David.

The limo stopped and the crew got out. Justin ran to Gail and Juan was eyeing Yolanda. Everyone was happy to see Justin.

David told Tonya to give him Daisy. She was getting big and had begun walking and repeating whatever she heard. Daisy was crazy about David, he had her spoiled from day one.

Justin put his bags upstairs and they all sat down and ate well.

Tonya had to go upstairs so David jumped up and followed her. She didn't see David behind her when she went into the bathroom. David went in his old bedroom and waited for her to come out. When she did David grabbed her arm and pulled her into the room. Tonya was trying to fight David off as she said stop boy! David threw her on the bed but she got mad because she had just got her hair done. David started kissing her and sucking on her neck. He reached under her summer dress and pulled her thong to the side as he started fingering her.

She was mad, but it had been three weeks, so her body was on fire and between her legs was wet. She stopped fighting.

David pulled down his pants and entered Tonya's wet spot. She let out a low moan as David was giving it to her. She started sucking on David's neck to keep from screaming when David started moving fast. She was trying to push him up because she was not on any pills and he didn't have on any protection. Tonya said, "Damn it!" As she put her legs on David's shoulders and let him have his way.

They got up and Tonya went to the bathroom where she saw all the passion marks on her neck. She told David he had to get her hair done over then she went down stairs.

Gail asked Tonya, "Where's David?"

Tonya lied and said, "I don't' know."

Gail and all the girls started laughing as David came down stairs.

Tonya said, "There he goes."

Gail said, "Boy where you been?"

"I was upstairs talking to Tonya," He answered.

Tonya covered her face and started laughing. She told David not to say anything else to her.

David walked up and hugged Tonya as Gail said, "Both of you are crazy as hell."

~ 137 ~

LINDA

Chad and Linda were sitting in the hotel talking when Linda told Chad that the money was good but she was not fucking with Lisa anymore because it was too much of a risk.

Linda said, "I love David but I'm not in love with him anymore. We just have a son together."

Chad said, "No matter what, I will do my all to protect you. I'm getting twenty kilos a week and I have the streets on lock. David is still getting more drugs than anyone in Hartford. Juan is still his number one man and Justice, her son, was making a lot of money too. Can I take you home?"

Linda said, "Yes." Then she grabbed her bags.

They walked out and got into Chad's grey and gold B.M.W. They headed for New Haven to Linda's condo.

Linda had on a white mini skirt and a short shirt to show off her flat belly. She was looking good.

Chad fired up a blunt as they headed out.

DAVID

David told everyone he had to make a run and he would be right back.

Juan said, "Man I'm fixing to go check on this money with Justice."

David said, "That's cool with me."

"I'm going up stairs to chill because I have a light head ache." Justin told them.

Tonya said, "David call me later on."

David kissed Daisy and jumped in the Chevy Impala so he could stay low key. He was headed to the Vill, over to Sherry's house.

LINDA

Linda and Chad pulled up in front of a big, nice, condo style house with a black gate surrounding it. It was clean.

Linda said to Chad, "This is it and don't ever tell anyone you came here."

Chad started smiling and said, "It's a blessing to me baby girl."

Linda got out of the car with her bags. She hit he code on the door and it opened. She went in first then Chad, the house looked like it belonged to a movie star. Trina or Lil-Kim, a rich hoe. It had a white leather Gucci couch, china cabinets and thick white carpet in every room.

When Chad and Linda got to her bedroom he saw the queen size bed with big fluffy pillows on it and mirrors all over the walls. Chad sat on the bed watching the 64 inch TV and Linda told him that she would be right back.

Chad got himself a drink of E & J and chilled. He waited about thirty minutes until Linda came out of the bathroom with a blue bra on and a matching thong. She was looking good from head to toe. Chad got up and started walking towards her.

Linda said, "Chill nigga'."

She got on the end of the bed and put lotion on her legs in front of Chad. Slowly she rubbed it up and down her legs and over her stomach. Chad got a hard on from the first look at Linda's legs. She knew what she was doing to him and Chad couldn't resist. He walked over and touched Linda.

She said, "Chad this is not that type of party baby. I'm a bottom bitch, ride or die not a cheap fuck!" Then she said, "If you want this, you got to put in work."

Chad said, "Baby I will do anything in the world for you. I have wanted you since the first time I set my eyes on you with David."

Linda said, "Talk is cheap. I'm like a house, you got to have a down payment."

He replied, "tomorrow we will hit the mall and from that point I will do my part as your nigga'."

"Cool, but step out while I get dressed," She said with a smile.

Chad walked to the living room smiling because he wanted Linda. David had told him years ago how good her candy was.

DAVID

David was headed to downtown Hartford. He was chilling when he turned and saw the all-black Chevy Blazer coming from the Hilton Hotel. He said to himself, 'that bitch Lisa is hiding in there somewhere.' A car blew its horn and took David out of his thoughts. He made a left and headed to the Hilton Hotel just to see.

He pulled the Impala into the parking lot of the hotel and got out. David checked to make sure he had his gun then he put a hat on and dark shades before he walked into the hotel. He knew his way around because he damn near grew up at the Hilton Hotel.

David walked around and talked to some old friends that had been working there for years. He ran into Gina Manson, a fine red-bone about 43 years old. She had been working at the Hilton about fifteen years.

She saw David and said, "What's up Bad Boy?"

David smiled and looked Gina up and down, she was fine like Tonya and Linda. David said, "I need you to do something for me."

Gina asked, "What could that be?"

He said, "Do you remember the Puerto Rican girl I use to run with named Lisa?"

Gina replied, "Yeah, real pretty."

David said, "Right, I want you to call me if you see her in this hotel. Tell Tammy Green and Kim Banks the same thing." He reached in his pocket and gave Gina five, one hundred dollar bills.

She smiled and said, "Will do!"

David gave her his cell phone number and his beeper number then he walked off. He went out of the hotel, got in his car and headed for the Vill.

JUSTIN

Justin was laying on David's old bed chilling, watching TV and eating some hot dogs. He looked on the table in the corner of the room and saw a yellow piece of paper. He jumped off the bed and looked at the paper, then read what was on it:

'To someone special from Ieasha Muhammad.'

It had her phone number, home address and a little heart drawing next to it. He walked to the phone and dialed the number. The phone rang three times before someone picked up and Justin said, "Can I speak to Ieasha?"

The voice on the other end said, "This is she."

Justin said, "How are you doing?"

She replied, "Fine Justin."

"How did you know it was me?" He asked.

"Because you are the only man, other than my father, who I gave my number to. My father doesn't call because I live with him," Ieasha said.

Justin said, "I feel special."

"You are special," She replied.

They both started laughing. Justin told Ieasha a little about him and his family. He told her that his grandmother Gail was going to take him car shopping tomorrow and that he was going to look for a Job.

Ieasha said, "That's good, but I want to drive your car."

"Okay, but what kind of car do you have?" He asked her.

"I have a Maxima," she told him.

Justin said, "I might get me another Lexus or a Cadillac truck."

Ieasha laughed and said, "It sounds like you already have a job."

"No but my grandma is going to take care of that. I'm going to come by the hospital to see you tomorrow on your lunch break," he said.

She said, "Okay."

When they hung up Justin was smiling because Ieasha was the only girl he had respect for. He wasn't sure about the Muslim stuff though.

CHAD AND LINDA

Chad went back to New Haven and picked Linda up to take her shopping. Linda came out of the house in a full body, cat suit, looking like a super star.

Chad got out and opened the door for her. She got in the car and kissed Chad in the mouth.

They got on the highway headed to New York City where no one could see them.

JUSTICE AND JUAN

Justice and Juan were riding out to the car wash in the meadows. Juan was driving the rental car fast when he saw the black Blazer.

Juan said, "Justice that's them punks who did that to Justin!

Justice said, "Let's get them!"

"We got to be smart, there's four of them and two of us," Juan said.

Justice said, "Let's follow them at least."

Juan was two cars away from the Blazer and they followed them to the Howard Johnson Hotel. The Blazer parked and four Hispanic men got out. They were all very healthy looking.

Juan got on his cell phone and called David.

David said, "What's popping?"

Juan said, "Howard Johnson Hotel."

"I was on my way to the Vill but that can chill until I get there," David replied and hung up.

Juan was checking his gun and so was Justice.

JUSTIN

Gail, Justin and Tonya went to the car lot on Albany Ave to get Justin a new car. He looked all around and finally found a car he loved. It was a brand new, money green, Lexus Coupe. Justin loved the Lexus cars, the only thing was that this time he ordered a special chip to make it super-fast.

Gail was smiling at him and so was Tonya. Tonya got in the car with Justin and they headed home. Gail was trailing them since Justin was driving fast.

Tonya said, "Boy you better slow down."

Justin said, "Grandma like that."

They both laughed.

CHAD

Linda and Chad were spending big money on diamond rings and gold chains. Chad got Linda a ten thousand dollar ring and two fur coats, along with some Gator boots. When he left New York he had spent over forty thousand dollars on a woman he had never slept with, but Chad had more money than he could count and money was still coming in every day, Linda knew that.

Linda liked Chad but she had other plans. They were headed back to New Haven chilling, listening to Gerald Lavert, "Mr. Too Dam Good."

DAVID

David pulled up in the Howard Johnson parking lot talking on the phone to Juan. He spotted the black Blazer and pulled up beside it. The man was going into the room. Juan was telling David on the cell phone that he was waiting to see what room the men were going to.

Juan said, "It's on! They are going to room 102."

David told Juan to rent a room next to the men and keep an eye on them. Juan went to the room and laid back. They heard a noise and everyone jumped, David started laughing when he saw it was his beeper going off.

He checked the number and said, "Damn. Who's this?"

He called the number and it ring one time then a voice said, "Bad Boy it's me, Mrs. Mason. Gina boy."

David said, "Okay, Okay. What's popping?"

Gina said, "I saw Lisa, she's on the second floor by herself in room 212."

David told her, "I'm going to give you five hundred more dollars and the other girls five hundred too."

Gina replied, "Cool, but come over to my house on Westland Street tomorrow at 8 pm."

"The same place you been staying?" David asked.

Gina said, "Yeah."

"I'll bring the money, but keep an eye on Lisa," He instructed.

David had been waiting to get some of Gina for some years. He hung the phone up smiling, Juan and Justice were half asleep. David said, "Watch them clowns, I'm going to make a run somewhere tomorrow but for now light that blunt up and lets smoke."

They all laid back and chilled, smoking good.

LISA

Lisa had called Lenny at the hotel, he picked up and Lisa told him that she made some calls and everything was good. She told Lenny the money was rolling in.

Lenny told Lisa things were also good on his end. He told Lisa that Justin was out of the hospital but he hadn't been seen.

Lisa told Lenny not to worry about him, she wanted David. Lisa said, "After we catch David you and I are going away." Lenny was on the other end smiling. Lisa said, "I'll talk to you later, four more men will be coming from New York to help hunt down the man who destroyed my family."

She hung up the phone with Lenny and laid back on the bed with nothing on but a pink thong. She was day dreaming about how good David made her feel when he manhandled her love box. He made love like a mad-man.

Lisa went to sleep with her finger in her wetness.

LINDA

Linda and Chad made it to her condo. He helped Linda bring all her bags in and she put most of the bags on her bed. Chad was chilling in the living room when Linda told him thank you. She said that she was looking forward to seeing him again.

Chad said, "I am just a phone call away."

Linda walked over to him while he was sitting on the sofa and unzipped her cat suit. She told him to lay down and he obediently did so. Linda sat right down on Chad's face. Chad was sucking on Linda's love box and juice was all over his face. Linda was moving up and down on Chad's tongue and moaning, she was telling Chad that she was coming. She came hard and a lot in Chad's mouth, then she got up, put her clothes on and was getting ready for him to go.

Chad was ready for more but Linda said, "Not tonight."

Chad got up and Linda walked him to the door.

She was smiling when she closed the door and picked the phone up as she walked to the shower. She called her friend Wynetta, who she had met when she first moved into her condo.

Wynetta picked her phone up and said, "Who is this?"

Linda replied, "What's up?"

Netta said, "Same old shit."

Netta was a very pretty girl at the age of 18 years old. She was a dime, fine to death and was a hustler who did whatever it took to stay on top.

"Girl you want to come over?" Linda asked.

Netta said, "Hell yeah!"

Before she hung up Linda said, "Bring a good movie with you."

She wanted David to meet Netta because she was real and needed a real nigga' on her team. David was the realest nigga' that Linda knew.

Chapter Ten

JUSTIN

It was a hot Friday and Justin had been laying low, he hadn't called Ieasha in a week because he was busy looking for a job. Justin found work at Pa-Pa's paints, where they painted all kinds of cars and that was Justin's love, painting cars. The shop was on Weather Field Ave. He was happy and so was the family. Justin had over a hundred thousand dollars saved up, so money was not a problem and his mother had five times more than that thanks to his father, David.

Justin was headed down Blue Hills Ave when he saw the hospital and Ieasha came to his mind. She might be on lunch break, he thought. He turned into the hospital parking lot and parked, then he got out and went in.

The lady at the desk said, "Can I help you?"

Justin said, "Yes. Can you call Ieasha to the desk?"

He sat down and was day-dreaming when someone touched him. He jumped and Ieasha said, "Hello." Justin got up and hugged her and she said, "Long time no see."

Justin said, "I been busy trying to find work. I found a job painting cars." Ieasha started smiling and he said, "I came to take you out for lunch."

Ieasha said, "That's nice but can I trust you?"

Justin said, "You can put your life in my hands and before I let you die, we will die together."

Ieasha said, "I'm convinced."

As she and Justin headed out she saw Justin's money green Lexus and said, "That is nice."

Justin asked, "Do you want to drive?"

She said, "Can I?"

Justin gave her the keys and they went to the Baskin Robbins in Bloomfield where they talked and ate ice-cream. Justin told Ieasha he was looking for his own place somewhere near his job. He also told her that he was letting the streets go.

He said he was happy working eight hours a day, five days a week.

Ieasha was happy, she told Justin that she would help him look for a place by going on the computer and looking in the newspaper.

"Justin there's something I've been waiting to ask you," she said.

Justin looked over at her and said, "What's that?"

Ieasha kept driving without saying a word. Justin was looking at how beautiful she was, even with her head covered she looked good. They pulled into the hospital parking lot where Ieasha said, "Thank you." Then opened the door to get out.

Justin grabbed her hand and looked her in the eyes. He said, "What's on your mind? I will respect whatever it is you want to ask."

Ieasha said, "What are you looking for in a woman, or should I say what kind of woman do you want Justin? It's just a question."

"I want a woman like my mother. A woman who has understanding, a woman who respects her man and respects him no matter where he's at. I want a woman who would kill for me if it came down to it. A woman who would hide me from the law and if I went to prison, I want a woman who would be there for me mentally and spiritually." Justin stopped talking, he had Ieasha in a daze. He looked in her eyes and said, "I want a woman like you."

Ieasha had tears in her eyes as she hugged Justin and said, "I am that woman and I would love to have a man like you."

Justin let Ieasha go and got in the driver seat of his car. He did not want Ieasha to see the tears in his eyes.

Ieasha said to herself that she would tell her daddy about Justin.

Justin pulled off with his mind wandering.

DAVID

David was headed to Westland Street to see Gina and take her the money, he was clean. Since Gina was older than David he wanted to show her that he was on point. He had on Polo pants, some black Gators and a Polo shirt to match, looking and smelling good. He was in the Impala to stay low key. He saw the white house and Gina's car so he pulled in the back.

Gina looked out the door in her U-Conn sweat pants and a t-shirt. She had her hair done up and was looking damn good.

David got out and said, "What's up?"

Gina hugged David and they walked in the house together. Gina had a nice house with no man and no kids, but she was real low key on a lot of things. Word was she liked women, but David's motto was all women like dick.

Gina told David to have a seat and as he sat down she brought him a drink of Remy Martin. They sipped their drinks and made small talk. He gave Gina the money for her and the girls. She started talking more, telling David how fine he was and that all the women wanted him. David was just smiling.

Gina said, "Nigga what time you got to be there?"

David said, "Bitch I'm the boss, ain't no time for me!"

Gina said, "Well you can stay with me tonight."

David laid back and Gina got up to jump in the shower. She told David, "You can go in my room if you want."

David got up and went to Gina's room, it was laid out. He laid across her queen size bed looking into the air. After Gina came out of the shower she walked into the room with nothing on but a towel. She put lotion on and got right then laid on the bed with David.

David rolled over, laid on top of Gina and said, "Damn you are soft!"

Gina was smiling at David as he started kissing her on the neck and working his way down between her legs. She was moaning and making all kinds of noises as David was licking her love box. He moved down and started sucking on her toes and licking the bottom of her feet.

He took his clothes off and Gina said, "Damn!" David was packing, he kept his eyes on Gina as he put ten inches inside her. Gina went crazy, she had not had sex with a man in two years. She was moaning, "Shit David! Fuck me! Oh! Oh!" Gina started begging David to stop.

David rolled Gina over and hit her from the back. He was ready to explode and Gina was good with David sucking on her back and neck to keep from moaning. He let his load off deep inside Gina.

They stayed in the bed all night making love. She couldn't believe how good David was at taking care of a woman in bed. Gina told David that he was the best she ever had. She wanted to see him more often.

David got dressed and told Gina to give him an extra key. She reached in her night stand and gave David the extra key.

He said "I might drop by anytime, what should I expect?"

Gina said, "Me, Kim or Janet. No man, don't worry you can handle the girls, they all know you."

David kissed Gina and walked out.

GINA

Gina went to work at the hotel smiling from ear to ear.

Kim said, "Gina you look like the sun, all shining."

Gina replied, "I got me a young dick last night."

They both started laughing and Kim asked, "Who was it?"

Janet was walking up when Gina said, "Take this and give Janet five hundred."

"Damn Bitch, you got marks all over you neck," Kim said.

Gina said, "David gave me some."

"You got down! All the girls used to talk about David," Kim replied.

Kim said, "I want some!"

Janet said, "Me too!"

"Guess what?" Gina said with a grin.

They said, "What?"

She replied, "I recorded it so you all can see it then I will trash it."

Gina told the girls to come over Friday then they laughed and went to work.

CHAD

Chad went back to the Vill and was chilling, talking to his young workers. Jerry and lil' Mike were smoking a blunt.

Chad told Jerry, "Man I got that bitch Linda. Man I ate that pussy hard last night!"

Jerry said, "What? Man, you lying. David will go crazy if he finds out!"

"Man fuck David, when I catch him he's dead! Jerry, I need for you to take this money to the safe house on Cleveland Ave," Chad said.

Jerry replied, "Cool."

No one other than Chad and Jerry knew about the safe house. That's where Chad kept all the money and drugs, his life was in that house.

JUSTICE AND JUAN

Justice was looking out the window when he saw two of the Puerto Rican men getting in the Blazer. He told Juan, "There's only two in the room, just two of them left."

Justice got on the phone and called David.

David picked up saying, "What's popping?"

Justice said, "David two of them just left, there's only two left in the hotel room."

He replied, "Good, just chill. I'm headed to the Hilton to pay Lisa a visit."

DAVID

David turned into the Hilton parking lot and put a hat on his head. He walked into the lobby and saw Kim. He said, "What's up Blacky?"

Kim said, "You." Then she smiled from ear to ear.

Kim was dark skinned, but built like a super star. She was about 37 years old and looking good, always running and staying in shape.

David asked, "Is Lisa still upstairs?"

She replied, "Yes."

David reached in his pocket and gave Kim five hundred dollars and said, "Give me the master key."

Kim said, "Okay."

David said, "Don't tell no one."

"You can trust me," she said. Kim went into the little room, then she came out and told David to meet her on the second floor in the laundry room.

David went up the stairs to the laundry room. It was dark so David made sure he had his gun. He heard a noise and jumped then looked up and saw it was Kim.

"Don't hurt no one," Kim said.

David smiled and said, "I won't."

He got the key and went looking for room 212. He found it and put his ear to the door but he didn't hear anything. He put the key in the lock and opened the door. Lisa was lying in the bed with just her bra and panties on, she was looking good. She had a 45 lying on the table next to the bed. David quietly locked the door and walked real slow to the table where he grabbed the 45. He unloaded it and laid it back down. He looked all around the room and saw a lot of money in a money bag, stacks and stacks of money.

David got a chair and sat in the middle of the floor, watching Lisa sleep. He got up and walked over to the bed. He touched Lisa's panties in the front, she jumped. She opened her eyes and saw it was David, her heart dropped.

She said, "What the fuck are you doing in here?"

David started laughing and said, "It's all a dream."

Lisa saw the gun was still on the table, but she was not going to try anything crazy because David loved to kill.

David told Lisa, "You are a fool. You can't hide from me in Hartford. I know every move you make baby."

Lisa said, "David, go ahead and do whatever you are going to do, I'm ready to die."

"Bitch! It's not about what you're ready for! It's about, why? It's about 2-DIE-4, it's about FOREVER, it's about love, family, respect, honor and loyalty." Lisa was looking crazy when David continued. "Who does all that money in that bag belong to?"

Lisa said, "It's a friend's."

David started laughing and Lisa jumped up.

"Bitch! Lay down before I fill you up with lead! Now look, I'm not going to kill you because you are not worth it, but what I want you to do is take off your bra and panties," David said.

Lisa did what she was told. David took his manhood out of his pants and walked up in between Lisa's legs. She let out a loud moan and David started moving fast. Lisa was moaning louder as David got ready to let off. He pulled out and put his manhood in Lisa's mouth where he let a load off.

Lisa was mad and David started laughing. David said to her, "Lenny must have a little dick!"

She didn't say anything. David grabbed the bag of money as someone knocked on the door. He grabbed his gun and told Lisa to look out the peep hole. When she looked out she saw it was Lenny and another one of her men.

David said, "Open the door."

Lisa opened the door and David put the gun to Lenny's head with the silencer on it. He told Lisa to check the other man. David sat the two men down and tied them up. Lisa was looking crazy because the 45 was still on the table.

David asked Lenny, "Where are the other men?"

Lenny said, "There's just us!"

"Don't lie to me ass hole!" David yelled.

Lenny started smiling and David got mad. He said, "You want to play hard in front of Lisa?" David pulled out his knife and said, "Lenny it's going to be painful because you want to be a smart ass."

Lenny was in love with Lisa. David gagged Lenny real good then called Lisa to him. He bent her over the table right in front of Lenny, he pulled out his manhood and went up inside Lisa slow. When all ten inches were deep inside her he pulled it out slowly and then put it all back in her real slow. Lisa was moaning because she never could handle all of David. Lenny was crying mad, he wanted to kill David.

David laid Lisa on the floor and spread her legs then put it in her. She was going crazy, the sad part about it was that she was loving it. Lisa had bust about three nuts when David made her get up, then handed her the knife. He walked over to Lenny and said, "Lisa is going to kill you for me." When he gave Lisa the order to kill Lenny, she was crying and shaking real bad. Lenny was trying to scream but it was useless. Lisa cut his throat and Lenny died before his head dropped. Lisa dropped the knife and hugged Lenny telling him how much she loved him.

The other man was in a state of shock. David asked him where the rest of the men were but he could not talk. David put two shots to his head then grabbed Lisa and told her to clean up the mess.

Lisa went to the bathroom to clean all the blood off of herself and David told her, "I'm going to let you live, but I want you to get out of Hartford."

Lisa was still crying when he kissed her on the mouth and walked out of the room. She was going crazy.

David gave Kim back the key and left. He had a lot on his mind, the feds were in town so he had to lay low. He knew deep down Lisa would coming back for blood, he should have killed her.

JUSTICE AND JUAN

Justice told Juan, "Let's get them now, that way we know they won't get away with what they did to Justin."

Juan said, "You got the gas Justice?"

Justice said, "Hell yeah!"

"Let's go," Juan replied.

They both walked up on the Blazer with their guns in hand and made the two men get out. The men didn't have time to reach for their guns, they were caught off guard. Justice and Juan tied them up, put them in the back seat of the Blazer and headed for Kenny Park.

When they got to Kenny Park the men were trying to talk but Justice and Juan got out, locked the doors and rolled all the windows up. They poured gas all over the Blazer and lit a match. The blazer went up in flames while Justice and Juan ran through Kenny Park woods and went to Tonya's mom's house.

They knocked on the door and Mrs. Weaver answered it. She said, "Hello Juan and Justice, what brings you two here so late?"

Juan told her, "My car broke down and I need a ride."

Mrs. Weaver always liked Juan. She was about 46 years old but looked real good. She could pass for 30 and she still partied on Saturdays.

Mrs. Weaver let the boys in, Justice got himself something to drink and she went to her room. Juan sat on the couch and grabbed the phone, he called David.

David picked up on the first ring, "What's popping?"

Juan said, "Man we need to see you! We're at Tonya's mom's house."

"It's cool, I'm on my way," said David.

Mrs. Weaver called Tonya and told her Justice and Juan were at her house. Tonya asked where David was. Mrs. Weaver told her that he was on his way.

Tonya said, "I am on my way."

Mrs. Weaver replied, "I don't need you over here Tonya."

They both started laughing and Tonya said, "Juan won't get none tonight and hung up laughing."

Juan went to Mrs. Weaver's room. She said, "Boy don't even go there with your young ass!"

Juan said, "Well you need to put something else on then young lady."

He sat on the bed and watched TV. His eyes kept wandering over to Mrs. Weaver and while he looked her up and down he realized just how sexy she was for her age.

DAVID

David was riding down Blue Hills Ave. when he saw all the police cars everywhere, lights flashing and the dogs. He knew something bad had happened so he pulled into the gas station where he went in and asked the lady that worked there what was going on.

She said, "Two people were found dead in a Blazer."

David got back in his car and said to himself, 'someone done got caught slipping in the game.'

TONYA

Tonya was on her way to her mother's house when a police car turned their lights on behind her, she pulled over. The officer asked her where she was coming from and if she had ID. Tonya showed him her driver's license and told him she was coming from home, headed to her mom's house. The officer asked her where her mom stayed and Tonya lied and said Bowels Park. She knew Justice and Juan were at her mom's house and she didn't want to lead the police anywhere near them.

The officer told Tonya to go on ahead. She went the Bowels Park way but kept going until she pulled into her mother's back yard. She got out and used her key to get in. When she walked in Justice jumped, he had been watching TV and didn't hear her.

Tonya asked, "Where's Juan?"

Justice lied and said, "I think he's upstairs."

Tonya went to her mother's room and Juan was sitting on the end of the bed talking shit to Mrs. Weaver. Tonya started laughing because Juan was like family and she knew her mother always wanted to sex up Juan's young, pretty, Puerto Rican ass.

Tonya said, "Boy there's police everywhere. They're looking for someone, where is David?"

Juan said, "David is on his way."

Tonya replied, "Call him and make sure he is alright."

Juan dialed the number and put the code in so David would know it was him. David picked up talking low, he said, "Juan I can't talk right now, police is everywhere. Tell Mrs. Weaver and Tonya to come get me I'm at the beauty salon on Blue Hills."

Juan told Tonya what David said and Mrs. Weaver said, "Oh My God! I hope David ain't in no trouble!"

Tonya said, "I am ready mom. Put some clothes on we are going to get him!"

Mrs. Weaver replied, "I know you're going, love will make you do right and love will make you do wrong."

Mrs. Weaver got dressed and was coming out of her room when Juan touched her on the butt. She turned around and started smiling.

Justice wanted to go and was arguing with Tonya but she said no!

Mrs. Weaver drove down Blue Hills Ave, police were still everywhere. Everyone knew Mrs. Weaver so they let her right bye. Mrs. Weaver pulled into the beauty salon and waited.

David came from around back with mud everywhere.

He jumped in the back and Tonya said, "Nigga' what have you done?"

David said, "I ain't done nothing! I was coming from Main and Tower."

Mrs. Weaver was driving the speed limit and being cautious.

Tonya asked David where his car was. He told her he left it in Bowels Park and he would send someone to get it tomorrow. Mrs. Weaver told David that Justin was doing well, he was working at a paint shop on Weather Field Ave and he was looking for a condo out that way.

David replied, "That's good, Justin is a smart kid and one day he is going to chill."

Mrs. Weaver pulled into her back yard and they all got out, Justice and Juan ran to the door and hugged David.

Justice said, "Tonya can I hold your car? I want to go over to my Grandma Gail's house."

Tonya gave him the keys and said, "Be careful."

Mrs. Weaver, Tonya, David and Juan went into the house. David told Tonya that he needed to take a shower and change clothes so he went upstairs and found something to wear and got in the shower.

Mrs. Weaver put on some short, shorts and Juan was looking and smiling.

Tonya said she had something to tell David so she went upstairs. When she got up there David had water and soap on his face. She pulled the shower curtain real hard and scared the shit out of David.

She said, "Nigga' where have you been the last few days?"

David said, "Girl I been taking care of things. The feds are in town and I'm lying low."

Tonya told him, "You need to!"

Juan was feeling all over Mrs. Weaver, she was wet and ready but didn't want to do anything while Tonya was in the house. Mrs. Weaver told Juan to come back when Tonya left. Juan continued playing in her love box, her wetness was all over his fingers and she was breathing hard. Tonya started coming down the stairs and they stopped.

Tonya said, "What you do in the dark will come to the light!"

Juan started laughing.

JUSTIN

Justin had found a nice condo off of Weather Field Ave on Earl Street. It had a nice back yard with a swimming pool and it already had new furniture in it. It had two bedrooms, a Jacuzzi in the master bedroom and half a bar. Everything was nice, Justin made a two thousand dollar payment and all he had to do was bring his clothes. He called David and Tonya and told them about the condo, they were both happy.

Justin had made a change in his life and his grandma Gail loved the way he had changed for the better.

JUSTICE

Justice was over at Gail's house, he had taken Tonya's car back to her. He called his mother Linda and they talked for a while, he told her about Lisa and some other things. He told his mother he would be over soon.

Linda told Justice she had some new friends and she wanted him to meet them. She said, "So come fresh like always."

Justice said, "I love you."

Linda replied, "Where's my other baby?"

Justice asked, "Who?"

"David!" Linda said.

Justice said, "He's at Juan's house laying low."

They both said love you and hung up.

LISA

Lisa was in New York lying in bed thinking of a master plan. She had tried everything to get David but nothing seem to work. She picked up the phone and said to herself, 'I will call a friend,' then she called someone she had met in Hartford, Jerry. Jerry was Chad's right hand man, but he was in love with Lisa so she was going to use him to find out what she wanted.

Lisa dialed his number, Jerry answered the phone. Lisa said, "What's up?"

Jerry knew who it was, he said, "Dam Girl! What makes you call me?"

Lisa lied and said, "Because you been on my mind," in a real sexy voice. Jerry was smiling and Lisa said, "I need to see you. I will be in Hartford Sunday, meet me at the Courtyard Hotel at 11 pm. I'm looking forward to seeing you," she said and hung up.

She had a big smile on her face, she was now about to start playing the game raw.

Chapter Eleven

NEW HAVEN CT.
LINDA

Linda and Netta had gotten real close, she had started bringing her friends over. April was one of her friends who was a real eye catcher. Pretty young thing, she was street smart at 17 years old. She carried herself like a 30 year old.

They were all sitting in Linda's living room watching the TV, smoking weed and drinking wine coolers. Linda was telling the younger girls things that she did at a young age with her son Justice. The girls were ready to meet Justice to see what Linda was talking about.

JUSTICE

Justice was headed to his mom's house, he had the Hummer H-2 out. It was clean and he was on point with the all-white G-unit boots and the Fifty pants on with a white G-unit shirt, he was fresh. He had a big carat in his ear to go along with his Rolex watch and chain. His pockets were fat and full of money. Justice had his hair braided in the A-1 style. He had a talk with Justin, his big brother and felt good that he was doing the right thing. Now that Justin had a condo Justice wanted one also.

The music was up loud when he pulled into his mother's yard. Justice saw someone looking out the window when he got out of the hummer.

April said, "Damn that nigga' is fine!"

Netta said, "Show you right!"

Justice opened the door and Linda jumped up to hug him. Linda turned around and said, "Netta this is my son Justice, the love of my life."

Netta said, "Hello."

Justice replied, "What's up?"

Linda turned to April and said, "This is Justice, my baby. When he was little I called him Demon because he stayed in some shit."

April said, "Well hello."

Justice looked April up and down and asked, "How old are you?"

"17 years old but ready for whatever!" She replied and put her hands on her hips.

Justice started laughing. He asked, "How old are you Netta?"

Netta said, "It's Wynetta, but you good anyway. I'm 18 years old, not many miles but love money!"

They all started laughing. They both asked Justice how old he was at the same time.

Justice had a slick mouth, he said, "I'm 17 years old, I got a sixty thousand dollar truck, money in a safe, a young face and I love women like bees love honey!"

They were all having fun and Linda passed Justice the blunt. April was eyeing him and he was doing the same with her. What she didn't know was Justice had been trained by the best. He got up and went over to sit next to April.

He leaned over to her ear and said, "I want to get to know you."

She said, "From all your mother done told me, I feel I know you already."

They started laughing. Linda was smiling because Justice was her little man and she felt safe with him like she did with David.

IEASHA

Ieasha was at home and she went into her daddy's room and told him she had something to talk to him about. Sabir Muhammad was a smart man, he had been in the marines for 20 years. He retired and opened up a computer store that was doing well. Sabir knew that Ieasha had something on her mind. She was a very smart young lady but she was spoiled.

Ieasha sat down and said, "Daddy I need you to answer something for me."

Sabir said, "What can I help you with baby?"

Ieasha said, "I have fallen in love with that patient that got shot that time. His name is Justin, the one I told you I spent a lot of time with."

Sabir asked, "Is he married?"

Ieasha replied, "No!"

"Is he Muslim?" Sabir asked.

Ieasha said, "No, but I am talking to him about that."

"Is he respectful?" Sabir asked her.

She replied, "Yes, but he's not Muslim."

Sabir said, "In due time."

"I want to bring him over for dinner Sunday," She said.

Sabir said, "That's fine, did you tell your mother?"

"Yes!" She said with excitement. "She told me to get with you."

DAVID

David had brought the 600-E Mercedes Benz out. It was cream colored and was dipped in gold everywhere. He dressed in some cream colored Gators and a three piece Brooks Brother's suit. He was cleaner than a new born baby. David was headed to New Haven Ct to see Linda and his son Justice. He had a bone to pick with Linda because word on the streets was she was dating Chad, one of David enemies.

David pulled up in the Benz and saw Justice come out of the house. He got out and hugged his son, then they both walked into the house.

Linda jumped up and hugged David and he grabbed a hand full of ass. She liked that and told Netta, "This is David."

Netta and April said at the same time, "Hello."

Linda said, "He is the realist nigga' alive."

The girls smiled and Netta had lust in her eyes.

David told Linda to come to the back so she followed him to her room and said, "What's up?"

David said, "So you been seeing Chad?"

Linda said, "Yeah. But it ain't nothing that's on our seed!"

David said, "That mother fucker tried to kill me!"

Linda said, "Come on baby, I'm not crazy, I know Chad isn't real."

"Did he get the pussy?" David asked.

Linda replied, "He can never get the pussy and you know better for asking me that shit. No one has got in here but you."

"Chad has been running his mouth so be careful," He warned her.

"It's cool, but I want you to get to know Netta better, she is a down ass bitch for whatever," She said.

David started laughing and said, "Girl you are something else and what you plan on doing?"

Linda said, "I will always be number one."

JUAN

Juan had been laying up over at his mother's house. It was around 10 pm when he pulled out his phone book and the first number he saw was Shandra Weaver, Tonya's mother's number. Juan said to himself, 'I am fixing to call her fine ass.' He dialed the number and the phone rang three times then someone picked up.

Juan asked, "Can I speak to Shandra?"

"This is her," she replied.

"You know who this is?" He asked.

Mrs. Weaver said, "Yes Juan."

He asked, "Can I come over?"

"Come on over," she said.

Juan told her, "I'm on my way."

Juan took a shower and got dressed, then he jumped in his rental car and headed to Shandra's house which took him about fifteen minutes to get there. He pulled up in the back yard and saw the porch light was on. He got out and knocked on the back door. After a minute Mrs. Weaver open the door in a white gown. She let Juan in and they sat on the couch watching TV together.

Juan slid closer to her and started where he left off a few days ago. He was kissing her neck and sucking he ears. Shandra was getting hot and told Juan to come to the bedroom. As soon as he went in she let her night gown fall to the floor and lay down on the bed.

Juan took all his clothes off and started kissing Shandra around the neck and sucking her chest. He licked her all the way down to her navel then went on down and started licking her love box. She jumped and started moaning, "Oh Baby! Shit!" Juan stayed down there working Shandra overtime until she had an orgasm, then she went out and came back, she was in heaven.

Juan laid himself on top of her and slid into her wetness. He was hitting her like she was a young girl. He turned her over and hit her from the back. Mrs. Weaver was a vet, she felt the young thug ready to bust. She used her years of skills and made him stand on his toes. Juan couldn't believe how good she was. He couldn't take it, he started moving fast and let loose inside Mrs. Weaver from the back.

They made love after that and then went to sleep. Shandra woke him up around 6 pm and told him that Tonya may be on her way.

He got up and got dressed then he gave Shandra a thousand dollars and said, "Go have some fun on me."

"Thank you," she replied.

Juan was headed out when he saw Tonya coming down the street. She didn't know it was Juan because he was in the rental. Tonya turned into her mom's driveway and got out with Daisy in her arms.

Daisy had gotten to be a big and bad girl. Tonya walked in and Daisy ran to her grandmother.

Tonya said, "What's up with you?"

Mrs. Weaver said, "Nothing," but she was smiling brightly.

Tonya replied, "Something is up, let me see."

She opened her mom's bedroom door and Mrs. Weaver said, "Girl get out of my room!"

Tonya said, "Who been over here?"

Mrs. Weaver told her, "I don't answer to you!"

"Juan been here and you got a big mark on your neck," She accused her mom.

"Where do I have marks on my neck?" She asked.

Tonya showed her and both of them started laughing. Tonya knew she needed that, it made Mrs. Weaver feel twenty years younger. Tonya said, "Okay now!"

JUSTIN

Justin was riding out to Avon, Connecticut to meet Ieasha's mother and father and to have dinner with them. He had the Lexus Coupe clean and he had on a blue and white Sean John suit with gold pin stripes and some white and gold snake skins. His Rolex was shining and he had an 8 carat diamond ring on his pinky. Both hands looked like they belonged to NFL players.

He had never been to Ieasha's house so he was looking for the number. The houses out that way were big and cost a lot of money. Justin found the number as he saw Ieasha's Maximum in the yard along with a Cadillac Escalade truck and a pretty BMW 520-I. He pulled his Lexus in the yard and waited.

He saw a tall man come out of the house, he had a cap on his head. Justin got out and said, "Does Ieasha live here?"

The man said, "Yes, get out and come in."

Justin left his gun in the car and when he walked in Ieasha was waiting.

She said, "Justin this is my father, Sabir Mohammad."

Justin shook his hand then he sat down and chilled. Sabir told Justin that he looked nice and Justin replied, "Thank you sir. You also look nice and so does your house."

Sabir asked Justin, "Where do you work?"

Justin said, "I work at Pa-Pa's Paint Shop off Weather Field Ave."

"I need to get some work done on my 64 Chevy, it's in the back yard, I already primed it up. How much you think a nice paint job will cost?" He asked Justin.

"Let me take a look at it," he responded.

Mr. Sabir and Justin walked out back to see the 64 Chevy. When they were out back Ieasha's mother said to her, "That's a nice looking young man. I love the way he dresses and the nice car he has."

Ieasha said, "One day mom, I am going to marry him. He has my heart, but I won't let him know that."

Sabir and Justin came back inside and Justin met Ieasha's mom. She told them to wash up the food was ready. Justin went to wash his hands and Ieasha came in behind him.

She said, "You need to dry your hands."

Justin looked her in the eyes and said, "Take this."

"What's this for?" She asked.

"It's the extra key to my house on Earl Street off Weather Field Ave," He said.

Ieasha started smiling. Justin hugged her and kissed her, putting his tongue in her mouth. He could tell she hadn't kissed that much because she was shaking, but she was so sweet.

Justin felt her butt, it was nice and fat. They heard a noise and Justin stopped, but Ieasha didn't want to stop. She was on fire, she had never had sex before but she was ready at 21 years old. She was burning from love.

They both went out and sat at the table next to each other. They had lamb chops, white rice, corn and pineapple cake with sweet tea for supper. Justin ate all of his food and said, "Now that was good!"

They watched a movie together until it started getting late and Justin told Ieasha he had to go. She walked him to the door, he got a quick kiss and said, "Come to my house tomorrow, I'm off work."

Ieasha said, "Okay."

Justin got in his car and headed out.

Ieasha ran to her dad and asked, "What do you think?"

Sabir said, "It's hard to impress me, but I am impressed. That could be a good brother, he's my type."

Ieasha said, "That's who I want!"

Sabir said, "The family stands behind you."

Ieasha was so happy she started crying, she knew a lot came with loving a Thomas man.

LISA

Lisa was back in Hartford going to meet up with Jerry, Chad's right hand man. She was pulling in the Courtyard hotel, looking good. She was on a mission and the place was packed, it was around 11:30 pm. She said to herself that Jerry should be there.

She spotted him coming down the lobby and said, "Gay-ba-so."

He said, "Tho! Gay-lean-do."

They walked to Lisa's room and she told Jerry she needed to get off some kilos' of cocaine and that she would give it to him for the low, low.

Jerry said, "Girl you know I got to ask Chad about that."

Lisa replied, "Don't ever tell Chad. Me and you never talked, use someone else's name, but never mine."

Jerry said, "Cool, is this where you are staying?"

Lisa said, "Yeah if anything changes I'll let you know."

THE FEDS IN TOWN

In the federal building across town, the feds were building a murder case against some big time drug dealers, king pens as they call them. David Thomas was their number one man. On his list was murder and drugs. CCI, Chad Smith and Juan Lopez were number two. David's son Justice Thomas was number three for drugs.

Special agent Ronald Smith was telling everyone that they had to be careful because David would run and he always carried a gun. Agent Smith said, "I want all of you to suit up, the first place is Stowe Village. Chad Smith, 95 Hampton St."

He showed them pictures of the building on an overhead screen. When they were done they all got into a UPS truck and headed to the place called the Vill.

LINDA

David called Netta in the room, she and Linda were talking. He told Netta he was going to take her to Hartford to show her around and Netta was all for it.

Justice was in his room giving it to April, she was moaning loud and Linda was smiling.

David started kissing on Linda and she came out of her clothes right in front of Netta. Linda bent over on the bed with her ass in the air so David went to work from behind. Linda was letting David have his way and Netta was getting wet as hell. David pulled out of Linda and told Netta to take off her clothes. Netta got naked and he walked over to her and started kissing her. She lay on the bed next to Linda and David started licking her click, she had never had that done before. He came up and kissed her on the mouth letting her taste her own juice from her wetness.

Linda grabbed Netta's legs and spread them open for David, he entered her love box and went to hitting her like a wild man. Netta was screaming because she had never had anything that big and long inside her, she couldn't take it all. Linda started kissing Netta on the mouth and she got wetter as David pounded her for about thirty minutes, then he rolled her over and rammed her from the back. David got ready to bust and he looked at Linda. She came over and he put it in her mouth. Linda was a pro, she told David to lie down and she got on his face, they had sex all day. They did everything, David was out of it, he took a shower and went to sleep.

Justice and April were laid up in bed too. Justice had April wide open.

STOWE VILLAGE FEDS

The kids were out playing in front of Hampton Street when they saw the brown UPS truck pull up. They kept playing not paying no attention it. The big white man got out and he had a bullet proof vest with F.B.I across his chest. He opened up the back door on the truck and twenty men dressed just like him ran into the building with their guns out. All you could hear was a loud noise, Boom! Boom!

Then there were nigga's everywhere. Chad had just gone up stairs and two F.B.I men came down with Chad in handcuffs. They put him in a small, unmarked, black car with tinted windows and sped off.

Channel 3 News Team was all over the place. The news was that the F.B.I. were in Stowe Village making some major busts.

JUAN

Juan was over at Sonya's house when he heard a knock on the door. He opened the door and they busted in. Juan started talking shit and they slammed him on the floor and put a foot in his back with guns to his head.

They searched Sonya's house then took Juan out and put him in an unmarked car and sped away.

Juan was in the back seat talking big shit, he was asking them what the charge was.

TONYA

Tonya was at her mom's house watching T.V. when Justin came over. The 12 o'clock news was coming on and they were showing pictures of Stowe Village and the arrests that had been made. Justin's heart dropped when he saw Juan's picture, Chad face was there also.

A wanted list came across the screen and David Thomas was #1 and his son Justice Thomas. Justin dropped to the floor because now it was up to him to make sure his dad and brother had the best lawyer and things were right on the streets.

Tonya called Gail and Gail told her she was watching the news.

Gail said, "Tonya them white folks are watching your house so be careful and tell David and Justice to turn their selves in before they hurt them. That's all them white folks want to do is kill a nigga' in the streets like an animal.

LINDA

Linda turned on the T.V. and saw David and Justice's pictures. She ran and woke David up. She told him that they were wanted by the F.B.I and they had Chad and Juan.

David said, "Damn!"

Justice went up and told April to chill. He said, "April if you stand by me, I promise we will get back together." April had tears in her eyes but Justice said, "This isn't over."

DAVID

David called the person he could depend on no matter what, his mother Gail. They talked and he told her that Jesse's company would back almost everything with the money he had. He told his mom he was going to turn himself in and she said, "Face it, that's the best thing. I love you and I will pray."

David called Tonya and said, "Where is Daisy?"

Tonya said, "Right here."

David said, "Stop crying it's that time, we had and got the best. They don't have shit on me. Meet me in New Haven at the Grand Inn Hotel and bring Daisy"

Tonya said, "I'm on my way. Justin will be with me also."

F.B.I.

The special agent had Chad in a room asking him where he got the cocaine connection from New York and who up there was bringing him over hundred kilos a week.

Chad said, "I don't know what you are talking about."

Agent Smith said, "Mother fucker I'm going to take everything you think you owned and make sure you never see the streets again." He threw his card in Chad's face and said, "Call me when this shit sinks in. Let me tell you before I walk out, your B.M.W. and Cadillac truck are out there in pawn and your motorcycle and gold is in the F.B.I safe. The money you had in the bank in your sister's name, I got a hold on that and she's on welfare so that's mine. Nigga' you are fucked unless you help me."

Agent Smith told the officer to get Chad out of his face.

Chad had a lot to think about, he did not want to lose everything he had risked his life for. All the blood and tears, his brother's death and his friend's dying.

JUAN

Juan was chilling when agent Smith came in the room. He had been through this before on a lower level so he said, "I don't want to talk, I have not hired a lawyer yet, so you can get the fuck on."

Agent Smith jacked Juan up and said, "I got your ass now. You need a lawyer."

He walked out and told the officers to leave him. The A.T.F. Agent Brooks wanted to talk to Juan but Juan told him the same thing and they were mad.

Agent Brooks said, "Take Juan Lopez to Morgan Street and leave him there."

Chapter Twelve

NEW HAVEN CONN
GRAND INN HOTEL

Tonya and her two kids were on their way to New Haven to see David. When Tonya turned into the hotel, she circled around to make sure no one was following her then she saw David standing in the hotel lobby. She parked and they all got out. Justin had Daisy's hand as they walked in.

David said, "What's up?"

Daisy ran to him, she was crazy about her dad. David led them to the room and they all went in. David sat Tonya down and told her what was up. Justin called Justice and told him that he was coming to see him.

David said, "Bring Justice back with you, we are going to turn ourselves in tomorrow."

Daisy fell asleep and David told Tonya he didn't know what they had on him, or who was going to fall weak. He told her that he expected her to be there every step of the way, 2-DIE-4. He prepared her for the rumors on the streets.

He said, "In the morning I want you to find me, Juan and Justice the best lawyer's money can buy."

Tonya laid on the bed with tears in her eyes. She said, "David promise me this is it, you don't need to sell no more drugs. We have four apartment buildings on Barbar Street, three houses in Connecticut, four houses in Georgia and over one hundred acres of land." Tonya was crying hard when she told David, "Promise me."

David said, "I don't make any promises, you can get Daisy and get out my life right now and there won't be no hard feelings. But don't ever ask me to make a promise I can't keep! I love you and respect you as my number one woman, but don't push it. I am going to always be real."

Tonya replied, "David you have had my mind, body and soul for years. I have never touched another man, I love you and when this is over I want to marry you."

David said, "Baby that's what I been waiting for."

They started kissing then David made love to Tonya like he would never see her again. Afterward she lay in his arms until he got up and played with Daisy.

Justin and Justice knocked on the door and then came in.

David told the boys, "Look we are all we got. Justice you got money put up and Linda is going to take care of it. Justin we are going to need you to stay low and follow orders."

Justin said, "Anything you want Dad, 2-DIE-4."

David said, "When I tell you to get a phone that can't be traced or billed, do it. Then you and I can talk about whatever."

Justin said, "Okay."

Tonya woke up and got out of the bed in her panties.

Justin said, "Mom."

Tonya said, "Damn." Then she started laughing. She put her pants on and grabbed Daisy. Tonya jumped on the phone and started calling some of the best lawyers in Connecticut. She called Rob Smith, David's old lawyer and told him about the case. He told Tonya he would take the case for David. She then called Johnny Fisher for Justice, Wayne Snow for Juan and Melissa Ford who was the family lawyer. These three lawyers were the best in the state. That was a bill of about a hundred and fifty dollars.

David called Timmy and Cheese to come pick him and Justice up from New Haven in a brand new limo Rolls Royce. He told Justin and Tonya to meet them down on Morgan Street then he said, "Are you ready Justice?"

Justice said, "Yeah let's get it over with."

JUAN

Juan was in his cell when the officer came out and told him he had a lawyer visit. Juan went out and saw an old white headed man sitting down with a brand new suit on, he looked like money.

Juan walked into the room and said, "What's up?"

Mr. Snow shook Juan's hand and said, "I was hired today and I am going to be looking into everything and do my best to free you. I need you to sign these papers so I can get a copy of everything they have on you." Juan signed the papers and Mr. Snow said, "This is a big case, it's the talk of the state of Connecticut."

Juan said, "I need to get out."

Mr. Snow said, "In due time. I will tell you everything as we go along.

JIMMY AND CHEESE

Jimmy pulled up in the stretch Rolls Royce limo to pick David and Justice up and take them to Morgan St. jail to turn themselves in.

David's lawyer, Rob Smith, had called and told the people that David Thomas was on his way and that he would be the lead lawyer on the case. He told them that he was hired by David Thomas along with Tina Braxton and David Pallard. Justice's lawyer was also there, Johnny Fisher.

When David and Justice pulled up in the limo Channel 3 News was there. David saw Gail, Jesse, Betty, Jasmine and Yolanda. Then he saw Justin who was standing there when the limo stopped.

Jimmy and Cheese got out and opened the door for David and Justice. The news people were trying to rush them but both Jimmy and Cheese were trained body guards, they knew how to handle crowds.

The news lady asked David, "Are you the King Pen? Have you ever had someone killed?"

David wouldn't say anything, he looked out at his family and smiled, trying to ease the mood.

Rob Smith and Johnny Fisher talked to the news people while David hugged Gail and his sisters. He kissed Tonya on the mouth and everyone was crying.

David and Justice went into the building and were booked. The special agent there didn't waste his time talking to David, he just threw a card at him and said, "If you want help call me." He did Justice the same way and they both replied, "Fuck you!"

IEASHA

Ieasha was at home watching TV when the news came on, they were talking about a crime family live from Morgan Street and she saw Justice going into the building. She said, "Oh my God that's Justin folks." Then they showed Justin who was standing there looking sad. Ieasha's heart dropped.

Her daddy, Sabir came into the living room and said, "You see that?"

Ieasha said, "Yes."

She started crying because she felt Justin's pain and she loved him. His hurt was hers and she prayed that Allah would have mercy on them all.

Sabir hugged his daughter and said, "Is Justin okay?"

"Yes, there he goes now," Ieasha said as she pointed to the TV.

The news showed Justin getting in a blue Corvette and driving away.

Sabir said, "That boy has changed but he use to deal with some heavy stuff. The word on the streets is that they are nothing to play with. Allah knows best and He is the only one that can lead a person on the right path. Hopefully one day Justin will be on that path."

TONYA

Tonya was on her way home one night and an unmarked car flashed its lights behind her. She pulled over and an F.B.I agent got out. As he was walking up, Tonya saw that it was Agent Smith. He made her get out of her vehicle, then he went through her car. He was a real ass and told Tonya that he was going to destroy her life and that it was a promise.

Tonya said, "I will make sure I destroy you first."

Agent Smith was mad because he couldn't find anything in Tonya's car.

David called her that night and she told him how Agent Smith had pulled her over and was harassing her. David told Tonya he would take care of it. She told David that everyone was talking about what happened at her job.

David said, "Baby I told you there would be talk, just be strong and raise Daisy."

MORGAN STREET JAIL
FED HOLDING

David was in the cell right down from Justice and Juan and Chad was on the other side. David told the boys to come to the gym so they could all talk. The officer came and got Justice out of the cell. He had a visit from his lawyer Mr. Fisher, who had come for Justice to sign some papers.

Justice went down to meet Mr. Fisher, he shook his hand and signed the papers. Mr. Fisher told him that he would have his first hearing on Monday.

Justice nodded his head, then got up and walked out where an officer took him back to his cell.

LISA

Jerry was telling Lisa that the Fed's got Chad, David, Justice and Juan. He told Lisa that he was laying low.

She told him, "I need you to find out who is where. Chad knows a lot about me and my family in New York."

Jerry said, "Girl they took all of Chad's shit and they're still finding some shit he had in other names of people in his family. I got to get him a lawyer and the money is slow."

Lisa said, "Call me if things change, I am still in Bloomfield."

JUSTIN

Justin was chilling at his condo on Weather Field Ave, laying on the couch. The door opened and he jumped up, it was Ieasha using her key. She came in the door with a big bag in her hand.

Justin said, "What's up?" Then he gave her a big hug.

"I saw the news," Ieasha replied.

"Yeah things are crazy right now," he told her.

Ieasha said, "I got some ice cream."

Justin made them both a bowl and they ate ice-cream while they watched a movie. Justin got real close to Ieasha and told her he was not easy to get.

Ieasha said, "And I am not easy to get either."

They both started laughing, then Justin started kissing Ieasha and rubbing on her legs. She moved closer and Justin sucked on her ear.

Ieasha got up and unwrapped her hair. She stood there and just looked at Justin then she said, "This never happened, promise me!"

Justin said, "I promise."

She started taking her clothes off and got down to her two piece swim suit.

Justin almost passed out when he saw her body. He asked her, "Why do you cover all that up with big clothes?"

Ieasha responded, "Because I want a man to want me for me, not my body."

He started feeling on Ieasha again and she started moving in close.

Justin kissed her ear and whispered, "Put your clothes back on, I can wait. I want you for you."

"Get it, do what you want," she told him.

"No," Justine replied then got up and walked to the back.

Ieasha was mad, but she was also glad that he wanted to wait for that moment. She knew that she really loved him. She walked to the back and hugged her man then said, "I would do anything for you and with you."

He smiled and said, "Now that's what I am talking about. Me and you for real, sex will come but for now let's enjoy each other."

They laughed and watched TV until it got late. Justin told Ieasha that his dad and brother had to be in court Monday. He said, "I got to be there because family always comes first. Loyalty and respect, 2-DIE-4, 4-ever!"

DOWN TOWN HARTFORD
FEDERAL COURT ROOM 3RD FLOOR

T.V. news people were everywhere, David, Juan and Justice were getting ready to make their first court appearance. Today everyone would find out what they were charged with and what the Fed's and state had on them.

David had on white, silk Brooks Brothers and some white and gold Sean John boots. Justice had on a blue Armada suit with a yellow tie and some yellow Armada boots. Juan had on a light gray Brooks Brothers suit with some black Gator boots. All the boys were looking good and when they walked into court all eyes were on them.

Everyone with a name in Connecticut was there. The girls from Stowe Village, Linda, Netta, April, Justin, Ieasha, Gail, Jesse and all of David's family, aunts and Tonya's family too.

David walked in first smiling and then Juan and Justice. Sonya and Ollie were sitting with Carmen, Juan's girl. Mrs. Weaver was there looking good in a silk pants suit. The Judge came out and everyone had to stand. The D.A. for the fed's was a real hot ass, her name was Mrs. Pat Stone and she was hard on drug dealers.

She got up and said, "Your honor today we bring before you the case of David Thomas, Juan Lopez and Justice Thomas VS. The United States. Charges are count 1, Conspiracy to traffic over a ton of cocaine from 1988 until 2004, count 2, murder for hire and count 3, trafficking weapons from Atlanta to Hartford. Your honor David Thomas also has an indictment alone on federal and state king pen statues for running an organized crime family called 2-DIE-4. Be advised your honor Justice Thomas was already out on bail for murder but the charges were later dropped because the eye witness came up dead."

David's lawyer Rob Smith, jumped up and said, "I object your honor. We can't try them together they are all different people."

Mrs. Stone said, "They are a crime family."

Mr. Smith said, "Prove it."

The judge hit the desk and said, "Order in the courtroom. Go ahead and speak Mr. Smith."

David's lawyer explained that all three men should not be tried together. The Judge said she agreed and Rob Smith got what he wanted.

Johnny Fisher told the Judge he wanted a bond hearing for his client and Mr. Snow said he wanted the same thing for his. The D.A. talked some more then the judge said a bond hearing would be at the next court hearing which would be a month from now. The Judge said for now everyone stays in jail.

Special agent's told the judge all kinds of stuff about David, Juan and Justice. He told the judge they would never hit the streets again and that's what made David make his decision. Mr. Ronald Smith was a walking dead man, he just did not know when or how.

David and the crew left the courtroom mad at the world. He had a lot on his mind, but he knew it might be over for him for a long time. He would die in prison before he would tell on anyone.

COUNTY-JAIL

David went back to the county and laid down, he was in a room by himself and so was everyone else, max 23 hour lock down. The officer shook the bars and David jumped.

Officer Webster said, "David Thomas A.K.A Lil-D, I have a box for you."

David jumped up and the officer slid the box through the bars.

David asked, "What's up?"

Officer Webster said, "Justin took care of me and walked off without saying another word."

David looked in the box and inside was three unlimited cell-phones that couldn't be traced. David smiled because his first born was on point. He called down the hall to Justice and Juan and said come to the gym tonight.

When David and the boys went to the gym, he gave each one a phone and told them to be careful. He told Juan and Justice that officer Webster was on their team then he went back to his cell and called Tonya.

She was happy that he was able to talk to her. David told her Justin did his job. Tonya told him that Agent Smith came to her job and was really getting out of hand.

David said, "Baby I'm going to take care of that."

He talked to Daisy, then he and Tonya talked a few minutes. He told her he would hit her up later, he had some calls to make.

David called Justin who picked up on the first ring. David said, "Good looking out son. Now I need for you to find out where Agent Ronald Smith lives and pay him a visit. He has been real hard on your mother and he is the lead agent in the case."

Justin said, "I will see agent Smith tonight. I know he stays in Avon, I'm on top of him. Ieasha and I will be going."

David said, "Don't slip."

Justin said, "I'm training Ieasha like you trained mom."

David started laughing and said, "Ieasha is a good girl, but make sure she understands it's 2-DIE-4, 4-ever, no turning back."

Justin said, "Dad I'm on that."

LINDA

Linda was on the phone talking to Justice, telling him about the shit that was going on in the streets. She told Justice that she was coming to see him just as soon as he could get a visit.

Justice said, "Bring April."

Linda said, "I will, she's been staying here with me, that's my girl."

Justice asked, "Mom have you seen Lisa?"

"Last I heard she was back in New York, but she comes to Hartford," she replied.

He said, "Watch her."

Linda said, "I don't leave home without my 9 mm and you know I will use it."

"You take care and I will call you later, much love," He said and hung up.

JUSTIN

Justin and Ieasha were sitting around and Justin said, "Ieasha I need you to drive me somewhere."

Ieasha said, "Okay."

He said, "You can't tell anyone. Just drop me off and wait for me, don't leave me."

Ieasha replied, "I would never leave you."

Justin went to the back room and changed clothes. He came back with all black on and a long black bag, he also had a cap on that turn into a ski mask.

He asked, "Baby are you ready?"

Ieasha said, "Yeah, let's go."

They went out and got into her Maxima then headed to Avon. Ieasha was driving and Justin was laying back behind the tinted windows. They were in the Avon Mountains when Justin said. "Help me look for Fox Street."

They found Fox Street and Justin said, "Let me out here and meet me on Nobel Street, there's some woods out there and a lot of trees."

Ieasha was a little scared, but she was down for her man. Justin was walking through the woods towards Mr. Smith's house.

Ronald Smith was staying alone, his wife had left him about four years ago because he never spent time with the family. He was always at work and she knew Smith was cheating on her. Mr. Smith was a drinker and loved to watch TV. He was up late looking over some paper work. He was close to making a big break in his case and that would keep David Thomas behind bars for the rest of his life. Mr. Smith started smiling on that thought.

Justin was on his back porch with a ski-mask on. He had a good shot from where he was, but he didn't take it, he wanted to make sure Mr. Smith died, no mistakes. He took the 270-Remington rifle out of the bag and looked through the scope, he had a good shot at Mr. Smith's head. Justin had the 9 mm on his waist and a hunting knife in his socks.

He knocked on the door and Mr. Smith was thinking it was the old man from next door wanting to talk at 2 am in the morning. Mr. Smith just opened the door, he never looked to see who it was.

Justin put the 9 mm to his head and said, "Don't' say shit. Take off all your clothes, slowly."

Mr. Smith got naked and Justin tied him up real good. Justin was looking at all the paper work then he put it all back in the suit case. He took the 9 mm and put two shots to agent Smith's head, he died on the spot.

Justin reached in his mouth, cut his tongue out and put it in his lap. He went out the back door into the woods and was waiting in the woods to see Ieasha's car. He said to himself,

~ 183 ~

'Ieasha should have been here.' When he looked up he saw her Maxima. Justin ran and jumped in then they headed back to his house on Weather Field Ave. Ieasha didn't ask any questions because she knew not to.

Justin said, "That's being loyal and respectful, you did well."

Ieasha started smiling. They pulled into Justin's yard, got out and went in the house. When they got inside Justin opened up the suit case and he and Ieasha looked over all the papers. They had seen all the names of the people who helped the state and Fed's build a case against David and his crew. Justin was hurt when he saw Lisa's name, she had been busted and was now working for the Fed's. He also saw Lil-Mike's name and Timmy, the limo driver was also working for the Fed's along with Cheese.

Justin said, "Damn!"

Chad had made a statement saying that all the drugs were David's and he was forced to sell it. He told them David had killed his brother over some drug money and that David and his crew were behind 94% of the murders that went on in Hartford, Connecticut.

DAVID

David was in his cell when the officer came and told him he had a visit, it was Rob Smith. David went out and talked to his lawyer. Mr. Smith told David they were still building a case against him and that special agent Ronald Smith was a monster. He was not going to stop until he got what he wanted.

David told his lawyer, "I need you to get me out and don't ever tell me about any deal, because I don't' make deals with the police."

Mr. Smith said, "Don't worry they won't ask me for no deal."

THE MOUNTAINS

AVON CONNECTICUT

Mr. John Bush walked over to Mr. Smith's house that morning at 6am, they always had a cup of coffee and talked about a case before Mr. Smith went to work. Mr. Bush knocked on the back door but no one answered. Mr. Bush knew he was home because the car and truck were still in the yard. He looked in the window and what he saw made his heart stop. He saw his friend naked on the floor.

He ran home and called 911. The police came fast because they knew rich people and important people stay out there. When they knocked, the door opened. Mr. Smith had been dead for over four hours.

Mr. Bush was hurt, he looked down and saw his friend's tongue in his lap. The news people were everywhere and FBI men were searching the woods. They felt that whoever did it was still around.

Mr. Bush said, "I told him to let go of that big case and go back to just a little agent. God bless his soul, he wanted whoever they were."

TONYA

Tonya was at home when the news came on TV. She said, "Oh My God! Someone killed that sorry motherfucker, Agent Rob Smith!"

She was not glad but she hated the way agent Smith was doing her. Tonya called David on his cell phone.

David said, "What's up baby?"

Tonya said, "Someone killed agent Smith last night in his home."

David said, "For real? Baby let me hit you back, I can't talk right now something going on."

David hung up and laid back on his bed. The news was music to his ears because a lot more bodies were going to fall for breaking the code, 2-DIE-4.

COUNTY JAIL

The news that special agent Ronald Smith was found dead spread fast. Every officer was talking about how someone cut his tongue out and shot him twice in the head. Everyone in jail was watching the news, they were showing agent Smith's house on TV. No witness, no arrest. The FBI were saying it was a clean hit. Head FBI agent Mr. Shay Bland was saying that Mr. Smith took down a big drug ring in Hartford and the next week he was found dead. They believed it was connected to the big take down. Now everyone wanted to know who killed special agent Ronald Smith.

LISA

Lisa was watching the TV when she said, "Damn David is still pulling moves!"

She started wondering to herself, who's out there doing David's dirty work? Then it hit her, David's oldest son came to her mind, Justin Thomas. He was just like David.

Lisa started thinking of a way to kill Justin before he came after her. She picked up the phone and called Jerry.

Jerry said, "What's up?"

Lisa said, "It's me, we need to fine Justin before he comes after us."

"Justin and I are cool. That young mother-fucker is a killer!" He replied.

"I know, I helped raise him! He was a baby when I met David," she told him.

Jerry said, "But for you I will help find him."

"We got to be careful because David trained him to track humans," she said.

DAVID

The officer came and got David out of his cell a long with two other inmates.

The officer said, "You are transferring to another holding prison."

David was headed to the Meadows on West Service Road. Justin had told David about everyone who had written statements against him. He told his son in time everyone must pay, 2-DIE-4.

David and the rest of the prisoners got on the bus. He was looking around for Justice and Juan, but they were nowhere to be found. David laid back and enjoyed the ride, he saw his old home the Vill.

GAIL

Gail had talked to Justin, she told him they were moving David and the boys to another prison and that they could go see him now. Justin was happy, he told his grandmother that he was still working and doing well. Gail had no idea that Justin was a killer.

Justin told his grandmother he loved her and hung up the phone.

LINDA

Linda was riding with Netta and April when they came across a young boy who was selling weed. Linda pulled over and they all started talking about how much green to get. Linda wanted to get enough so she could take Justice some when she went to see him. She got two ounces from the kid then Linda and the girls went home and were chilling.

Justice called and told Linda that they transferred him to Bridge Port, Connecticut on 1106 N. Ave. He told his mom it was rough but he could handle it.

Linda said, "April and I are coming to see you."

He said, "Bring me some T-Shirts, socks, boxers and new pair of Jordan's."

Linda replied, "Boy I got you."

"I got six thousand dollars on the books," he told her.

She said, "Cool I love you."

Justice said, "I love you too baby girl."

DAVID

David was in F-block and everyone in Hartford knew him so things were cool. Juan was in D-block, he had got in a fight with some kid from Albany Ave. David was working out and eating well. He and Juan had about nine thousand dollars on the books. New Jordan's, silk everything and much respect.

David was thinking about Justice. He was in Bridgeport, a rough prison for anyone. David knew Justice could handle it. They were scheduled to go to court in twenty days.

AGENT

Agent Marvin Harris was in charge of the big case in Hartford. He went to the Meadows Jail to talk to Juan. He felt he had something on Juan and maybe they could make a deal. Mr. Harris walked into the Meadows and told the officer to get Juan Lopez.

The officer went to get him and Juan came into the room. Mr. Harris said, "Hello Mr. Lopez."

Juan said, "What's up?"

Mr. Harris said, "I am not here to bullshit you."

He put some pictures in front of Juan's face and said, "They have you for a murder a year ago."

Juan was thinking, 'damn that's me and they got me!'

Mr. Harris was telling Juan everything Lisa had told him. All the stuff she and Juan had done together. Mr. Harris said, "Save yourself Mr. Lopez or you will never see your mom and sister again." He gave Juan his card and said, "Don't be no one's fool."

Mr. Harris walked out without saying another word.

Juan had a lot to think about, he and David were like brothers. David's two sons were like his own, they were family. For the first time in years, Juan was scared. He had tears in his eyes. His mother needed him, his sister needed him, but David had made him rich and was closer than family. They shared so much, 2-DIE-4, 4-ever 140!!!!!!

PART TWO:

THE FALL OF THE FAMILY 2-DIE-4

Chapter Thirteen

DISLOYALTY & DISTRUST
JUAN

Juan went back to his cell and called his mother. Ollie Lopez was glad to hear her only son's voice.

Juan said, "Mom I talked to a special agent, Mr. Harris. They got me down bad." Ollie started crying and Juan said, "Mom you got to be strong. I want you to call my lawyer and see what kind of deal Mr. Harris has." Juan said to himself, 'I got to break the code 2-DIE-4.'

He and David grew up together, but now it was a choice, him or David. Juan called his sister Sonya.

She said, "What's up Lil bro?"

Juan said, "They got me down bad, but the agent said he would make a deal if I worked with him."

Sonya said, "Save yourself, you never know what David will do. He may blame everything on you."

Juan knew in his heart that David would never tell on anyone, he was one of the realest nigga's alive. But Juan told her that he was not fixing to take a charge for anyone, plus the game was over. Juan wanted to win by any means.

Sonya said, "Boy are you still there?"

Juan said, "Yeah, I got a lot on my mind. I am going to save my ass."

Sonya said, "You better, I will see you soon."

Juan laid back with tears in his eyes. It was over. 2-DIE-4. He promised David 2-DIE-4, he would never cross him. Damn!"

JUSTICE

Linda had come to visit Justice, she had April with her and she brought Justice an ounce of weed.

Justice was looking good, he worked out every day and had been reading law books.

Justin and Ieasha had been to see him. Justin told his little brother things were going to be okay, but he had to be strong, it takes time.

Linda told her son she would be back every week.

Justice was kissing all over April before visitation ended. Then he hugged his mom and said, "Be careful."

DAVID

David and Juan were in church and David asked Juan what Agent Harris was talking about.

Juan lied and said, "The same old shit. I didn't tell him shit."

David felt hurt because Juan couldn't look him in the eye. David didn't say anything else and Juan did all the talking. David got up and hugged Juan, he had tears in his eyes.

David said, "I love you like the two brothers I lost, its 2-DIE-4. But if you break the code, I will hate you like an enemy."

David walked out of the church and never looked back at Juan.

It didn't matter, Juan's mind was made up, he was not going to prison for the rest of his life.

LAWYER SNOW

Lawyer Snow and Agent Harris had made a deal, Juan would tell on David and get the charges dropped and Agent Harris would get Juan an eighty thousand dollar bond after he made the statement on what all he knew.

Mr. Harris went back to the Meadows to see Juan. Juan wrote a statement concerning David and Justice's involvement. He told Mr. Harris about unsolved murders and big drug deals, the connection from New York, D.C., L.A. and CA.

Juan had broken the code 2-DIE-4. He said to himself, 'I can protect me, I'm not worried so now it's whatever!'

JUSTIN

Justin was at the Super 8 Hotel parking lot dressed in all black. Ieasha was driving and they were in a rental car. He spotted Jimmy and Cheese getting out of Jimmy's white 73 Impala. He got out with his bag and he laid in the grass.

He had the scope on Jimmy's head. Justin was a great shooter, he learned a lot in the school Marine R.O.T.C. He was the best in his class with a rifle. Justin shot Jimmy in the head and he never knew what hit him.

Cheese pulled out his gun and started looking around.

Justin shot Cheese between the eyes and he never knew what hit him either. His head split in half. Justin ran and got into the car with Ieasha. He kissed her and she drove off like nothing had happen.

LISA

Lisa was riding around asking people what they knew about Justin, but everyone played crazy because they were thinking Lisa was the police, plus she looked white. Lisa was mad, she wanted Justin bad and she knew her days were limited.

She had talked to Agent Harris, he asked her if she wanted some protection.

Lisa said, "No." But really she didn't know what to do.

Monday was the bond hearing for all the boys, they would be back on Morgan Street in Hartford in no time.

BOND HEARING

David, Justice and Juan were all back on Morgan St. waiting to go to court for a bond hearing. David and Juan didn't talk. Justice was telling David that Linda and April came to see him.

Justice asked, "What's up with Juan, he is not talking."

David said, "I don't know, he may have a lot on his mind."

The officer came and got the boys, they were headed to the 3rd floor Federal Courtroom. When they got there, they all sat down.

Judge Bond walked in and everyone stood up. Mrs. Pat Stone the D.A was looking evil. She took the floor first.

She said, "Your honor I need extra time on the case because the lead agent was found murdered at his home."

Judge Bond said, "Yes ma'am we understand that."

Mrs. Stone sat down and went to writing on a pad.

Mr. Snow stood up and said, "Your honor I had made a request to have a bond set for my client Mr. Juan Lopez. He is not a risk and Mr. Lopez doesn't have a history of run in's with the law."

Judge Bond said, "I grant Mr. Lopez a bond of one hundred thousand dollars. He is not to leave the state of Connecticut."

Juan's lawyer said, "Will do, we thank you, your honor."

David's lawyer got up and told Judge Bond that David should get a bond because he was part owner of a family company and he would not run because he had no reason to.

DA Mrs. Stone jumped up and said, "David Thomas should not get a bond because he has been charged before for a violent crime."

The judge said, "Bond denied for David Thomas."

Justice's lawyer, Mr. Fisher told his side about Justice, trying to get him a bond. Mr. Fisher told the judge that Justice had a murder charge, but it was dropped. He told the judge that Justice was a good kid.

Mrs. Stone jumped up and said, "Your honor Justice Thomas is also on the Fed watch list."

Judge Bond said, "Bond denied until trial."

Everyone was mad but Juan's family was happy. Ollie was smiling because she loved her only son and Sonya was happy too.

Gail and Tonya were crying but David told them it would be okay. Linda was crying for her son and David.

Juan did not look David's way at all. The bail man came to get him and they went down stairs.

David was hurt because with all he and Juan had been through, he couldn't believe Juan fell weak.

David's lawyer came over and told David, "I have something to show you."

He and his lawyer went into a little room where Mr. Smith showed David a statement by Juan Lopez. David read it and his heart turned cold as ice. Juan had turned state on him and Justice.

"What do you want me to do?" David asked.

Mr. Smith replied, "From me to you, handle it in the streets. He don't need to show up at your trial."

David walked out and when he and Justice were on the van headed back, David told him everything. Justice was hurt because he loved Juan too.

David said, "It's cool, but it's going to really hurt Justin when I tell him, because that's his God father."

David went back to the Meadows and Justice was headed back to Bridge Port. David had seen the news, Jimmy and Cheese were found dead in the Super-8 parking lot and the FBI were on the case.

David called Justice on his cell phone.

Justice said, "Damn!"

They talked and David told Justice to stay strong and in the end it will pay off.

JUSTIN

Justin and Ieasha were at his house, Justin had got Ieasha a 9 mm and she was good with it. Justin told Ieasha to keep it with her for protection.

Ieasha said, "Baby I want to move in with you for protection."

Justin asked, "What you waiting on?"

Ieasha already had a lot of clothes at Justin's house anyway.

LINDA

Linda had gone home, she had been hanging with some known crack heads, Kim and Sha-Sha. Linda had smoked some crack for the first time, Kim told her it would help her forget her problems. Linda was feeling funny from the drug, but she had plenty of money, fifty thousand dollars in the safe.

Justice never told her where his money was but she had smoked up two thousand dollars' worth of crack with her friends. Netta and April didn't know Linda was now smoking, so she had to hide it from them.

LISA

Lisa had gone and talked to agent Harris, she was telling him about a lot of stuff. She told him about Linda and that Linda knew everything about David. She also told him that Linda had helped commit a lot of crimes.

Mr. Harris said, "Do you know where Linda is at?"

Lisa said, "Word on the street is that she is somewhere in New Haven."

Agent Harris got on the phone and put the word out.

JUAN

Juan was in the holding cell waiting to get out. The officer came and said, "Mr. Lopez you are free to go."

He opened the door and Juan walked out of Morgan Street a free man.

Mr. Harris was waiting on Juan, he said, "I'm cool."

His mother and sister were waiting on him. He got in the car and they headed home to his mother's house where he would lay low.

DAVID & TONYA

Tonya had went to see David, she said, "Juan is out but he's lying low, no one has seen him."

David said, with tears in his eyes, "Juan broke the code, ain't no more love for Juan."

Tonya said, "I feel you baby."

David looked up and Justin and Ieasha had walked into the visiting room. David was smiling, he loved Justin because they were just alike. Everyone talked and ate, David was playing with Daisy but she was sleepy.

David said, "Will you girls pardon us? I need to tell Justin something." The girls walked off and David said, "Juan turned on me, he wrote a statement." Justin started crying. David hugged his son and said, "Only the real last, the ones who tell die fast!"

Justin looked his daddy in the eyes and said, "I'm going to handle this."

"Be careful," David told him.

Justin said, "Dad Ieasha is like Tonya and I love her."

David said, "That's cool train her well. But watch agent Harris and check on Linda."

"The word on the street of New Haven is that Linda is smoking crack," Justin said.

David was hurt, he told Justin not to tell Justice.

Justin said, "I won't. Ieasha and I are trying to get him back to Hartford jail, by next week."

CHAD

Chad was still trying to make some deals he wanted to get out bad, but he didn't want to tell on his New York people. He told the Feds, that David had the drugs coming into Hartford for years and he was a killer.

Chad was going for a bond hearing next week and most likely he was going to get out because of the deal he made. Agent Harris told Chad that he would help him with most of the charges, but Chad had to come to court when David's trial started.

Chad said, "That's a deal."

He wrote another statement telling it all.

LISA

Lisa had found out where Linda was staying. Four of her men had come down from New York and they were headed to Linda's house.

Linda was in the house high as a kite, she was in another world smoking so much crack.

Lisa and her men pulled up in front of Linda's house in a black SUV. Lisa said, "Two of you come with me and two stay in the SUV."

She got out and knocked on Linda's door. Linda was so high she didn't look out the peep hole, she just opened the door.

Lisa and her men pushed passed her and Lisa told her two men to check the house and kill whoever was in here.

Linda said in a low voice, "Bitch, what are you doing?"

"You ran away from me," Lisa said.

Linda was getting ready to reach under the couch for her gun, but the drugs made her move slow. Lisa grabbed her hand and the men came back in the front room. They told Lisa the house was clear.

Lisa look Linda in the eyes and said, "I loved you like a sister, we had it all, seen it all." Lisa was crying, she said, "But everything in life has an ending." Lisa pulled out a needle and ordered the two men to hold Linda down.

Linda was pleading, but not the kind of pleading a person would plead close to death. Linda's last words to Lisa were, "Coward Bitch! I will see you in hell!"

Lisa injected the poisoned drugs into Linda's arm. Linda moved but to no avail, her heart stopped in just two minutes.

Lisa took it hard, she had tears in her eyes. It hurt but that was the code of the streets, pain is love.

JUSTICE

When the news got to Justice that Linda had died of a drug overdose, he could not believe it. Something told him that someone killed his mother. Justice was in pain, he cried for the first time from the pits of his soul. He cried for all the young black girls and boys who had lost their mother before him. He cried for the last time. He knew someone killed his mother and the first person that came to his mind was Lisa.

Justice made his mother a promise as he prayed to God. He was going to kill that bitch Lisa. He knew he had to be strong so he laid back and went to sleep, the world had stolen the closest love he knew, his mother.

TONYA

Tonya, Gail and the whole family had gone to see Justice. He was a strong kid and he understood what it was like to be in a world without your mom. April took the news hard and so did Wynetta. Justice told his grandmother Gail, that he didn't want to go to the funeral because he would not come back to jail.

Gail hugged him and said, "I understand."

The state wouldn't let David go because of his case. But everyone else would get a chance to pay their respects to a thug girl who had it all.

Everyone in Hartford knew Linda, she had been getting money for a long time and if you were about money you knew Linda. She was a legend in Hartford, AKA 'The Heartbeat.'

DAVID

David was sad, he wanted to know who had done that to Linda. He made some powerful phone calls from prison. The word on the streets was Lisa was back in town. David said to himself, 'I should have killed that bitch.' David knew Lisa was a cold hearted person, he also knew that Lisa would kill with no remorse.

JUSTIN

Justin and Ieasha had been up looking over paper work. Justin told Ieasha that Linda was like a mom to him and whoever did that would pay dearly, 2-DIE-4, 4-ever, 140. He told Ieasha that Juan had turned state on David and that Juan was Justice's God father.

Ieasha asked, "Are you going to the funeral?"

Justin said, "Hell yeah, I got to pay my respects, its 2-DIE-4. Linda showed me so much about the streets. How to save money and how to treat a real woman."

Ieasha hugged Justin and said, "She did a good job on showing you how to treat a real woman."

Justin just smiled.

JUAN

Juan was at his mom's house in East Hartford, laying low. He knew David would soon find out that he turned state on him and Justice. But Juan was a killer also, he kept a 45 magnum with him at all times. He was not going into no witness protection program.

Sonya was bringing all kinds of girls over to see him, Juan had money saved up sky high, thanks to David. But deep in Juan's heart he knew his time on earth was limited. He was going to have to kill or someone was going to try and kill him.

Juan said to himself, 'I am ready. I won't slip.' He had seen many people die from orders David had given. He was going to have fun until that time came. He could not change what had been done. 2-DIE-4 was what he lived, but now he had broken the code.

THE FUNERAL

The funeral was held on Barbour St. in a big white church. Everyone was there, all colors of people, white, black, Jamaican and Hispanic.

Justin was one of the pallbearers. Gail, Jasmine, Betty and Yolanda were on the front row along with Jesse. Tonya came along because she respected Linda.

The pastor was Rev. Raymond Black, he spoke and told the people in church, you never know when God's going to call you home. He started preaching. "This was a young lady who had seen the world, she had the finest things on this earth. She lived a movie star life, but don't any of that matter to God when he calls you home. Money, cars, clothes don't mean a thing. You can't buy life. Can I get an amen? People you better get your life together, the end is nearer than you think."

Everyone in the church was crying. Justin was hurt, he had Ieasha on his side. After the funeral everyone went their way. Justin and Ieasha were riding together.

Juan was a no show and that hurt Justin even more because Juan and Linda were family. Juan showed no love or respect, which made Justin's heart turn cold. Instead of tears he had blood in his eyes for Juan. A man he used to love, his God father, 2-DIE-4.

~ 201 ~

LISA

Lisa was chilling with the four men she had brought from New York. She watched the whole funeral, she could have killed Justin but she was thinking about what she had done to a very close friend. She started crying, she wanted all of this to be over with.

David had caused so much pain in Lisa's life, she wanted him to pay. Lisa was still doing her thing, even after she agreed to tell on David to the Fed's. Agent Harris had Lisa write a statement on David to keep her freedom. Lisa had heard that Juan had rolled on David and Justice, she felt better, but she knew both their days were limited for crossing David.

JUSTICE

Justice was transferred back to Hartford, he was in the Meadows with his daddy David. David was asleep when Justice came into D-block. David was in cell 123, Justice was in cell 127.

Justice asked one of the inmates if he knew David or Lil-D.

The inmate said, "Man who don't? He is in cell 123."

Justice walked in the one man cell and said, "Man get up!"

David rolled over and said, "What's popping son?"

Justice said. "How'd you know it was me?"

David said, "Someone had told me before you got here. Plus no one can just walk in my room." He got up and hugged Justice.

David brushed his teeth and washed his face. They sat down and talked.

David said, "Bro I'm sorry about what happened to Linda."

Justice was fixing to say something but got a lump in his throat.

David put his hand up and said, "I feel your pain. But you got to move on, there is no place on this earth for a weak man. Death will come to us all one day. You still have a family that loves you dearly." David went on and changed the subject, he asked, "How is April doing?"

Justice said, "She has been doing good, coming to see me, taking care of what I need to be done."

David said, "That's love, she is just like your mother, so you can love her better."

Justice started smiling.

CHAD

Chad was sad about what happened to Linda because he was falling in love with her. Chad was fixing to get ready to get a bond. He had made a deal with the feds and his court day was Monday. Everyone knew Chad was going to get out. Word on the streets was that he was telling.

That Monday the judge gave Chad a hundred thousand dollar bond. Chad was ready to get out. He was happy his lawyer told him he wouldn't do a day in prison, Chad had given him a lot of money.

JUSTIN

Ieasha was with Justin, they were chilling. Justin knew Chad would make bond today and he told Ieasha we need to make a run before it gets too late.

Ieasha said, "Okay baby, but promise me that when we get back home you are going to make love to me."

Justin said he promised and kissed Ieasha on the mouth. He went into his room, changed clothes, put all black on and grabbed his bag. He and Ieasha got in the rental car and headed for Morgan St. jail to lay low on Chad.

Justin was in a garage waiting. Ieasha was parked in the Hilton Hotel parking lot. She had her cell phone in her hand.

When Justin called that meant to come get him from the spot, he had been waiting almost an hour. His legs were hurting, but pain was love. He had to take care of this today. Justin saw a black limo pull up in front of the jail. He picked up the riffle and put the scope on the car.

The driver got out and walked into the building but there were some more people in the car. Three minutes later Justin spotted Chad coming out of the Morgan St jail with the driver of the limo.

Justin had the scope in between Chad eyes and he pulled the trigger. Chad's head exploded, the driver walking next to him had no idea what had hit Chad. All he saw was blood and brains, everyone ran out of the building and the Police had guns out.

Justin dialed the number. Ieasha wasted no time to pull up at the spot. Justin got in the car staying low and told Ieasha to drive to East Hartford. As they were riding the police and the ambulance went flying by, going to Morgan St.

When they got to East Hartford, Justin told Ieasha where to go. They rented a hotel room at the Ramada Inn. Ieasha told the lady she wanted the room for a week.

Justin wanted to find Juan and kill him because this was personal, 2-DIE-4.

Ieasha and Justin went to their room. Justin turned on the TV and Ieasha went and took a shower. While she was in the shower Justin made a few phone calls. He called David's cell phone and David picked right up.

David knew it was Justin, he said, "Good job son I see the news." David told Justin that Justice was there with him. Justice got on the phone and told his brother he loved him, they talked a few minutes and Justin told them he had to go.

Ieasha came out of the bathroom and asked Justin to put some oil on her. Justin laid her on the bed and put cherry oil on her. He kissed her from head to toe. Justin was licking Ieasha's whole body and worked his way down to her womanhood. She was wet as the Connecticut River, he had her going wild. He entered Ieasha's world, a place where no man had ever been and they made love that night.

Justin went to sleep and when he woke up, Ieasha was sitting up watching the news. It was talking about a man who was shot in the head in front of Morgan St jail after making bond. Ieasha knew Justin had done it but love made her not care.

Justin walked up on her and said, "What's up pretty woman?"

Ieasha smiled and said, "Nothing sexy man."

"Ieasha are you ready for 2-DIE-4? Are you ready to live by this code?" Justin asked her.

She said, "Yes I am."

"Promise me you won't ever cross me, or my family," he said. Ieasha got ready to say something as Justin said, "Hold up, I'm not finished. Promise me you will be there for me even if I go broke or go to prison for life. Promise me you will give me that mental support." Justin said with tears in his eyes.

Ieasha told him, "I promise you all of the above. I am in this with you for life."

Justin kissed Ieasha and said, "There's no turning back. The only thing that can take the promise back is death."

Ieasha got into bed and lifted the blankets for Justin to get in. She and Justin made love then fell asleep in each other's arms.

LISA

Jerry called Lisa and told her that Chad had got killed.

Lisa said, "What! Who the fuck had the heart to kill Chad at the police department? There's only one mother fucker who could have had that done! I think David has the police doing the killings for him. Let me call you back."

Lisa hung up with Jerry and called Agent Harris. She told him to watch all the police officers because she had a feeling that David may have someone in that department doing the killings for him.

Mr. Harris told Lisa that the FBI was on the case and they were looking into all the murders to see if there was a connection. He told Lisa to call him if she found out anything for sure.

TONYA

Tonya was at the house playing with Daisy, she had gotten so big. Tonya had to start taking her to school. Justin had called Tonya, she was worried because Justin and Ieasha were hanging tight and now Chad was dead. She didn't want to believe it was her only son who was doing the killings, but she knew he had a part of David in him. She said a prayer, asking God to have mercy on her son.

SABIR MOHAMMED

Sabir was telling his wife that Ieasha didn't come to Jumuah every Friday like she had before and she had been acting funny, not like the girl that he raised. Sabir told his wife that he was going to look into something because he had friends who worked for the FBI that could tell him about anybody with a name, living or dead. There were a few people he wanted to run a check on.

JUSTIN

Justin and Ieasha were in the bed chilling. Justin got up early that morning and told Ieasha he would be right back. He grabbed his 45 and a Rambo knife then headed out of the hotel room. He got into the rental car and headed to Juan's mother's house.

It took him about ten minutes to get there, then he pulled in the back where no one could see him and waited. Justin saw Juan pull up with some fine ass girl. He knew he had to get the jump on Juan because Juan was a killer also, plus Juan was smart.

Justin got out of the car and walked to the back of the house, he put his ski mask on and some gloves. Justin walked to the back door and checked it, the door was unlocked. He said to himself, 'Juan is slipping, pussy will make any tender dick nigga' slip.' He walked in the house, heard the shower running and he pulled out his gun. He put the silencer on it and looked in the room where he saw the fine ass girl. Looked like he had seen her somewhere before, but what the hell she had to die, right place at the wrong time. Justin put two shots in her chest and she fell to the floor. Justin stood over her and cut her throat.

Juan was still in the shower. When he got out he felt like something was off, but he was thinking it was his mom coming back home. As soon as he walked into his room and dropped his towel Justin put four shots in him, two in the head and two in the chest. Justin reached down and pulled his tongue out, cut if off and put it in his hand.

Out of all the killings this one was personal. Justin looked around and found the safe. He opened it and took all the money, over two hundred thousand dollars in cash. Justin made it out of the house and drove back to the hotel.

Ieasha was waiting on him, she had started feeling scared when Justin walked in the door and told her it was time to go. She packed both of their things and they headed out.

OLLIE LOPEZ

Ollie and her friends had just came back home from shopping. Ollie went to her back door and saw it was open. She knew her son Juan had to be home, she told her friends they could go. Ollie walked in, sat the bags on the kitchen table and went into the living room. She saw the pretty girl lying there and what she saw next almost made her heart stop. Blood was coming from the girl's neck.

Ollie screamed and grabbed the phone, dialing 911. She told the operator to get someone there. Mrs. Lopez was going crazy, they told her someone was on the way. She dialed Sonya's phone number and told her to come over.

The police got there and Mrs. Lopez's friends from next door came to comfort her. The police came in and checked the house. When they got to Juan's room the officer jumped and covered his mouth. Mrs. Lopez passed out, the room was ugly.

The officer said, "Take her out, there's two dead bodies in here."

The news reporters were everywhere. Sonya had made it there and she was going crazy, she could not believe that someone would do her brother like that. She was crying and asking, "God why?" Juan was all she had, her only brother, he had spoiled her for years now he is dead.

JUSTIN

Justin was at his house, he had taken Ieasha home and was sitting back watching the news. The Channel 3 News was talking about two dead bodies that were found in East Hartford. Both victims were shot in the head one victim's tongue was cut out of his head. The FBI said it could be linked to a big case that got an agent killed along with four other people. They said they had no witnesses or suspects, it's a cold case. Agent Harris got on TV and said they were not ruling out anyone. He said that it's hard to get a break in a case like this because people are afraid to come forward.

DAVID

The word was out that Juan had been killed two days after Chad. David said to himself that Justin was a beast. He was thinking to himself when Justice came and said, "Dad, Justin is not playing, him and that girl are on it."

David said, "That's family love, 2-DIE-4. Nigga's got to follow the rules or die like ducks. Son the only way the hunter kills the duck is when he quacks, he don't open his mouth he lives."

Justice said, "I never thought about that with the duck, but I'm going to always be the hunter."

IEASHA

When Ieasha got home her father Sabir was waiting. As soon as she walked in the door Sabir said, "Baby girl what is wrong with you, don't you fear Allah?"

Ieasha said, "Yes." She continued walking to her room.

Sabir stood in front of the door and said, "Well you need to start back going to Jumuah on Fridays."

Ieasha said, "Daddy I only missed one Jumuah, Justin and I were out of town."

Sabir said, "Baby that boy Justin is into some heavy stuff and you need to watch yourself."

Ieasha replied, "Daddy I love him and I am not going to let him go."

"Allah knows best," Sabir said and walked off leaving Ieasha day dreaming about the love Justin had put on her earlier that day.

AGENT HARRIS

Mr. Harris called David out of his cell, he knew David wouldn't tell him anything but he wanted to let David know something. Mr. Harris said, "Mr. David Thomas, I know you ordered the hits on all those people."

David didn't say anything, he looked at agent Harris like he was crazy.

Mr. Harris got in David face and told him that he was going to die in prison.

David got mad and spoke his mind. He said, "Man fuck you and who ever had you! I ain't did shit! Prove it!" He then got up and walked out.

Mr. Harris said, "I will see you in court next week sucker."

David yelled back at him, "Yeah, talk to one of my four lawyers sucker."

They took David back to his cell.

JUSTICE

Justice's lawyer had told him that he talked to the judge and that he would be getting a bond, but he could not leave the state of Connecticut for any reason.

Justice was happy to hear the news, he told his lawyer that he would be staying in New Haven, Connecticut. Justice wanted David to be free also, so part of him was still sad.

COURT DAY

David and Justice were brought to Lafayette Street for federal court on the ninth floor. Justice was telling David about his lawyer saying that he would get a bond.

David said, "That's good, but when you get out watch out for all the people around you."

Justice said, "Dad you know I'm on my job. I'm going to get this money and keep our respect in the streets."

David was smiling, he said, "Take care of Daisy, one day she will be a woman and we don't want anything but the best. Warrior blood line, no lames."

Justice and David walked into the court room together. The bail bondsman called Justice Thomas' name. The DA told the judge that the state would allow for Justice Thomas to get a bond due to mishandling of the case. Justice's lawyer spoke a few words about the motion he filed to dismiss the whole case but the judge said he had to make a ruling. He sat Justice's bond at one hundred thousand dollars. Justice sat down and smiled.

The DA call David Thomas to the stand and stood up with him. One of David's lawyers were arguing with the DA about the FBI agent Mr. Harris harassing David while he was in jail. He also was asking the judge for bond.

Agent Harris got up and talked to the judge about David. The judge told David he would stay in prison until the trial date. David had the poker face, he was not going to show them crackers that they were in control. He was cool, he had everything in prison but his car. Tonya came to see him every week and he paid officers to let them get a few hours alone.

Everyone got up and hugged David. He picked up his baby girl Daisy and kissed her. She was fat and pretty, David told all his family and friends that he was cool.

Justice said, "Tonya make sure you all come get me, I will stay with you until I go to New Haven."

Tonya said, "Okay."

MORGAN ST. COUNTY JAIL

Justice was waiting for Tonya and the family to come get him. He had been in the holding cell for about an hour and started wondering what was going on. He knew the money was not a problem, but what was the hold up.

He had on a white, silk Brooks Brothers suit with white and gold Polo boots that had one carat gold buckles and a gold silk tie. He was clean as a pimp trying to catch his first hoe, dressed to impress. He was daydreaming when the officer came and said, "Mr. Thomas your ride is here."

Justice jumped up and grabbed a small bag with his bible and pictures of his mom and family. He threw away all the letters when he walked out of the jail. An all-white stretch Cadillac escalade was waiting. Justin jumped out and hugged his little brother, he had a bottle of Moet with him.

They toasted his release and had a drink for the good times to come. Justin reached in his pocket and gave his baby brother a fresh twenty thousand dollars.

Justice could not do anything but smile as the limo pulled up in front of the house. They drove into the back yard where everyone was waiting and food was being cooked on the grill.

April was standing out there looking good. When Justice got out everyone showed some love and Gail had tears in her eyes. Tears of joy, because she knew how the system worked against young blacks.

They all took pictures and chilled for the day.

LISA

Lisa was chilling, laying low because the word was out that Justice had made bond. Lisa had made up her mind that she did not want to kill Linda's only son. She still had four of her men with her, they was staying at her favorite hotel. The Hilton downtown Hartford, Conn. But Lisa was still running the streets chasing that money.

SABIR

Sabir had called one of his friends with the FBI because he wanted to know what kind of person Justin Thomas was. The man his Muslim daughter was so in love with. He also wanted to know what his mom and dad did for a living.

He dialed a number and Agent Marvin Harris picked up, Sabir said, "What's going on Marvin."

Mr. Harris said, "Nothing much long time no hear. What's the problem, because that's the only time you want to call me is to check someone out. We need to start back to going fishing."

Sabir said, "Work has been good so I haven't had much free time. I need you to check out this name for me."

Agent Harris asked, "What's the name?"

Sabir said, "Justin Thomas.

Mr. Harris said, "Drug family. Probably a killer. His daddy is David Thomas, the one who just got taken down, they are dangerous men. They have a strong family. Everything I just told you was off of the top of my head, I'm on the case. But don't you say anything to anyone because you could be risking your life and your family's as well."

Mr. Sabir lied and said, "It's nothing with me, I saw their name on T.V, and just wanted to know if they were real gangsters or wanksters."

Mr. Harris said, "They are the real deal, the kind that were around in the 60's and 70's."

Mr. Sabir told him, "Thank you, one day we will go fishing when I get time off."

Then they hung up and Sabir said, "Oh Allah you know best. My daughter is in love with a thug! Have mercy on her and lead her to the path that you have bestowed. Favor not the paths of those who go astray." He walked off wondering what the future held for him and his beloved daughter. One thing was for sure, he was not going to run her off. He had seen girls who hate their father's because he didn't like the boyfriend and plus he liked Justin.

Chapter Fourteen

DISLOYAL AND BETRAYED

Justin had been living with Ieasha for a while, she was still working at the hospital and they were happy but Justin had one problem. David had pled out to 20 years for drugs and guns. He was now doing time in an Atlanta federal prison a long way from home.

Gail had family in Atlanta. A brother who made sure David got visits and the things he wanted.

Justice had lost the condo in New Haven. He and April had broken up, she was supposed to be pregnant. Justice was not happy with the world because his mother was gone. He stayed alone and never smiled.

Lisa had gotten off on the federal charges and she was in hiding. She didn't go to trial since Chad and Juan were dead and the case was weak.

For two sad days the whole city was hurt, but they understood the street code. More nigga's had to step up and keep it real. 2-DIE-4, 4-ever, 140 the code of the streets.

TONYA

Tonya was laying out back in her big back yard, chilling. She had been swimming all day, Daisy was at her Grandma Gail's house. She saw an SUV pull into her back yard and realized it was Justice in his baby blue Land Rover. It had gold 26" inch rims with a TV on each of the back head rests. The music was blasting loud.

Tonya had on a two piece Victoria Secret bathing suit.

Justice jumped out of the truck and said, "What's up girl?"

He never called Tonya mom, or step mom because it was never like that, they were more like street friends. He was

David's son, Justin's brother and Daisy's brother, but he was really nothing to her.

Tonya said, "Hello bad boy where have you been?"

Justice looked behind him playfully and Tonya started laughing.

He asked her, "Do you want to go out tonight?"

She asked, "To where? I don't do them outlaw clubs, I'm too old for that."

Justice said, "No woman, they just opened this new joint in Manchester. It's a big boy club. Broke nigga's can't come in and they have off duty police working security."

Tonya said, "Boy it better be nice."

Justice replied, "Girl I am coming to pick you up at 9 pm. I'm fixing to go over to Park Street and pick up some money."

Tonya said, "Okay."

Justice jumped in the truck and left.

Tonya was ready to get out of the house, it had been a long time. She had not done anything in some years now that David was in the Feds in Atlanta. The sex was rare, she was like a hot 16 year old girl. She had to rub between her legs to make sure she was still a woman. She said to herself, 'maybe it's a good idea to get out of the house and have some fun.'

LISA

Lisa had moved out to Bloomfield and was staying on Dumont Street. She had a real nice house that she had built from the ground up. She was laying back by herself, the men she had with her went back to New York. If she needed them they were a phone call away.

She was looking at the number on a piece of paper, she had the devil in her and she wanted to play with fire. She called the number and Justin said, "Hello?"

Lisa said, "Who am I speaking with?"

Justin asked, "Who is this?"

She waited and then said, "This is Lisa."

Justin said, "Long time no see, this is Justin. What makes you call me?"

Lisa said, "I wanted to let you know I got a house built in Bloomfield on Dumont Street. Come over so we can talk."

Justin wrote the address down and said, "I just might do that."

Lisa said, "Its safe," and they hung up.

Lisa had always liked both of David's boys, they were both good looking and young. For her to get one would kill David, if he found out and pictures were worth a thousand words.

Lisa had installed little cameras in the walls, you couldn't see them if you weren't looking. She wanted to show David that she could still fuck with him through his first born. She had to show this nigga' he was not made of steel.

JUSTIN

Justin was laying back on his king size bed thinking, he had so much on his mind. All the murders, the money, his father and Lisa. Ieasha had been bitching about him not working any more. It was cool because he loved Ieasha and she wanted what was best for him. She had gotten into two fights over Justin and his cheating.

Justin looked at Lisa's address and smiled. He went and took a shower and got fresh, he was going to pay Lisa a visit. He had always liked her body and she was a fine girl, nice suntan just like J-lo. But a darker tan, she was a dime all day, even at 35 years old. She had class like a boss bitch is supposed to. She would kill you before God got the news.

JUSTICE

Justice was leaving Park Street, he had picked his money up from Lil-Ricky and D-Rock. Justice had started using the drug's he sold. The drug that made his father the Heartbeat Don. Justice got high to get his mother off his mind.

He drove over to his condo over on Magnolia Street and took a shower. He got fresh, so he could get Tonya, they were going to have fun.

TONYA

Tonya was sitting in the living room of her house waiting on Justice, she felt like a young girl in school waiting on her first date. She was looking good in her yellow Gucci mini skirt and white silk Gucci blouse, letting her cleavage show. She had on white Armani Gator pumps.

She heard the music when Justice pulled up in his Land Rover, Tonya sprayed on some White Diamond perfume and went to the door, she looked out then went to the truck and got in with Justice.

Justice said, "Girl you look good."

Tonya started smiling, they were headed to the grand opening of the new club in Manchester called 20 Love. They were both looking good.

CLUB 20-LOVE

When Justice pulled up at the 20-Love all eyes were on his baby blue Land Rover. He drove through the crowded parking lot and parked in the back. He and Tonya got out and went into the club. The VIP section was already waiting on them in the VIP room with two bottles of Moet chilling. The music was playing and the weed was burning. Justice was already high off the cocaine and the Moet just took him farther there.

Tonya was sipping her drink and laughing. She had hit the blunt a few times, something she hadn't done in years. R. Kelly was coming on bump and grind, throw back. Justice and

Tonya went to the dance floor. They were dancing and having fun, until Justice started grinding on Tonya kind of hard.

Tonya could feel he was rising up on the inside of his pants. She didn't move, she was feeling good. She was starting to get wet because no other man had touched her like that but David and now she was wet over his baby son.

The music stopped and Tonya went and sat at the table. Justice walked over to the bar and Tonya was feeling good and hot.

He came back and said, "Hey girl you okay?"

Tonya said, "I can handle me are you okay?" Then she started smiling.

The club was closing and Justice asked Tonya to drive because he was a little over the limit.

JUSTIN

Justin put his clothes on and was headed out the door when he turned around and got his bullet proof vest and his gun. He was headed to Bloomfield on Dumont Street. He was going to pay Lisa a visit. He saw that Dumont Street's lights weren't broken and all the cars in the driveways were nice, Benz's, BMW's and Rang Rover's.

Justin found #316, it was a nice size brick house with pink trimming around all the windows. A rental car was parked in the front driveway. Justin pulled up behind the car and got out. He went up to the door and knocked.

He was in a day dream when Lisa opened the door. She had on her night gown and said, "Come in."

Justin walked in and loved the way Lisa had her house laid out. His eyes could not stay off Lisa's body, this was one fine Puerto Rican chick. Justin sat down and Lisa started telling him she had no problem with him or his family. She told Justin that David started all this shit over money.

Justin said, "I respect you and hope that you stay loyal to me, but don't ever tell anyone that I came by your house. If you do, we both might get killed because you know David ain't having this shit. We can be cool, but I need you to help me out. I fucked up a hundred thousand dollars in about nine months."

Lisa said, "You don't have to explain I'll look out, I have more money than I can spend."

Lisa and Justin talked for about two hours and smoked some weed. They were laughing and talking about the old days. Justin was high as hell and Lisa started rubbing on his leg. He was feeling his manhood grow when Lisa kissed him and said, "Is it in you?"

Justin did not say anything. He was ready for Lisa, he had always dreamed about her. He laid Lisa back on the couch and licked her all over. Her eyes were rolling back in her head because this young man was a pro. He started licking Lisa in her wet spot and playing the lick game with her. She was going crazy.

Justin took his clothes off and Lisa was impressed with what she saw. He entered her wet world and it was on fire. Lisa started moaning and moving with the motion of the young man who was on top of her. He was ready to explode when he backed out. Lisa wrapped her long legs around his waist and he let loose of his seed in her warm world.

They made love all night and talked. Lisa told Justin a lot of stuff, but Justin saw Lisa's weak side. She would be easy to kill, but he was not going to hurt her. He wouldn't do that right now, he wanted the money and good honey.

JERRY

Jerry was mad as hell with Lisa because she tried to play him. He was telling Little Man about what happened. Jerry was saying he was going to get that bitch. Chuck-D and Woody were laughing because they had been in the game a long time and they told Jerry that Lisa was a slick hoe and she was gangster.

They all smoked a blunt and chilled, getting money like always.

GAIL

Gail was telling Betty that April had called and she said that she was eight months pregnant with Justice's baby. Gail was telling Betty she had not seen Justice in about two weeks and that Ieasha called looking for Justin because he hadn't come home last night.

He had called and told Gail he was okay but Gail said, "I was not going to tell Ieasha shit. I got all my boys back."

Betty said, "Ieasha is a good girl. Justin need's to keep her."

Gail said, "She's okay, but what's that stuff they practice. She is all covered up all the time."

Betty said, "They are Muslim."

Gail said, "Them are some respectful people."

Gail and Betty talked some more and watch the young and the restless.

TONYA'S HOUSE

Tonya pulled the Land Rover in her back yard. Justice had fallen asleep from the long ride. Tonya woke him up and said, "Boy you can stay here tonight because you ain't ready to drive."

Tonya and Justice went in the house where Justice went and sat down on the couch.

Tonya said, "You can chill, I'm fixing to go get in the shower."

Justice turned on the TV and started watching some videos. He fired up a blunt and smoked some good weed.

Tonya was out of the shower and in her room sitting on the bed, putting on that apple oil. Justice got up off the couch to go to the kitchen, he looked in Tonya's room and saw that she did not have any clothes on. Justice couldn't believe how fine Tonya was, he wanted a close up look.

He walked to the door and asked, "Girl you want to hit this blunt?"

Tonya had her head down, she didn't know Justice was standing at the door. She said, "Yeah and boy I don't have no clothes on."

Justice walked in as Tonya grabbed her robe and put it on, but she had nothing else on under it.

Justice asked, "What kind of oil is that?"

Tonya said, "Apple. I need you to put some on my back."

Justice started laughing and said, "Okay I'm going to turn my back, lay on the bed and let the robe down to where just your back is showing."

Tonya lay down and Justice got the oil and rubbed some in his hand, the oil smelled so good. He started rubbing Tonya's back, her skin was soft and pretty like caramel. Her round ass was in the air. As Justice was rubbing away. He pulled her robe down some more and now he could see the crack of Tonya's ass.

Tonya said, "Boy rub the shit, you acting scared."

Justice went ham, he started rubbing Tonya all over even reaching under her and rubbing in her breasts. He dropped to Tonya's butt and she jumped. He had taken the robe all the way off of Tonya, and her whole body was showing. She closed her eyes, she was not going to turn around because she had tears in her eyes. She had been loyal to David, but she had no control, it had been so long.

Justice started sucking on Tonya neck and she started moaning, she was on fire. He was licking her all the way down her back. He got to the crack of her ass and kept licking. Tonya was wiggling and going wild. She raised her ass up in the doggy style, she was not going to look back. Justice was licking her womanhood from the back as he stood and took his pants off. Tonya did not move, she was still in the doggy style with her head down moaning. Justice pulled her to the end of the bed where he entered a world that no man but David had ever been in.

Justice was longer and bigger than his daddy. Tonya buried her head in the pillow and Justice went to work, he was not taking it easy. She was making noise and mumbling, "I, please, I am about, oh I'm coming!"

Justice could not hear anything, he was gone. He rolled Tonya over so he could see her face. She had her eyes closed but when Justice put both her legs on his shoulders she opened her eyes because she was having an orgasm. She was letting go and she started throwing it back to Justice calling his name and telling him to give it to her. Justice started kissing Tonya on the mouth, he was about to let go, he was moving fast. Tonya could not tell him not to cum in her and Justice let a load off inside her.

He lay on top of Tonya, they were both sweating and smiling.

Tonya said, "Boy you got to take this to your grave."

Justice said, "I know."

Tonya said, "I want some more, I love the way you did me."

Justice was lying on his back and Tonya rolled on top of him and went to work. She had drained herself and Justice fell to sleep. Between Tonya's legs was sore but she was feeling like a new woman.

They heard a knock at the door and they both jumped out of bed. Justice ran upstairs to the guest room and put his clothes on, he was thinking, 'close call.' He felt bad, that was his dad's first love, damn!

IEASHA

Ieasha was at her dad's house. She was mad because Justin didn't come home. She was not saying much so her dad came over and sat down next to her.

He said, "Baby a man is going to be a man. That boy is out in them streets, anything goes. So don't worry about him just pray and stay strong always. Have his back."

Ieasha said, "I want to punch him in the face."

Sabir started laughing because he knew how women could get and the things they said when they got mad. Mr. Sabir said, "Baby I feel you, but don't ever put your hands on someone to harm them, not the one you love."

She smiled and went to talk to her mother. They had some girl stuff to talk about.

JUSTIN

Justin had stayed with Lisa all night, he called Ieasha on her cell phone.

Ieasha picked up and asked, "Where you are?"

Justin said, "Baby I ran into some problems so I stayed over at my brother Justice's house."

Ieasha said, "Well I'm at my dad's house and I am fixing to go to work. You need to be home when I get there."

Justin said, "Calm down mommy I got this. I'm over at my mom's house, I will be home. But I don't promise to be home when you get there."

Ieasha said, "Well you need to be home with me tonight. I'm not trying to demand nothing, I know you are the man in this relationship. I'm not going to lose you to no one, not even the streets." She stopped and said, "Do you hear me Justin?"

Justin said, "I am going to be home."

Ieasha said, "I promised you it was 2-DIE-4 and that's what it is. But baby you got to hold me down also."

Justin said, "We will talk about that. I will see you tonight, I love you and can't wait to get home."

Ieasha said, "I feel the same way about you but ten times more. It's new to me." Justin was laughing. Ieasha said, "It's not funny, you got me doing stuff I said I would never do."

Justin said, "You got me the same way, that's why I'm coming home, that's new to me."

TONYA'S HOUSE

Justin pulled up at his mother house, he said to himself damn I forgot my key. He knocked on the door for about five minutes before his mother came to the door. He walked in and said, "What's up?"

Tonya said, "Boy I'm fixing to get in the shower."

Justice was coming down the stairs and he was dressed fresh.

Justin said, "What's up Bro?"

Justice replied, "Just cooling."

"Man my money is low, I borrowed fifty thousand from your grandma," Justin said.

Justice said, "Damn man what the fuck are you doing with your money?"

Justin replied, "I got some from my men and I fucked up about ten G's. I got to get that up.

"Nigga' don't' let the streets bite you in the ass," Justice told him.

Justin said, "What's up?"

"I got you but nigga' chill on the way you do things. I got a little bread put away and plus I am good. Got Lil-Ricky, D-Rock and crew doing their thing, about fifty thousand a day and I got shit going on with me. I bring in about sixty-five thousand dollars a week, so it's good little bro," Justice said.

Justin said, "Man I got something to tell you. But you can't tell anyone Justice."

"Man it's my word, come on bro we are twins," replied Justice.

Justin said, "Man I fucked Lisa!"

Justice said, "What? Man what the fuck you just said?"

"I fucked the shit out of Lisa nigga'," Justin said.

"Damn!" Justice said. "That's cool, I don't give a fuck, just tell me where is she. Did you kill her?"

Justin replied, "No man, she thinks she can play me, but it's all for you bro."

"I want you to kill that bitch, but take your time. Make her believe you are cool," Justice told him.

Justin was laughing and said, "Shit fuck her. The pussy is good she a vet."

Justice asked, "Where does she stay?"

Justin said, "Bloomfield on Dumont Street 316."

Justice got the address then Tonya walked in and they both stop talking.

Tonya said, "What you two devils up to? Yeah okay, I am fixing to go get Daisy." Then she walked out.

Justice was looking at her ass and Justin caught him, Justin said, "Damn nigga' don't be looking at my mom's ass like that!"

Justice started laughing then ran and grabbed Justin, they had not play fought in a long time.

Justin stood up and said, "Lil-Bro."

Justice said, "Man don't start that sad shit!"

Justin said, "I ain't, shit nigga' you always had an eye for Tonya."

Justice said, "Bro I'm just living and in life. There's going to be things that will happen we may not understand. The pain, the love, so let's just get off that and move on to the bigger problems in life."

Justin said, "Man I love you and I showed what you mean to me, just don't let your feelings lead you."

JUSTIN

When Justin got home Ieasha was in the kitchen cooking. Justin eased up behind her and covered her eyes, but he could not fool Ieasha because she knew his smell. That's why she bought him the Muslim oil called, 'Makkah.' It had a special smell.

She said, "Hi baby." Ieasha turned around and kissed Justin on the mouth, she looked him up and down then said, "My daddy said hello and my mom said they still have the same address."

Justin said, "I'm going to see them, I've just been running a bit, but it's going to get better."

Justin walked to the bathroom and closed the door, he pulled out a small bag and then he pulled out a needle. He put heroin in it, held his arm tight by the shirt and shot himself up with the drug that brought the best of the best to their knees. A drug that loved nothing but your soul. Over the last year the drug was getting the best of Justin. His money was going fast, he had five cars, a Benz, BMW, Corvette, Jag and a Porsche. Now all he had was his money green Lexus. He even sold the BMW that he had gotten for Ieasha and she was back to driving her old car.

He was sitting on the edge of the bathtub, thinking about a lot when Ieasha came and hit the door. Justin did not realize he had been back there an hour. The noise from Ieasha's hard hit made Justin jump out of his mood.

Ieasha said, "Open the door!"

Justin opened the door and Ieasha knew from the look on his face that he was super high.

Ieasha said, "Don't overdo it."

He replied, "I am just a little stressed out, but I'm good."

They both walked to the kitchen and ate. Ieasha said, "I'm going to the doctor because I have been sick for the past month."

Ieasha had been throwing up at work and going to sleep, she told Justin she was taking off work Friday to get checked out.

Justin said, "I will take you. Like you were saying on the phone I'm going to do my part. Anything having to do with you and your health I am there with you every step of the way."

"Thank you baby," She said.

They went to the bedroom and Justin made love to Ieasha. She had a smile on her face, she was so in love she didn't see she was getting off the path from which Allah had bestowed favor.

JUSTIN

Justin was riding through the Vill checking things out, he saw Little-man and Woody. He knew them OGs' from his Dad. The Vill was his second home, he waved and kept riding. He turned down Cleveland Ave and he had April on his mind, so he headed to New Haven. April was pregnant and Justice was ready for a child. He wanted a boy because that's what his mom always wanted him to have.

LISA

Lisa was on the phone telling one of her men in New York that she was in the game, she now had protection in Hartford. She told her man in New York to tell Lucy to meet her at the airport.

Lucy was a fine Puerto Rican girl around 25 years old. She grew up on the streets of New York. Lisa took her in when she was young and gave her some boss game. Lucy could fool you, she was a killer from the heart. She loved no man. At ten years old she was coming from school when two grown men grabbed her and raped her bad. She killed one by cutting his throat with a razor, then the other one she got three weeks later. She tricked him in the hallway by making it seem like they were about to have sex but she cut his manhood off. He died in great pain.

Lucy was known for being a cold bitch, but she would still sleep with a man for a reason. Now Lisa needed her on her team.

NEW HAVEN CONNECTICUT

Justice pulled up at April's house on the south side of New Haven. It was a nice house with the yard cut real neat, a very respectful place. Justice didn't get out, he blew the horn and April came to the door. He got out and thought April was looking good, her stomach was big.

Justice said, "What's up sexy lady?"

"You, where have you been?" April asked.

Justice replied, "I had to handle some things."

"This is my eighth month, I will have the baby next month in November," she told him.

He reached in his pocket and gave her two thousand dollars. April's mom was watching, she liked Justice because he was so respectful.

Justice said, "Call me if you need anything."

She told him, "You need to get your shit together and leave them streets alone."

"I'm cool, don't worry about anything. If something happens to me, your child will be taken care of," he said.

"I don't want anything to happen," she replied.

Justice said, "It won't."

He kisses April on the mouth then grabbed her butt. She backed up smiling and Justice got in the truck headed for Hartford.

IEASHA'S CHECK UP

Justin and Ieasha pulled up at the clinic and went in holding hands. Ieasha loved Justin for that, because he had so much love for family.

She gave the woman at the desk her name and told her she was there for an appointment. The woman gave Ieasha a cup to pee in and she went to the ladies room. She filled the cup half way and came back out where she and Justin sat and waited.

He was playing with Ieasha ear and they had waited about ten minutes when the lady at the desk called, "Ieasha Muhammad, to Doctor Newton's office please."

Justin didn't go in with her, she was in there about twenty minutes then she came out the door smiling. Justin jumped up and said, "What's up?"

Ieasha said, "You wonder why I am getting fat?"

Justin said, "I noticed that."

Ieasha playfully hit him on the arm and said, "You did not notice. I am having a baby!"

Justin hugged her and they laughed together. Ieasha was not showing much, her mother had been the same way.

Ieasha said, "Take me by my daddy's house."

Justin asked her, "What you want, boy or girl?"

"It don't matter long as it's healthy and has a good spirit," she replied.

Justin drove the rest of the way to Ieasha's dad's house thinking about what he was going to do now that his baby was on the way. That was one more problem added to the rest of the ones he had to deal with. He needed some more drugs.

LISA

Lisa was almost in Hartford, her and Lucy were riding, listening to music. Lisa saw a pretty blue and gold Land Rover and she said to herself, 'I saw that Rover somewhere on Blue Hill Ave.' She got up alongside of the truck but couldn't see in the dark limo tint.

Justin looked over and saw Lisa and another girl in the car next to him, he played it cool. Lisa didn't know the streets of Hartford like Justice did. He turned off on a side street and met back up with Lisa farther up. By this time he was about four cars behind her.

He followed Lisa all the way to Bloomfield where he watched her pull up at the house on Dumont Street 316. Justice said to himself, 'I got that bitch.'

Lisa was telling Lucy that she had seen that truck before but she couldn't make out who it was. She said, "I think I'll call Justin because he knows everyone in Hartford that got money. I love the way this place look, we are going to get money and live like true queens."

SABIR'S HOUSE

Justin pulled up at Ieasha's dad's house. They got out and went inside. Ieasha's mom Khadijah, was sitting on the couch reading, "The sealed nectar" a Biography of the Noble Prophet.

Ieasha said, "As-salaamu alaikum."

Her mother replied, "Wa alaikum As-salaam."

Ieasha saw her daddy come to the living room and she said, "Have a seat."

Her daddy gave her a look and said, "So you the boss now?"

Sabir could tell Ieasha was happy, he had not seen her like that in some months. He sat down next to his wife.

Ieasha said, "Okay, I just came from the doctor today and I am one month pregnant."

Sabir replied, "You know that lying and joking in Islam is not allowed."

Ieasha said, "For real dad."

He started smiling.

Justin said, "She is for real."

"Well you need to sit down," Sabir said.

Everyone was happy but Sabir wanted to ask Justin a few things. He asked Justin, "Now do you plan on marrying my daughter?"

Justin had plans on marrying her but not right now his money was not right. But he said, "Yes sir."

Mr. Sabir said, "I will approve."

Ieasha was smiling.

Khadijah said, "Ieasha, we need to start planning."

"Yes Mom we do," Ieasha said. "I am going to let my job know."

Khadijah was not worried about what her friends might say, she loved her daughter and had her back. No one was perfect.

TONYA AND DAISY

Tonya was in the kitchen cooking breakfast when Daisy walked up and put her hand over her mother's eyes'. They had a good relationship.

Tonya said, "It's Daisy."

Daisy replied, "You ain't no fun!"

"Guess what?" Tonya said.

She asked, "What?"

Tonya said, "Your daddy has been moved to Enfield and we are going to see him next week."

"Okay, I can't wait," she replied.

Tonya told her, "I'm going to tell him you got boys calling the house after 11pm at night."

Daisy said, "I don't like that boy, he be buying me stuff at school so I get his money."

"Baby, boys come last. You got to get good grades so you can have a job that will pay you your worth," Tonya said.

"I love school and I expect an A in my classes. Anything under that and I work harder," Daisy said.

Tonya said, "That's good, because you remind me of me at 16 years old. Just be careful because your looks are going to have all kinds of men wanting to talk. They don't care about your age, but don't ever let a man make you do anything you don't want to do."

Daisy said, "That's where my karate comes in, I will break a nigga's neck."

"Okay you got a lot of your daddy David in you too," Tonya said.

Daisy told her, "And I will fight them girls in school, know that."

JUSTICE

Justice pulled his Land Rover up in Tonya's yard. He had been snorting powder all morning and he was high as a kite. He was happy though because he had Lisa's address. He got out and used his key to go in the back door, but Tonya already had the door open.

Justice walked in the house and said, "Hello young ladies."

Tonya said, "What's up young man?"

Daisy said, "Give me some money."

Daisy was crazy about her brothers and she knew how they lived in the streets. Justice reached in his pocket and gave his baby sister ten one hundred dollar bills.

Daisy said, "Thank you, now Mom can I use the car? I will put the gas back in it."

Tonya said, "Go head just be careful."

Daisy got the keys and headed out of the house.

Tonya said, "What's on your mind Justice?"

Justice said, "I just came from over at April's house, she's eight months pregnant."

"You go boy." Tonya said.

"What you think?" He asked her.

Tonya said, "That's good. You got to man up, take care of what's yours. April is a good woman and it's not the woman, it's the man instilled in the woman. She's no stronger than the man she is with. If you don't teach her shit, she won't know shit. Feel me?"

Justice said, "Yeah, I feel you sexy."

Tonya said, "You a mess." Then she went back to washing dishes. She was over the sink with her back turn to Justice and she had on a bright yellow sun dress.

Justice walked up behind her. Tonya said, "Don't try me Justice." But she was smiling.

Justice started rubbing on her butt and sticking his tongue in her ear. Tonya just stood there with her eyes closed.

She turned around and said, "Justice don't think what we did last night was for anybody. I have never cheated on David."

Justice said, "I'm not worrying about that, I can handle me."

Tonya turned her back to him, smiling.

Justice had his manhood out and he reached over and pulled her dress up from the back. She had on a thong. Justice

~ 232 ~

moved it to the side and slid into Tonya's wetness as she held on to the sink. She let Justice sink every inch of his manhood into her wetness. He was pounding her and the cocaine high had him moving fast. Tonya was about to explode and Justice was about to cum too when she pulled him out and dropped to her knees. She put Justice's dick in her mouth and his knees started shaking.

Tonya was a pro, Justice had a lot to learn about her. He exploded inside her mouth and she never even looked up. She got off her knees and went to the bedroom.

Justice stood in that spot in a daze with lust for his dad's bottom bitch.

JUSTIN

Justin's phone went to singing, 'We are taking over' and he picked up saying hello.

"What's up baby boy?" Lisa asked.

Justin said, "Shit what's up with you?"

Lisa said, "I just got back from the airport, had to pick up a friend."

"Do I know her?" He asked.

"You remember Lucy, from New York, Sanchez?" She asked him.

Justin said, "I heard of her but never got to meet her. My brother asked about you."

Lisa said, "You can bring Justice over, that's still my baby. Tell him he needs to come see me sometimes."

DAISY

Daisy had went to the Vill in Tonya's BMW. All the boys down there wanted to get in her pants, but she was after the man with the most money and that was Jerry. Daisy spotted Jerry as he spotted her and came to the car.

He said, "What's up baby girl? What brings you to the hood?"

Daisy said, "The hood is in my bloodline. So I love being around hood nigga's."

Jerry started laughing, he said, "Park the car and chill with me."

Daisy said, "No, why you don't get in the car with me and we turn a block."

Jerry got in the car. Him and Daisy road around the block chilling and talking about everything. Jerry went to telling Daisy about the old days when her daddy was the Heartbeat Don.

Daisy said, "I done heard so much."

He asked, "Do you have a boyfriend?"

"I can't find the right one. Don't too many men want to spoil young ladies, they pockets ain't right," she said.

"You just ain't looked the right way." He told her.

Daisy said, "I can see that. I hope age won't be the reason."

"What would be the reason for you giving me your number?" Jerry got out of the car in the Vill and he told Daisy, "I am going to spoil you."

Daisy said, "We will see."

She smiled as she drove away. She liked Jerry, but money made her cum and she was already wet.

Chapter Fifteen

DAVID

David was waiting on a visit, he had been talking on the cell phone to some friends who were telling David that Justin and Justice were messing up a lot of money. David was day dreaming when the officer called his name for visitation.

He was fresh and smelling good, ready to see his baby's mom and daughter. Tonya and Daisy were sitting at the table waiting on David, they both looked good. Dressed with the best clothes money could buy. David walked in and went to the table. He hugged Tonya and then Daisy as he sat down and went to drilling Tonya.

David said, "What have you lost control of the family? I expect for you to get things back together."

Tonya said, "I'm going to talk to everyone. David that's all I can do!"

David said, "Well then do that!"

"What else do you want to eat" She asked him.

David told her and she got up to get it. Daisy and David were sitting alone and David said, "Baby girl you all I got and you have a lot of my DNA, my last seed. I need you to stay real, 2-DIE-4 is in you. Your brothers have fucked up a lot of money. I'm trying to get an appeals lawyer out of West Hartford named Kenny Harden. He wants one hundred thousand dollars. I have it but I need to handle some other things."

Daisy asked, "Dad what's up with that Puerto Rican boy from the Vill name Jerry? He's after me."

David said, "What? Well he is street smart and word is he is getting big money out there. He was Chad's right hand man."

Daisy said, "I got his ticket. I'm going to break him. Don't let the look fool you Dad, I am tough."

Tonya came back to the table and said, "David, April and Ieasha are having babies, they are both eight months pregnant."

David replied, "What? Damn I feel old. I am fixing to be a granddaddy!" He was smiling, happy to hear the family was growing, in his mind he wanted boys, but girls would do. David asked Tonya, "How much money was in the safe?"

Tonya said, "About three hundred thousand dollars."

David said, "Cool, but it's going fast."

"You still have a safe at the house in Avon," she said.

"I know but I done spent the money in all the other safes. Tell Justice and Justin that I need to see them real soon, like the next visitation day."

Daisy and Tonya talked to David about family matters until visitation was over. Then they left and David was taken back to his cell.

JUSTICE

Justice was riding low, waiting on the right time to catch Lisa because he wanted to pay her back for what she did to his mother. His cell phone went off and he looked at the number, it was his big brother Justin.

Justice answered and said, "What's popping Big Bro?"

Justin replied, "Man I need some money."

Justice said, "Bro how much?"

"Two thousand dollars," He told his brother.

Justice said, "Damn Bro!"

Justin had not been home in two weeks, he had lost his condo and Ieasha was pregnant and was back at her parent's house.

Justice had sold his Lexus for a little of nothing. He told Justin to meet him on Clark Street next to the school, He hung up and drove to meet his big brother. When he pulled up he spotted his brother on the corner and pulled up next to him.

He said, "Get in."

Justin's clothes were dirty and he looked bad. He wasn't on top of anything.

"You need to clean yourself up," said Justice.

Justin said, "Man I'm sick!"

"Let me take you to a private doctor," Justice begged.

"No lil' Bro it's that heroin," Justin told him.

Justice said, "Why you tried that shit?" He had tears in his eyes.

Justin said, "Bro I can't sleep with all them murders on my mind. Heroin is the only way my mind stays clear."

Justice pulled up at the house on Magnolia St. They both got out and went inside. Justice went to the back and got his brother some fresh clothes to put on. Justin took a shower and got clean. Justice gave his brother two G's, he didn't know what for. They both walked out of the house and got in the truck headed for Garden St. Justin told his brother to let him out.

Justice stopped to let his brother out. He said, "Big Bro be careful, everyone is worried about you."

Justin said, "Yeah I know."

Justice pulled off with a lot on his mind. He hated that drugs took his big brother down. He hated that drugs were the cause of his mother's death. He hated that drugs were the reason his Dad was in prison and he hated that drugs were what made him rich. Justin had done a lot of killing for the family so he had to stay strong, along with his brother no matter what. He was going to see to that.

DAISY

Daisy was telling her mother that David needed extra money for the appeal lawyer.

Tonya said, "David fucked up a lot of money on bull shit, but you will never know how much money he has. He never tells about all of what he's got. He always keeps an ace in the hole."

Daisy said, "I'm going to help him out. These suckers out there got to pay. They want me? Bring on the money."

Tonya said, "Just don't fall for that love shit."

Daisy said, "Never that! It's 2-DIE-4, family that's who got my love."

Tonya said, "Girl you are so much like your daddy."

JERRY

Jerry was on Cleveland Ave. at the stash house. No one knew about the money that was inside the house, but him and Chad. Chad was dead. The master bed room was filled with money. It was inside of Nike bags, over a million in cash and more was coming in day by day.

Jerry had Daisy on his mind. She was a dime all the way around, the baddest and thuggest girl in town. Her dad was well respected and now his sons are well respected. Her mother was raised up in the game too. Jerry said to himself, 'damn I want to get in them pants.' Jerry still wanted to get Lisa for tricking him, but he had time, right now he wanted to exercise his game. He picked up the phone and called Daisy.

GAIL

Gail had been talking to Ieasha a lot, they had become friends and Ieasha was telling her what Islam was like and what they believed in. She told Gail that Justin had not been around in three weeks and that he lost their condo.

Gail said, "Damn! Girl Justin is on something else. But don't worry he is strong and he will get himself back together."

Gail was crazy about Justin because he was the first grandchild. But Gail was old school, she knew Justin was on a heavy drug. He had borrowed money from her and never came back around. All the signs were there.

Ieasha told Gail she would talk later, she had to get to work because her break time was over.

JERRY AND DAISY

Daisy's phone went off, she picked up and said, "Hello Jerry, what's up?"

Jerry asked, "What are you doing?"

Daisy said, "Nothing."

Jerry asked, "How did you know it was me?"

Daisy said, "Because don't no other man call me. It's hard to get my number."

Jerry was smiling on the other side of the phone. He said, "Well can I come and take you out to chill?"

"It depends on where we are going," she told him.

Jerry said, "Shopping,"

Daisy said, "That's cool. Meet me on Blue Hills Ave, in front of the hospital." They hung up and Daisy said, "Mom I'm fixing to go shopping."

Tonya asked her, "Girl where you get money from?"

"It's on Jerry, he's doing the buying," Daisy said.

Tonya said, "You be careful."

Daisy walked out the front door looking good. She was standing in front of the hospital when the white and gold Benz 400-E pulled up. He was playing 50 cent, 21 questions.

Daisy hopped in after Jerry let down the driver side window. He was looking at her and said, "Damn! Girl you are fly."

Daisy had on a Baby Phat mini skirt and a white Phat blouse to match with the white pumps. She looked better than Melissa Ford in the King Magazine.

Jerry said, "We are headed to Enfield Mall to spend some money!" He could not keep his eyes off Daisy. The mini skirt had slid back and a lot of her inner thigh was showing, he could almost see her panties.

"So Jerry, tell me how many women you have," she said.

Jerry started smiling and said, "None, don't got time for hoes. There's only money on my mind."

~ 239 ~

Daisy said, "That a good one, but I feel the same way. I don't have a man because every nigga' wants pussy for free."

"Not me," he said.

They both start laughing.

Daisy said, "Not saying that like I'm a hoe, because Jerry you know my family. I can get anything I want. Don't need any nigga's money. But I am not fixing to fuck with no broke nigga' either."

"I feel you and that's why I want you to be my right hand girl. That means the girl I can trust," he told her.

Daisy said, "You can trust me long as you don't cross me."

"Damn you are so much like your dad," he said.

"I hear that a lot. I try to just be me, I can never be like my Dad," she replied.

Jerry said, "I have a lot of respect for David."

Daisy said, "You are starting off good."

They both busted out laughing.

JUSTIN

Justin was broke and didn't have any drugs. He and Black Rob were hanging tight. Black Rob use to have money back in the days, but drugs had taken over his life too. Justin use to look up to Black Rob, Cash Mike, Woody, Chad money, 1-2 Evil, Book man, Learch, Daddy Yump Diamond, Buzz-Rock, Monster, Mark Curtlen, Big Ed Curtlen, Mega Fu, Travis T-Bone, Tuff-Toke Buck, Bozack, Sam-Dog 808, Sharvin 40, Lil-Ricky, Jerry and Tato Gothe. These were the legends around Hartford.

The Vill, Westland and St. Albany Ave. Justin use to run routes for these players, but Black Rob had let the drugs control him. He was telling Justin there was a store on the corner of Enfield he wanted to rob. He had an old 38 special with one bullet, he told Justin they wouldn't have to hurt no one. The old man at the store only had a bat behind the counter. Everyone knew Mr. Green so robbing him was out. But drugs had Black

Rob and Justin planning to rob Mr. Green Friday before it closed.

JUSTICE

Justice was headed out to Bloomfield to pay Lisa a visit because she had hurt him for the rest of his life by killing his mother. He had the world on his mind, his daddy wanted him and his brother to come visit him. David was upset about how fast the money was going. But Justice wanted to see his Daddy. They were close and that was his love. His money was looking real good now, Park Street, Nelson Court, Dutch point and Bowels Park was paying off.

As Justice got closer to the house, he got right in front and something came to his mind, he pulled off. His brother Justin was on his mind, drugs had made them split up. Drugs had stolen his big brother, his role model. He had to get his brother some help. Ieasha had not called him back and he had not heard from her in two weeks.

LISA

Lisa and Lucy were lying across her queen size bed counting money by the thousands. Lisa was telling Lucy that word on the street was Justin had started using drugs.

She said, "I can't believe that because he is a strong seed, we spoiled that boy growing up."

That made Lisa think about her best friend Linda and what she had done.

Lucy looked up and saw Lisa crying. Lucy said, "What's wrong? You can tell me, I'll understand."

"I killed Linda," Lisa said.

Lucy said, "Its okay baby, just think about the good times."

"Linda was jealous of Justin, but she loved him. That was David's first son and to hear he is on drugs is terrible. I am going to do all I can to help him. If he comes here I won't turn him down.

JUSTICE

Justice was riding down Blue Hills Ave headed to Garden St. He was going to get his big brother some help.

JUSTIN AND BLACK ROB

The store on the corner of the hood was getting ready to close when Black Rob and Justin were coming up from the back. Black Rob told Justin to come in after him. When Black Rob went in the store Mr. Green said, "Hello." Black Rob reached in his coat pocket and pulled out the gun, Mr. Green's eyes got big and he said, "Please! Don't hurt me." Justin walked in, went behind the counter and got the money. Mr. Green gave Justin the other money he had in his pocket.

Justin and Black Rob ran out to the street and headed down Garden St. Black Rob had plans and Justin was not a part of them. They went to one of the hoods crack houses, but the place was closed. The lady Mrs. Tiny, had got put out and Justin said, "We got to split the money."

Black Rob said, "Yeah its coming."

Black Rob had no plans of splitting the money. He always had greed in him, which was his down fall. That's what took him from being a King Pin and getting fifty thousand a day, to using about five thousand a day and living on the streets. He wanted it all and got ahold of the wrong thing.

When they got in back of the laundromat Black Rob pulled the gun on Justin and said, "give me the bag nigga'."

Justin said, "Come on Rob don't go there."

Rob said, "Nigga', I will smoke your black ass."

Justin could not believe a dope fiend done tried him. The only thing on his mind was killing this nigga' that he once had so much respect for. Justin knew Black Rob was going to kill him because of who he was. If Justin lived, Rob knew he would die.

Justin started thinking back over his life, his mother, his sister, grandma, the fun, the hurt and the pain. Justin asked God to forgive him. He told himself if he came out of this alive he would seek help for his drug problem because it had gotten out of hand. Justin wanted to live to see his first seed born.

When he spoke he said, "Why Black Rob?"

Black Rob said, "Nigga' you question me? You ain't shit no more, you let drugs bring you down to an ant."

Justin was so hurt at what life had become, he got ready to jump at Black Rob but some lights caught both of them. Justin saw the blue Land Rover and he knew it was his little brother. Damn! He needed that. God is real he answered Justin's prayers!

Justice had seen two men standing in the spot. He could tell one of the dudes was his big brother so he pulled up. He saw the other man pull a gun on his big brother, then he realized the other dude was Black Rob. Justice jumped out of his truck with his 44 in his hand. He shot Black Rob two times in the head before he could speak. The one bullet Black Rob had was no use, he was dead before he hit the ground.

Justice told his big brother to jump in. Justin ran over and got the bag out of Black Rob's hand. It had all the money in it. They both got in the truck and headed out.

Justice asked, "You okay?"

Justin said, "Man its cool, I needed you and thank you man you came just in time."

Justice said, "Man its cool, but you can't get yourself in shit like that again."

They were headed to Magnolia St to Justice's house. When they got to the house, they both went upstairs. Justin sat on the couch thinking and Justice sat across from him.

Justice asked, "What's in that brown bag?"

Justin said, "Money."

He told Justice what he and Black Rob had done. Justice heard Mr. Green's name he grabbed the bag and headed out of the house. He was headed to Mr. Green's store on the corner of Garden St. When he pulled up and went in Mr. Green was sitting down talking to his wife.

When Justice walked in they said, "Hello Justice."

They respected Justice for being loyal at a young age. They watched him grow up.

Justice said, "Are you okay?"

Mr. Green said, "This is the first time someone has robbed me in 30 years."

Justice said, "I handled that you will never have to worry about him anymore."

Mr. Green smiled a sad smile but he understood the street talk, he was an old, old player. Justice gave the brown bag to Mr. Green and headed out of the store.

Mr. Green said, "Justice, your day on earth has just got longer. God is going to bless you and your family, thank you son."

Justice did not like what Black Rob had done. You don't take from your own kind, we are all already broke. Justice got back to his house and Justin had been in the shower and got clean in some of Justice's new clothes.

Justin told Justice, "Man I need some help! I got to get off this shit, I promised God if I got out of that shit with Black Rob I was going to get some help with my drug problem."

Justice said, "I am going to help now."

He picked up the phone and called some private rehabs numbers, some of the best in the world, right there in Connecticut. No one will never know. Justice got his big brother to go to the rehab in West Hartford, they used a false name Danny Wright. Justin was ready to live with no more drugs. The next morning Justice and Justin were headed to West Hartford, to the Harvey and Mattie Rehab Center.

Justin checked in under Danny Wright, it was a 30 day program at a hundred dollars a day. Some of the best had been there, movie stars, actors and rappers. They went there if they were on drugs and did not want it to get out, it was very expensive and it was very private. Justice was not worried about the money, he wanted for his brother what he wanted for himself, the best in life. Justice promised his brother that no one would know, they could guess but he wouldn't tell a soul. They hugged each other, Justice didn't want to leave his big brother. They both looked at each other with tears in their eyes.

Justice said, "I love you man."

Justin said, "It's the same here. You check on the family, hold them down and let me get my shit back together."

Justice turned and walked out the door, headed to a world he did not understand. A world that would eat you if you are weak, a world where love was hard to hold on to.

ENFIELD MALL

Jerry and Daisy had been all over the mall, he had let Daisy go wild with the shopping. She got name brand everything. Jerry also got Daisy two princess cut, 14 carat diamond rings, priced at five thousand a piece. She had ten pairs of female Reptiles, Gator, Elephant and Lizard boots. Jerry was holding Daisy's hand as they walked out of the mall.

Daisy knew Jerry wanted her and a part of her wanted him, but Jerry had to wait. He had to prove he could help her and her Dad. Daisy had already made up her mind, she wouldn't go out cheap. Plus she was a virgin and a lot of guys didn't know that.

Jerry and Daisy got in the car and headed out, back to Hartford. On the way back he was touching on Daisy's legs, but Jerry was a fast driver. Daisy had just gotten into the feeling when Jerry pulled up at her house.

Tonya was out back hanging out clothes when Jerry got out and opened Daisy's door. He let the trunk up and there were bags everywhere. Tonya was watching and thinking back, she remembered those days, not so long ago.

Tonya walked over to Jerry and said, "What's up?"

Jerry said, "Chilling."

Tonya said, "I see you got a few things for my girl."

Jerry started laughing as Tonya grabbed some bags and helped them into the house.

"Yo Daisy I will call you later," Jerry said.

"Do that," she replied.

Jerry got in his car and headed back to the Vill. He had never spent money like that on a female that he had never touched, but he called it an investment. He wanted Daisy at whatever the cost.

JUSTICE

Justice pulled up at Tonya's house with the music blasting. He had not seen Tonya in about three weeks. Tonya had called and told him that his daddy wanted to see him and Justin both, A.S.A.P.!

Justice walked in the house and Daisy had stuff all over the place. Justice said, "Damn! Girl you spend it all? You must have hit the lotto!"

Daisy said, "Something like that. Only thing is, I didn't have to wait on my money, it came to me!"

Justice said, "Okay player," and they both started laughing.

Tonya walked out of her room in her short shorts looking good.

Justice said, "What's up lady?"

"Nothing much. Where is Justin?" She asked.

Justice lied and said, "He's in New York handling some things."

Tonya said, "For real?"

She knew Justice was lying, but she knew her son was okay. The streets were telling her that Justin was on drugs and that hurt Tonya.

Justice went over to Daisy and asked, "Who is he?"

"Jerry from the Vill. We been kickin' it," Daisy told him.

Justice said, "'Good move, he about that money."

Tonya was looking crazy because she wanted to know what Daisy and Justice were talking about.

Daisy said, "I'll see you later, I got something to do." She went upstairs to her room.

Tonya waited until Daisy was in her room and she said, "Justice what's your fucking problem? It's been three weeks, you haven't called or even come by!" Tonya's feelings were starting to show.

Justice said, "Damn Lady! I have been out getting money."

Tonya was mad, she walked off and went to her room. Justice pulled out his cell phone and called Lil-Ricky on Park-Street, he ask Lil-Ricky what was up and Lil-Ricky told him the money was coming fast and they needed more products. He told Justice that Book-Man had a house in Stowe Village and he was moving weight fast.

Justice said, "Look bro, I'll meet you Friday at Main and Tower, have that paper."

Lil-Ricky replied, "I got you," and they hung up.

Tonya was laying across her bed when Justice walked in and stood there looking at her round ass.

Justice said to himself, 'this is a bad woman.' He walked over and lay on Tonya, she was wiggling and telling Justice to get up off of her. Justice started kissing her behind the neck and sticking his tongue in and out of her ear. She was falling weak and she stopped fighting. Justice undid her shorts, slide them down and saw the blue thong. He started licking Tonya down her back, which was really her weakness. That was how they first had sex, Tonya fell weak for the tongue. She started moaning loud and moving. She got on her knees in the middle of the bed and Justice was behind her with his head buried in her sweetness. She knew it was very risky because Daisy was upstairs, but she was too far gone to stop. She went to shaking and let the honey juice flow into Justice's mouth and he didn't stop.

Daisy had got off the phone and was walking to the kitchen. She heard some moaning and listened closely. She had never had sex before but she knew that noise from watching movies. The sound was coming from her mother's room. She looked out the window and saw Justice's truck was still there and she tip toed to her mother's door. The moaning got louder, Daisy had got excited because she had not seen or heard real sex before, but she was ready. She put her ear to the door and what she heard on the other side made her want to see.

Her Mother was calling all kinds of words out. She heard, "Baby it feels so good!" Daisy checked to see if the door was locked, she turned the knob and to her surprise it was unlocked. She eased it open and what she seen almost made her faint? Justice was behind her mother licking her butt. Daisy was shocked but curious, she wanted to know how it felt.

Tonya and Justice had no idea she was watching. Daisy was a big girl now and for the first time she felt something wet between her legs. She put her hand down between her womanhood and felt something sticky. Daisy stood there with her finger between her legs. She was watching hard, she saw Justice stand up and take off all his clothes. She saw her step brother's manhood and was in shock. Tonya had backed up to the end of the bed and was waiting on Justice to go up inside her world.

Daisy was at the door masturbating for the first time, but not the last. She said to herself she would never tell her dad, because he would kill Tonya and Justice. She knew that she and Justice were half siblings and she loved and respected him, so she was going to take what she had seen to the grave along with the other stuff she had seen or heard.

Tonya had her eyes closed and was enjoying what Justice was doing to her. She was moaning louder and louder. Justice was hitting Tonya from the back with no mercy while Daisy was at the door watching. She put two of her fingers in her wetness, she was into it. The faster Justice went, so were her fingers. Daisy felt a rush and out of nowhere she made a noise, no one heard it but her. Her knees got weak and she ease the door closed then went upstairs to her room. She lay across her bed, thinking about all she had seen and Justice was on her mind.

Tonya heard a noise and tried to move, she looked back and saw the door move, she knew it was Daisy, but she was having an orgasm and did not care. She was in heaven. Justice had let a load go and fell on top of Tonya.

She said, "We got to stop."

She jumped up and put her shorts on. She was leaving as the phone rang, she picked it up and it was her mother. She pointed for Justice to get dressed and Justice followed orders. Mrs. Weaver wanted Tonya to come over to her house. Justice kissed Tonya on the mouth and headed out the door.

Daisy got up and looked out the window her mind was on sex.

Tonya hung up the phone and went upstairs to Daisy's room, she knew Daisy had seen her and Justice but she wanted to see what she had to say. When Tonya opened the door Daisy jumped.

Tonya said, "What's up girl?"

Daisy said, "Nothing," like a little girl.

Tonya lied and said, "You must have been sleeping, I been calling you."

Daisy said to herself, 'yeah right.' She said, "No I was watching a movie on TV."

Tonya just smiled and said, "I'm going over to my mother's house and chill after I get out of the shower.'

Daisy said, "I'm going to stay here and do my homework."

Tonya hugged her baby girl and walked out.

JUSTICE

Justice was headed to Lisa's house in Bloomfield. When he got there the lights were on, so he pulled up in the drive way and got out.

Lisa heard the door close. She looked out the window and saw the blue Land Rover. She said, "Lucy that's the truck we saw the other day.'

Lucy looked out and said, "Yes it is."

Lisa grabbed her 357 mag and waited. She spotted Justice coming to the porch and said, "Lucy that's Justice, he's Justin's baby brother, Linda's son."

Lucy said, "Damn! He is good looking."

Lisa said, "He's a killer just like his mother, brother and daddy."

Justice knocked on the door and Lisa was waiting. She opened the door and said, "Hello Justice, how are you doing?"

Justice said, "Good."

Lisa said, "Come on in and have a seat." Justice went and sat on the couch and Lisa asked, "You want a drink?"

Justice said, "No I need to talk to you."

"Go ahead and talk," she replied. Justice looked over at Lucy and Lisa said, "Oh this is my friend Lucy. She's from New York, I raised her so whatever we talk about is not going anywhere."

Justice said, "I'm trying to get a bigger connection because it's in demand. I'm making money all over Hartford.

Lisa said, "I can tell you are doing well, how much you want?"

Justice said, "A hundred kilos a week for starters, at wholesale price."

"No problem, money first," she said.

Justice said, "Half and the other half when I get the shit."

They talked about the prices and Justice agreed to her price. He told her that Daisy and Justin would be his man.

Lisa said, "I would like to meet your sister Daisy."

Justice said, "I will let you two meet soon."

"How is Justin?" She asked.

Justice was eyeing Lucy and that fine ass she had. Lisa saw Justice had an eye for her girl so she said, "Justice you can come by when you get ready. Lucy and I will be here chilling.'

Justice replied, "I got to run." He hugged Lisa and then he hugged Lucy and he let his hand drop to touch her ass.

Lucy smiled, but didn't let Lisa see it.

Justice walked out and got in his truck, he was feeling good. He was about to make a big move and get the money all the way right, 2-DIE-4.

LISA

When Justice pulled off Lisa said, "Damn! That boy has grown up to be good looking!"

Lucy said, "I want to get to know him better."

Lisa said, "I want some of him."

"Me too," Lucy replied.

Lisa had told Lucy what she had done to Justice's mother years ago, but Justice had never disrespected her and she respected him. Lisa was also the first person to touch Justice after the doctor. He was born in Jamaica. Lisa told Lucy, "Those were the good old days."

IEASHA

Justin and Ieasha had been talking on the phone almost every day. Things were coming along fine. Ieasha was telling Justin that agent Marvin Harris was back on the trail, he had been questioning her about where Justin was.

Justin said, "I will see you soon, don't worry about him. Don't let them white folks trick you into saying nothing."

Ieasha said, "Baby I will never say anything because I don't know anything. Get ready for your first born, 2-DIE-4."

Justin was laughing, he said, "I love you and will see you soon."

TONYA

Tonya had gone over to her mother's house. She got out of the car and used her key to let herself in the back door. Mrs. Weaver was sitting on the couch, reading the Hartford Courant. She had just come back from her morning run, she was in real good shape. Her body was like a young woman, like Gavelle Voin, her legs were firm and her butt was tight. She was nice and round, no stomach and her breasts were still standing.

Tonya walked in and said, "Hello young lady."

Her mother said, "Where is my granddaughter?"

"She done got too grown to come by. That girl got a boyfriend that spends thousands on her at the mall."

Mrs. Weaver said, "You and her are just alike, she's just a little lighter."

Tonya said, "I love her to death. I haven't seen Justin in about thirty days, but he's okay."

"That Justice is growing up to be a fine young man, what you think?" Mrs. Weaver asked.

Tonya lied and said, "He is okay." But deep in her heart she was falling in love with Justice, David's baby son.

Mrs. Weaver said, "Girl you know that boy look good. He is David's son not yours." They both started laughing. Mrs. Weaver said, "Girl they say them girls is crazy about his young behind."

Tonya said, "I be hearing about him."

JERRY

Jerry was chilling in the Vill, getting that money he had been collecting all day. His cell phone went off and he answered, "Yo!"

Bozack said, "What's up nigga?"

Jerry said, "Nothing fool! What's up with you?"

Bozack said, "Man you know Lil-Ricky got a trap in the Vill on Hampton St?"

Jerry said, "What?"

Bozack said, "Book-Man is selling weight."

Jerry knew Lil-Ricky worked for Justice so to keep the peace he said, "Bozack just chill, I'll take care of that."

Jerry hung up, he had a plan to be the first man to fuck Daisy and then take her baby brother to war. He had already heard Justin was on drugs. Jerry had Bozack on standby and he was a killer. When he showed up someone was going to die. Bozack grew up with David and knew his sons, but Bozack was his own man and he killed to eat. He stayed in a five hundred thousand dollar house overlooking Windsor. He drove a Benz, or an Austin Martin and flew to the Keys or Jamaica twice a week. Now he was in Hartford waiting on the final call because whatever command his boss gave, that's who would die.

But to go up against David's boys was a hard job, they were rich killers.

Chapter Sixteen

FRESH START
JUSTICE

Justice was headed to West Hartford to the rehab center to pick his big brother Justin up. He was feeling good, this was like a fresh start. His big brother was coming home. Justice was smoking a blunt, he had not snorted any cocaine in three months. He was not fucking with that no more. Justice had a lot to do, his daddy David wanted to see him and Justin and he understood the order to make it happen.

When he pulled up at the rehab, all eyes were on him, white folks were everywhere and Justice walked into the center with a Nike bag in hand. His big brother had got his weight up and was looking good. Justice hugged him and didn't try to hide the tears of joy. He gave Justin the bag and Justin went in the back. About ten minutes later he came out looking like a star. He had on a blue and white Giorgio Armani shirt and white jeans to go with it. He had on some blue low cut Gucci boots, he was looking good.

Justice said, "Damn boy, you look like new money!"

Justin said, "Well let's go spend some!"

"There's a big party going on at Main and Tower next week," Justice said.

"We will be there," Justin told him.

Justice said, "What kind of car you want?"

"No car right now I want that new Cadillac truck," Justin said.

They got in Justice's truck and headed to the Cadillac dealership on Albany Ave. When they pulled up Justice saw his man Mr. Kevin Shaw. He always dealt with Kevin. He was a good white man who loved cocaine, but he handled it well at first, like everyone did from the start. Kevin was so far gone now, he was making deals with his daddy in-law's cars.

Justice and Justin got out and Mr. Shaw came over and shook Justice's hand and then shook Justin's hand. He said, "Can I help you Justice?"

Justice said, "Yeah my brother is looking for a Cadillac truck."

Mr. Shaw said, "Look around son, get what you want."

Justin was already looking, he passed a few good looking trucks until he spotted a brand new pearl, white Escalade with 24" rims. He called Mr. Shaw over and he ran over there like he was on fire.

Justin said, "I want that truck."

Justice came over and said, "You want that Bro?"

Justin replied, "Hell yea!"

Mr. Shaw opened the door and pulled up the rug, He got both sets of keys and threw them to Justin then said, "It's yours."

Justin was happy, it had been years since he felt that good.

Justice walked over to his brother and said, "Let's do what we be known to do. Let's get this money!"

He gave Justin about ten thousand dollars and said, "Follow me to Grandma's house."

GAIL

Gail and all her girls were sitting around playing cards and telling jokes. They heard some loud music playing and Jasmine got up and looked out the window. She saw Justice's Land Rover but she didn't know who was driving the pretty pearl white, Escalade truck because the windows were super dark.

Justice got out first, then Justin got out and all the girls ran out of the house to hug the boys. Everyone gave Justin a little money.

Gail asked, "You okay?"

Justin said, "Yes ma'am!"

Gail said, "Stay on top of your game, don't let the game get on top of you player!"

Everyone started laughing, but Gail was telling him some real shit.

Justice said, "I'm going up stairs to chill."

Justin said, "I'm going to see Tonya and my other Grandma, grandma number two.

"Okay then, because I am Grandma number one," Gail replied.

They laughed and Justin talked for a while, then he got in his truck and headed to see his other family. They were all close, but Justin favored David's side of the family, they were more down home, real people.

JUSTIN

Justin was headed down Albany Ave. and all eyes were on him in his pearl white, Cadillac Escalade on gold rims. The girls on the avenue were checking to see who the new truck belonged to.

Justin pulled up in Mrs. Weaver's back yard. When he got out his mother, Tonya came running to the door. When she saw her son get out of the truck she ran and hugged him. He was looking good and smelling good. He had picked up about twenty pounds.

Mrs. Weaver came out and hugged her grandson. They were all happy, Justin was telling them about the things he had seen and the plans he had for after Ieasha had the baby.

Tonya said, "Baby I just want you to be safe and stay out of trouble."

Justin said, "I'm cool."

When they all went in the house, he said, "I need to call Ieasha and he picked up the phone to dial her number. He didn't get an answer so he sat on the couch and talked to his mom and grandma for about two hours. They laughed and talked about the old days.

Then Justin said, "I got to pull out, but I'll be around. I need to go check on Ieasha."

Tonya and Mrs. Weaver hugged him as he got in his truck and headed for Avon, Conn.

LISA

The news had gotten to Lisa that Justin was back in town and had a brand new Cadillac Escalade, riding good and looking good. Lisa was happy to hear that, but she was ready to make one of her biggest deals with Justice for a hundred kilos. That was the biggest since her and David were rolling together. She was living well with Lucy on her side, living the life in the style that Lisa was showing her. Concerts, movies, great dinners, the best wine, the best clothes and not to forget, they were on some freaky shit together. But now they had Justice, Justin and soon, Daisy. Lisa laidback in front of her swimming pool and enjoyed the sun tan she was getting. She was thinking about what lay ahead for a boss bitch.

IEASHA

Ieasha and her family were sitting in their front yard cooking out. All her family had come down from New York and Boston. Her aunts and cousins had heard about Justin but had never gotten to meet him. Sabir and the men of the family were sitting around talking about football. Justin pulled up in his Cadillac truck and everyone froze. The windows were so dark you couldn't see inside and the gold rims were shining. Justin saw Ieasha, he opened the door and stepped out. All eyes were on him, now he knew how 2-Pac felt when he wrote that song.

Ieasha spotted her man, she ran and hugged Justin and kissed him on the mouth.

Justin said, "I missed you baby."

Ieasha said, "I missed you too."

Mr. Sabir came over and shook Justin's hand then her mother came over and hugged him. She let leasha introduce Justin to the rest of the family and Justin spoke to everyone. He started rubbing on leasha stomach telling everyone it had to be a boy.

leasha said, "It doesn't matter."

Justin said, "I know the Feds are watching me but that's their job, I'm clean."

"Give me a month and things will be back on track," he told her.

"No matter what I will always stay loyal to you, it's 2-DIE-4, 4-ever," she told him.

Justin gave her an emotional hug. She was still looking good even with the big belly. He said, "Baby just chill."

leasha got ready to say something and Justin's cell phone started ringing. It was his brother Justice, he told Justin to meet him at Tonya's house they all needed to talk.

Justin said, "I am on my way."

leasha held Justin's hand until he got in his truck. She kissed him on the mouth and said, "I love you."

Justin said, "I love you little mama!"

THE ROYAL FAMILY

Justice had got some rest and was headed to Tonya's house to lay down the law. It didn't matter that he was next to the baby. He had the brain and the money, so he was stepping up to lead the family. Daisy was sitting around talking on the phone with her boyfriend Jerry, he was madly in love with Daisy and she was playing hard to get.

Daisy heard some music outside, she looked out the window and saw it was Justice. He got out and Daisy opened the door to hug her brother. Daisy was thinking about the night she saw him having sex with her mom.

Justice said, "What's up?"

Daisy jumped out of the day dream. She said nothing, just smiled. They sat down on the couch and Daisy hung the phone up and turned the TV up when they heard someone pull in the drive way. Daisy got up and saw the white Cadillac truck.

"Boy that's a nice ass truck just pulled up," she said.

Justice said, "Girl that's your brother Justin."

Daisy ran out to meet him and they hugged each other. Justin came in and they all sat down while Justin fired up a blunt and passed it around.

Justice said, "We all we got. We are family, let's get back what our Dad had. Let's get this money!"

Daisy said, "I'm ready."

Justin said, "You know me, it's 2-DIE-4, 4-ever."

Justice said, "Here's the plan. Lisa wants to meet Daisy, she wants to get to know you."

Daisy said, "That bitch can meet me because I want to meet her."

Justice said, "Lisa is slick baby girl, so be careful."

"She ain't seen slick, it's in my blood," she replied.

They all laughed and Justice said, "Well Friday I'm going to get a hundred kilos of coke from her. But we ain't going to deal with her forever."

Justin said, "Bro you lead the way, me and Daisy are going to follow orders."

Daisy said, "I got Jerry taking real good care of me."

Justice said, "That nigga' is spending well."

Justin said, "We all got to be ready for the party at Main and Tower Friday."

Daisy said, "The Royal Family will be there."

JUSTIN

Justin left the meeting, got in his truck and headed for Bloomfield, over to Lisa's house. He had Daisy in the truck with him. When they pulled up at Lisa's house she was on the front porch. Justin got out and Lisa ran over and hugged him. She looked him up and down then said, "Boy you are looking good."

Justin said, "Baby girl you still look damn good too."

Lisa started smiling and asked, "Who is that pretty girl with you?"

Justin said, "That's my sister Daisy."

Daisy said, "Hello," and shook Lisa's hand.

Lisa had heard about Daisy but didn't know she looked that good. They all walked inside Lisa's house and Justin said, "Where is Lucy?"

Lisa said, "Her lazy ass is asleep."

Every one sat down and Lisa sked, "How old you are Daisy?"

She said, "16."

Justin got up and went to Lucy's room. Lisa was staring at Daisy like she was a piece of steak. Lisa was a freak, she loved eating pussy and turning young girls out. Daisy had caught her eye.

Lisa said, "So Daisy do you have a boyfriend?" Daisy was not going to tell Lisa she was with Jerry for the money. Lisa said, "Here is my number you can call me anytime and we can have a girls night out."

Justin had woken Lucy up. She came out the room and Lisa said, "Lucy this is Daisy, Daisy this is my best friend Lucy."

Lucy came and sat on the couch, they talked girl talk while Justin sat and listened. He enjoyed them.

Justin said, "We got to go, Justice is waiting on us."

Lisa and Lucy hugged them as they were leaving. Daisy turned around and said, "I'll give you a call."

Lisa said, "Do that."

JUSTICE AND TONYA

Justice was back at Tonya's house waiting on Justin and Daisy to get back. Tonya came out of the room and Justice said, "What's up and hit Tonya on her back side."

Tonya turned around and said, "Look baby boy we need to chill, I believe Daisy heard us that night having sex."

Justice said, "She's a smart girl, but she won't do nothing to hurt me, you or David, because she loves us all."

Justice walked up on Tonya and pinned her to the wall kissing her on the mouth. They heard Justin pulling up and they both jumped then went their separate ways as Justin and Daisy walked in.

Justin said, "What's up family?"

Justin told Justice that he took Daisy to meet Lisa, he told them that they all had to see David this week, everyone said okay.

Tonya went to see David every week, he had about twenty thousand dollars on the books. He had a cell phone, DVDS and he paid off officers to let him and Tonya chill for about thirty minutes when the time was right. But David wanted out, he needed that lawyer for his appeal.

Justice was getting ready to leave and Daisy's phone went off. It was Jerry, he asked Daisy if she wanted to go out, she said cool and Jerry told her he would pick her up at 9pm then they hung up

Justin got ready to go to Ieasha house.

BACK ON TOP OF THE GAME

Justin had bought a house in Windsor. A nice big house with the swimming pool in back and a guest house. It had two acres of nothing but yard with big pine trees. Ieasha had a brand new Porsche and she was happy, expecting to have her baby any day.

The Fed's had been hanging around a lot. Justice and Lisa were doing good business but Justice was still plotting against her. He had made Lisa drop her guard.

Daisy and Jerry were still dating and he was still spending big money but getting no sex.

The family was back making money and everyone was saving for the rainy days.

Tonya and Justice had stopped messing around with each other, but they still flirted when they were around each other. Betty and Jesse were doing well. David's sisters were living well also and it was almost like the old days.

But nothing last forever, every hustler knows that.

JUSTIN

Justin was in his brand new Benz headed to his mom's house, Tonya had been calling him all day. He pulled up and went in the house where Tonya was sitting at the kitchen table.

Justin asked, "What's up?"

Tonya said, "Boy I told you to come over here an hour ago, don't make me," she raised her hand. Justin started laughing because she still treated him like a baby. Tonya said, "Justin you got to be careful because everyone is talking about how good you and Justice are doing."

Justin said, "Okay, I'm moving slow and I got money in about four different spots. I'm going to tell you so if something happens to me you can handle the money."

Tonya said, "The money is cool, but I want you to stop and chill. You have everything money can buy."

Justin said, "I'm going to get out of the game mom, just chill."

"Boy don't tell me to chill, I ain't doing shit," she said.

Daisy walked down stairs as Tonya and Justin asked at the same time, "Where are you going?"

Daisy had on a white mini skirt, a blue blouse with the matching pumps. She said, "I'm going to see someone, I'll be back later." She hugged Justin and her mom.

Tonya said, "Be careful."

Daisy had a purple and gold Lexus coupe, it was the talk of the town. On the front plate it said "Hot to Handle." She walked out the door headed to Lisa's house, she didn't want her mother to know. Anyway she was a big girl now and she could handle herself.

JUSTICE

Justice was riding slow feeling good, he was coming from Park Street. He had been drinking and smoking weed and he was feeling horny. He was headed home but went the long way. As he was riding he ended up on Tonya's mom's side of town. He decided to stop by Mrs. Weaver's house, he called her by her first name Shandra, because she was not his grandmother, plus she was fine to him for her age.

Justice pulled up in the back yard and knocked on the back door. Mrs. Weaver came to the door with her night gown on.

She said, "Come on in Justice."

Justice went in and sat on the couch. He said, "What's up Shandra?"

She said, "Nothing much, just got out of the shower, I was watching a movie."

Justice said, "What's the movie?"

Mrs. Weaver said, "Belly."

Justice replied, "Cool."

Mrs. Weaver said, "You a mess," and walked to her room.

Justice jumped up and got close up behind her and said, "What you say woman?"

Mrs. Weaver said, "Boy don't make me spank you."

They were so close Mrs. Weaver felt Justice's chest touching her and she started breathing hard. They looked each other in the eyes playfully and Justice grabbed her by the shoulders and started kissing her on the mouth. Mrs. Weaver wanted to fight him off, but lust had taken control. Justice started playing with Mrs. Weaver ears and running his hand under her gown.

For 52 years old Mrs. Weaver had the body of a 25 year old. She ran and worked out every day and it paid off. Mrs. Weaver was a dime, her tits stood up all natural. She had pretty caramel skin and hazel brown eyes.

Justice pulled her gown over her head, she did not have on a bra but had a hot pink thong on and Justice laid her across the bed and started kissing her from head to toe. He sucked on her tits one at a time, licking her like she was some candy. Mrs. Weaver was gone, her eyes had rolled In the back of her head. It had been years since she had gotten the full body treatment. Justice was working his way down her stomach, sticking his tongue in and out of her navel. He went on down and pulled the thong loose, Mrs. Weaver was on fire, she lay there with her eyes closed and Justin came out of all of his clothes. He got on his knees at the end of the bed and Mrs. Weaver felt something moving at a fast pace. Her body went to jumping and she was moaning and out of control, trying to move Justice's head with both of her hands. She closed her eyes and saw stars. She was having an orgasm for the first time in her life.

Justice had juice all over his face as he stood up and look down at Mrs. Weaver. Her legs were spread wide open and she was breathing hard and loud. Justice took her left leg and put it on his shoulder and slid all eleven inches up in her. She was wet and tight but Justice did his thing, she was so good he was about to go there, so he pulled back when Mrs. Weaver looked at him and said, "Give it to me."

Justice slide in her and went off like she was a young girl. She was calling his name and digging at his back. She put her other leg on Justice's shoulder and was throwing it back. Justice was about to cum and she used her skills, she locked on him and made him tell her it was good. Justice let a load go in Mrs. Weaver and fell on top of her.

He said, "Damn!"

They made love all night. Mrs. Weaver was a freak and Justice had made it come out. Early that morning Justice woke Mrs. Weaver up with his manhood in her mouth going to work, he just laid back and enjoyed, she was a pro. He was about to cum when he moved her head. She got off the bed to stand up, thinking Justice didn't want no more, but to her surprise Justice bent her over and she put both her hands on the dresser while Justice pounded her pussy from the back. She was throwing it back as she came hard and so did Justice, they were both sweaty and spent.

Mrs. Weaver turned around and said, "Boy you a mess, but you know Tonya, she be watching and asking about us a lot."

Justice was getting dressed, he said, "Don't worry I don't kiss and tell." Mrs. Weaver started smiling. Justice said, "If you need me to do something just say the word."

Mrs. Weaver said, "Boy you know I'm going to want some more. Just tell me I can get some more sometime."

Justice walked over and kissed her on the mouth, he backed up and said, "You can get it whenever you're ready."

Mrs. Weaver said, "Boy I want you to be careful because there's all kinds of stuff in them streets."

Justice started laughing. He said, "You are safe with me. I don't play where I eat, in other words I get dirty money in the streets. I'm not fixing to get no dirty woman. That's why you were on my mind on my way home."

They both laughed and Justice headed out the door, he was on the way home again.

APRIL

April was telling her mother to call Justice because she was in pain.

Her mother said, "I'm going to call 911 first."

She picked up the phone and dialed 911. The operator said, "Can I help you?"

April's mother, Kassie said, "My daughter is pregnant and I think she's fixing to have the baby!"

The operator said, "Calm down, we will have an ambulance in route."

Kassie dialed Justice's number and told him that April was fixing to have the baby.

Justice said on the other end, "I'm on my way."

IEASHA

Ieasha was riding with her daddy when she started having sharp pains. She started crying and Mr. Sabir knew what it was, he said, "Just hold on baby."

He pushed the Range Rover to speeds he only did alone. He was wide open coming down Blue Hill Ave. He pulled up to the emergency room at Saint Francis hospital. He ran in and got some help.

The nurse came out fast because they knew Ieasha, she was once their boss. They rolled her in and put her in a private room. She got V.I.P treatment.

Ieasha told Sabir to call Justin. He called Justin and told him. They knew that he and Tonya were on the way.

JUSTICE

Justice had made it just in time, April was at the hospital in down town New Haven. When he walked in April's mother Kassie was waiting on him.

She said, "April is in the room ready to have the baby."

Justice put on his scrubs and walked in the room, April was laid back with both legs in the air. He walked over and grabbed her hand. April was happy to see her child's father because so many women had told her about their baby's father not being there and how it made it hard to have a baby. The doctor was telling April to push and April was yelling and holding Justice's hand.

He backed up to see when the baby came out and he got sick. He could not believe what he was seeing, a baby being born was something new to him and it touched Justice in away only a dad would know. The joy, the love and the pain. When the baby came out Justice was yelling louder than April, he scared everyone.

The doctor said, "It's a boy!"

He was a big nine pounds and ten ounces. The doctor cleaned the baby and gave him to April.

Justice said, "I have a name, Kareem Elliot Thomas."

April said, "That's nice."

They rolled her to a private room and checked the baby out fully. Justice was one happy man, a son was a blessing.

BABY BORN
JUSTIN

Justin and Tonya had made it to the hospital just in time. Mr. Sabir greeted them and told Justin Ieasha was in labor. The nurse gave Justin a set of scrubs and led him to the room. Tonya sat down in the waiting room, she was about to be a grandmother. Her phone went off and it was Justice, yelling and telling Tonya that about ten minutes ago April had a boy.

Tonya said, "Boy Ieasha is having her baby now."

Justice told her the baby's name and said he would be in town soon.

The doctor was telling Ieasha to push, Justin was standing back shaking. He saw the baby come out and almost lost his breath. All the murders came back to him, the love a father has for his son, the pain a mother goes through and for someone to kill a human being was cold blooded, it was hurtful. He saw his baby boy eight and a half pounds and nine ounces.

Justin said, "His name is Raheem Otis Thomas."

Ieasha said, "I love that name."

The Royal Family was happy, two boys born ten minutes apart. Betty and all the girls was happy, so was Tonya and Mrs. Weaver. Khadijah always wanted a boy now she had one to spoil rotten. Sabir was all smiles, he said the 'Al-Fatihah' in the baby's ear.

DAISY

Daisy, Lisa and Lucy had gotten the news of both Justice and Justin having baby boys just minutes apart. They fired up a blunt and popped some Moet. They were feeling good, they started joking and acting silly.

Jerry had been calling Daisy all day but she didn't answer her phone. She had about five girls selling drugs for her in Nelson Court, a weed trap that cleared about six thousand dollars on a slow day. Tasha Smith was her main girl, but she went to school with the rest of them, Regina White, Diane Jones, Missy Johnson and Tammy Melton. Daisy was on top of her game. Lisa gave her half price on everything. Justin had showed Daisy how to shoot all kinds of guns. She kept a 38-special on her and would use it.

Lisa put in a DVD and they sat back and chilled. Lucy was feeling freaky, so she went and got in the shower. Lisa and Daisy were still drinking when Lucy came out of the shower and told Lisa to put some strawberry oil on her. She was naked and Daisy was looking crazy but she stayed calm, she didn't want to let the girls know she was lame to sex.

Lucy laid a blanket on the floor and lay down on her stomach while Lisa rubbed oil all over her back and legs. Lisa was rubbing real slowly and softly, then she started kissing Lucy around the neck. Lisa turned around and looked at Daisy. Daisy started smiling and Lucy rolled over on her back. Lisa stood up and got naked. She had a body that would make a blind man see, she was super fine. She went back to kissing on Lucy, licking her down her stomach and Lucy started moaning.

Daisy remembered that same noise when Justice was giving it to her mother. She took off all her clothes but Lisa didn't notice it because she had her head in Lucy's honey nest. Lisa looked up and saw Daisy naked. She we shocked, the body Daisy had was perfect, no scares, no stretch marks and her tits were small and round. She had a body like no other.

Lucy and Lisa got up off the blanket and told Daisy to lay down. They were about to freak her and Daisy was scared, but she laid down on her back and closed her eyes. Lucy kissed Daisy on the mouth, pushing her tongue in and out. Lisa was sucking on Daisy's breasts and it was feeling good to Daisy who still had her eyes closed, until Lisa hit her clit. She was putting her tongue in Daisy's wetness. It felt so good Daisy had to look up and see what she was doing.

Lisa was a pro, Daisy started moving and moaning, "Shit! Oh shit! Oh, oh, wooooh. Damn!"

A feeling took her like no other, she was coming hard, shaking and breathing hard. Lucy sat on Daisy face, she had her tongue out and licked Lucy while Lisa was still sucking in her juice. They showed Daisy a few tricks with the tongue and after about two hours Daisy was a pro, she made both girls cum.

Daisy had enjoyed it. She got dressed because it was time to go, Tonya would be worried.

Lisa said, "We don't tell anyone what we do."

Daisy said, "I am not a baby. No one will ever get me to say nothing about nothing."

Lucy said, "I like that, you are a bad girl."

Daisy walked out to get in her car and headed home with mixed emotions. No matter what she did a man was always what she wanted. A woman could not do what she wanted done to her. She smiled and thought about Jerry.

JERRY

Jerry had a lot on his mind, the money was slowing up because Justice and his brother had things on lock in Hartford. He was calling a meeting with his crew, he was ready to take Justice to war. He called for his crew to meet him on Hampton Street, that's where Lil-Ricky had been letting his boy trap out. He ordered the house to be robbed.

JUSTICE

Justice didn't know that the house had been robbed, he was still in New Haven. He called his sister Daisy and told her to meet him at Main and Tower they needed to talk.

Daisy said, "I'll be there."

Justice didn't tell Justin because he was laying low. The feds were in town and they were coming to hand out an indictment for drugs and guns. He believed his brother's name was on the list, so he was not going to chance that.

MAIN AND TOWER

Daisy pulled in the Main and Tower parking lot, she parked all the way in the back and Justice pulled up in a rental car. He got out and got in the car with Daisy.

Justice said, "Look Daisy, Jerry ordered for the house we got on Hampton Street to get robbed."

Daisy said, "What? That mother fucker crossed the family?"

Justice replied, "Yes, he did!"

Daisy said, "I will handle it."

"Lil-Ricky is at the Hilton Hotel, he's for whatever," Justice told her.

Daisy dialed Jerry's number, he picked up and Daisy said in a sexy voice, "Hello baby, where are you?"

Jerry told her, "I'm chilling at the Howard Johnson Hotel."

"Well can I see you?" She asked.

Jerry said, "Hell yeah, I'm in room 102."

"Look for me," Daisy said.

Jerry was ready to see what he had spent so much money on.

Justice said, "Be careful Lil-Sis."

She replied, "I got this."

Justice got in his car and rode off.

JERRY

Jerry was headed back to the Howard Johnson Hotel to wait on Daisy. He had just put some more money in his safe house and he had the key with him because that was the only one. He was feeling good, smoking that good weed. He had

Daisy on his mind. He always wanted to get some of that hot ass. She was the baddest girl he had seen in some years.

Jerry pulled into the Howard Johnson and went to his room feeling like a boss player. Things were going to get back on track. Fuck Justice and his family.

But in the back of Jerry's mind he always wondered what was ahead for him.

DAISY

Daisy was on her way to meet Jerry and show him she was the main blood line of David. He would be her first kill. Daisy had to show Justice that she was no little girl. She had worked hard to get the lawyer, Kenny Harden, the money to work around the clock to get David out on an appeal bond.

Daisy checked her gun and made sure she could reach her knife. She pulled up into the Howard Johnson Hotel parking lot looking for room 102. She found the room and parked at the end. She got out and looked around to make sure no one saw her go to the room. She knocked on the door but stood at 103.

Jerry hurried to the door and opened it. Daisy walked in and hugged him. The room smelled like weed. She sat her pocket book on the night stand and Jerry rushed over to her and started kissing her on the mouth. He was rubbing all over Daisy and he started taking his clothes off. Jerry got naked and lay across the bed while Daisy turned the light off. She pulled her pocket book close to her and started taking off her clothes.

He could see from the light coming in the window and Daisy's body made him hard on site. Daisy lay on top of Jerry and was kissing him around the neck. She reached her other hand over to her pocket book and pulled out her knife. Jerry had his eyes closed, laying naked on his back. She was licking his neck and then he felt cold steel. He jumped but it was too late, Daisy had cut his throat and he died with a hard on.

Daisy got a rush. She got up and said, "I told you it was 2-DIE-4, you scum bag!"

She checked the room and found ten thousand dollars in Jerry's coat pocket and a key with an address on it. Daisy took it all and walked out of the room never looking back.

That was her first kill but not her last.

JUSTICE

Justice had told Lisa he was coming over because he needed another load of drugs, but tonight Justice was doing this for his mother Linda. He had a needle in his pocket which was full of poison. Lisa had to pay for what she did.

Justice pulled up and Lucy came to the door and let him in. Lisa was laying on the couch watching TV and when Justice came in she got up to give him a hug.

Lisa said, "You ready?"

Justice said, "Like no other."

Lucy went back to her room, Lisa got up and went behind the couch. She had about fifty kilos in a grab bag back there.

Justice said, "You know me and you have gotten real close, but in life turns are made and we don't always understand."

"Boy what you talking about?" She asked.

Justice said, "Life and 2-DIE-4."

Lisa said, "I understand."

Justice pulled out his gun and Lisa was ready to scream but Justice said, "Don't scream because you won't do anything but cause me to kill Lucy too and this is not about Lucy. Lisa you killed Linda, did you think I was going to let you get away with that?"

Lisa was crying quietly, she was thinking of what she should do or say. She said, "Your mother crossed me!"

Justice asked, "Why did you poison her?" Lisa couldn't say anything, Justice said, "I'm going to poison you the same way."

He pulled out the needle with the poison in it and Lisa knew she was going to die. Her whole life flashed in front of her.

All the money she made, all the men she had tricked, all the young girls she had turned out on drugs and sex. Daisy came to her mind and she wanted her one more time.

Lisa looked up at Justice and said, "Fuck you!"

Justice slapped her with the gun knocking her out. He stuck the needle in her neck and laid her back on the couch. He had tears in his eyes, it was joy.

He went to his mother's grave and told her years ago that he would get Lisa. Lisa had slipped and the game had bit her in the ass. He walked out the door with all the drugs, he was headed for New Haven to see his son Kareem. That was his pride and joy.

DAISY

Daisy headed to the Hilton Hotel to find Lil-Ricky, his room was upstairs.

Daisy parked her car in a low key spot and got out. She went in and got on the elevator and was headed to the third floor to find room 326. She was walking cool, she found the door and took a deep breath before she knocked. She knocked lightly and Lil-Ricky came to the door.

Daisy said, "Are you Lil-Ricky?"

He said, "Yeah."

"Justice sent me to you," she said.

Lil-Ricky said, "Come on in."

Lil-Ricky was a thug hustler. He was a good looking Puerto Rican kid at 21 years old. He had been in the streets since he was 12. Daisy had always liked him because he was always fresh and she had heard the girls on the streets talk about how he put down the thug passion.

Daisy said, "What's up?"

Lil-Ricky said, "Chill, china doll."

"Boy I need to take a shower," She said.

Lil-Ricky showed her where everything was and Daisy got the stuff out of her bag and went to the shower. He was laying on the bed watching TV when Daisy walked out of the bathroom with a two piece bathing suit on.

He said, "Girl where the hell are you going?"

"To bed, I can't sleep with all those clothes on," she said.

Lil-Ricky jumped up off the bed. When he saw Daisy's body he liked to fell out. No wonder Jerry had spent over fifty thousand and got no sex. But Lil-Ricky was no sucker, fuck how fine Daisy was he had game. Lil-Ricky was up chilling, it had got late and he said to himself, 'I am not sleeping on no fucking floor.' He got down to his silk boxers and took his shirt off. He slid under the cover next to Daisy. When he lifted the cover up he saw Daisy's body and got a hard on instantly.

Daisy was not fully asleep. She was thinking about what could be in the house that the key she got from Jerry went to. One day soon she would check. Lil-Ricky moved close to Daisy and she felt his body touching hers. She started moving up a little because she could feel Lil-Ricky's manhood growing.

He said, "Daisy, Daisy, Daisy fuck!"

"What's up?" She asked.

Lil-Ricky said, "Are you sleep?"

Daisy rolled over and said, "How can I sleep with your shit all on my ass?" She was laughing.

Lil-Ricky playfully rolled on top of her and looked her in the eyes. She had pretty, light brown eyes, almost hazel like her mom. Daisy was looking at him and Lil-Ricky started kissing her on the mouth.

Daisy said to herself, 'I'm going to let him have his way.'

Lil-Ricky started rubbing on Daisy tits and took the top of her swim suit off. He was licking Daisy all the way down her belly and Daisy got hot. He took the bottom part of her bathing suit off and she was naked. Lil-Ricky start sucking between Daisy legs, she went wild, moaning and moving crazy. She had Lisa do the same thing but Lil-Ricky was doing it better. She was more into it now too. Lil-Ricky was putting one finger at a time in Daisy wetness, she was so tight. Lil-Ricky took his time, he went back up and started kissing Daisy on the mouth. He propped one of her legs up to open her up wider and he guided his manhood into her wetness. He felt Daisy jump

She closed her eyes and was biting down on her lip. Lil-Ricky took it easy when he slid into her. She let out a loud moan and that was when it came to Lil-Ricky that Daisy was a virgin. He took slow strokes until he felt her open then Lil-Ricky had Daisy in another world, she was feeling good. She was clawing Lil-Ricky's back and moving with his every move. Lil-Ricky was enjoying the wet sweet, tight pussy that Daisy had. She was calling his name and going crazy. He was about to go there and he started moving fast. Daisy was trying to get lose but he let his seed go all up in Daisy's new found world.

They hugged and kissed and Lil-Ricky made love to Daisy all day. She was happy, she loved the sex life.

JUSTIN

Justin was enjoying the family life, he and Ieasha were happy with their son Rahim. Justin was spending a lot of time with him, but things had changed. FBI Agent Marvin Harris had gotten up enough evidence to get an arrest warrant on Justin for drugs and guns.

Justin was in the room playing with his son when he heard cars driving up real fast. He looked out the window and saw the house was surrounded by FBI agents.

Ieasha came to the room crying and Justin said, "Baby this is it, I told you one day my past would catch up."

Ieasha said, "Do you have a gun?"

Justin said, "Baby I plan on getting out and coming back to you and my son. I am not going to do nothing crazy."

Ieasha said, "I love you."

They both heard a loud knock on the door. Mr. Harris was nice to Ieasha and her son because of her daddy. He told her to sit on the couch while they searched the house. They handcuffed Justin and walked him to the car.

The search came up clean, Justin had beat Mr. Harris again. He was expecting to find something.

Ieasha got on the phone and called her dad. She told him what was going on and Mr. Sabir told her he was on the way.

She was heartbroken, just when life seemed so right, everything was going wrong.

LUCY

Lucy woke up in the middle of the night and saw that Lisa was not in the bed. She jumped up and went to the living room where she saw Lisa laying on the couch, but something white was coming out of the side of her mouth. Lucy went crazy, she was yelling, crying and shaking Lisa, asking her to please wake up. But Lisa had gone to meet her maker, she was at peace.

Lucy called 911 and was screaming, that the ambulance could not save her. Lucy had all the money and drugs, but she had lost her best friend and lover. Lisa had done so much good and bad. Lucy was thinking that Lisa took an overdose, she didn't know Justice had killed her for killing his mother.

TONYA

Tonya had gotten the call from Justin, they had booked him for guns and drugs and they were looking at murder charges. Justin's name and face was all over TV and on the front page of the Hartford Courant. He had a big trial ahead on Federal and State charges. They wanted to give Justin life without parole, but he hired the best lawyers money could buy.

DAISY

Daisy was chilling, she had fallen in love with Lil-Ricky. They took trips all over the world, Paris, Jamaica and Canada. Daisy was Lil-Ricky's down ass chick. They had a big five hundred thousand dollar house in New London. It was a nice two acres of land with a water fall. They were laying low, spending money and having hot sex.

JERRY

Jerry was found dead at the Howard Johnson Hotel, it was all over the news and the streets had gone crazy. Hoods were at war, Nelson court, Chappell Garden, Bowels Park, Chater Oak and Dutch Point. People were dying and the Fed's had to come to town.

The streets knew Jerry had got Justice's house robbed, so they knew who was tied to his murder, 2-DIE-4.

JUSTICE

Justice and April were staying together and they were doing well. Justice owned about four apartment complexes in Hartford, he also had a chain of night clubs MMM, Money Making Men. The clubs were in New York, Texas, Miami, Hartford and Atlanta. Justice also had some people on his team that could save his brother Justin.

DAVID

Kenny Harden lost David's case to the high court on the appeal, but he had more plans for David and Daisy was a lot of help. They were going to get David out of that prison one way or another.

David was chilling, he had everything in prison. Now it was about the wait.

BETTY

Betty had about five houses being rented out all over Connecticut from Hartford to New Britain. She had moved back to Atlanta, Georgia where she had a chain of day care centers called 'We Care Day Care.' They were all over Connecticut too, the girls were living good and doing fine.

SABIR, KADIJAH, IEASHA

The Muhammad family had convinced Justin to convert to Islam and he became a Muslim. He was helping the younger brothers in prison stay on a positive track.

Justin's case was put to the side because the DA came up dead, 2-DIE-4.

4-EVER
TO BE CONTINUED

Other Books by Life After death Publicationz.

Visit us online at…
www.lifeafterdeathpublicationz.com

Secretly Secured
By Kelvin Scott
After being abandoned by his father and thrown into the foster system following his mother's death, De' Angelo Smith -better known as Dezzy- finds himself drawn to the streets. His path crosses with Diamond, who is also a product of the foster system. But after a wild night in Tallahassee, Florida, Diamond and her friends become the focus of a very dangerous hunting game. Fate brings them together as they encounter true love for the first time, but just as quickly fate will tear them apart. Will they ever be reunited? Will Dezzy keep the promises he made?

Cable
By BornTrue Bethea

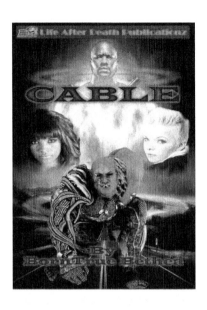

MONSTERS ARE NOT BORN... THEY ARE MADE!!!
In the year 2015, the world is overrun by a terrorist group known as S.C.A.R. The last piece of freedom is a little part of the United States' west coast that has been renamed the Free World. The only thing that is stopping S.C.A.R. from overrunning the Free World is their super-soldier Cable. He is a half-man, half-machine who has found only one purpose in life, to kill any threat he sees, by any means possible. During one of their missions, Cable and his men come across a time machine made by the enemy. Knowing the location of one of their experiential sites, Cable volunteers himself to go back in time to stop the terrorist group before it starts. Before he can find what he's looking for, he discovers that the enemy also has a time machine along with vital information that can stop Cable. Will S.C.A.R. complete their mission of world domination, or will the terrorist group crumble by the hands of Cable?

Jack Boyz
By True King

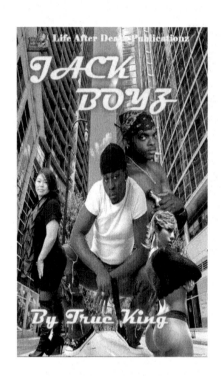

Malaki is a self-proclaimed Muslim on the outside, but on the inside he is a stone cold killer and a Jack Boy who is followed by his infamous crew, the Black Out Boyz. Their reign of terror is unstoppable and touches every dope boy with a sack. He has every girl around dropping to their knees before him and he greedily indulges himself. But Malaki's heart belongs to Jazmine, the good Muslim girl whose father thinks Malaki is evil. Everything is all good until one of the Black Out Boyz's enemies decides to hit back. Now Malaki and his crew will be forced into an all-out war or risk losing everything. Who can he trust and who must he get rid of? The loss will be great but the big question is, have the Jack Boyz bitten off more than they can chew?

http://www.amazon.com/dp/B00YCYCYDG/ref=cm_sw_r_fa_dp_eRZzvb1HJJRMH

https://www.createspace.com/5517475

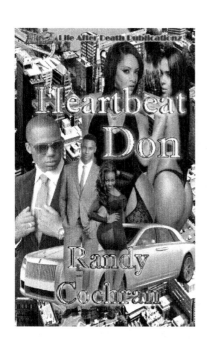

Heartbeat Don
By Randy
Cochran

David was young, innately intelligent, charming, well dressed and filthy rich. He frequented posh clubs and hotels, owned posh houses, luxury cars, and anything anyone had a craving for. Women desired to be with him and men wanted to be like him. He was the Don of Hartford, Connecticut. A rogue, but a respected guy in the streets who had the money and power to demand that respect. He and his men were the objects of fear, they had a resolve to kill without mercy in order protect their own interests. The Don had come a far cry from the boy he was. Raised in Atlanta, Georgia by his grandmother, together with his two sisters, he was taught to be good and god-fearing. The gentle boy's life began to change abruptly when he, his sisters and his mother moved to Hartford, Connecticut to reunite with his stepfather and other siblings. Not only was he living with a stepfather who was an alcoholic and wife-beater, he also lived in a town where crime and belligerence ruled. Soon he surrounded himself with friends who, in one way or another, spent time in juvenile detention. Then one night he met his first Don. The don supplied the highest quality drugs known to the streets of Stowe Village, business was booming. David realized that he wanted to be the Don and to do that he would have to get rid of the reigning Don. In no time, he becomes the object of vengeance and hatred from the Under Lords of New York. What will David give up to achieve his dreams?

http://www.amazon.com/dp/B00ZE6LAOA/ref=cm_sw_r_fa_dp_fJ3E vb13K957P

https://www.createspace.com/5553152

Mixed Stories
The Full View
By Chucky J

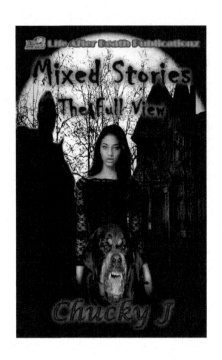

Copeland is a War veteran who likes to mind his own business, until one night when he sees things he shouldn't have and becomes a witness to a horrific murder. His race to escape the monster that's after him leads him into a new relationship and deep within himself. He fights to protect his innocent friend Tiffany, who has her own monster to chase, and to kill what is after him. Will he be able to escape the demon or will it catch up with him?

Sandra has had a very rough life growing up. The death of her parent's in such a terrible way left her alone, except for her dog Jackal. They are headed out on their own to start a new life until Jackal takes her along another path and the blackouts Sandra has been having get worse. She begins to hear from her parents and discovers secrets from her past. Her Mother has her own malicious agenda and uses Jackal and Sandra to carry out her unfinished business. When Sandra and Jackal finally make it back home things take a strange and twisted turn.

http://www.amazon.com/dp/B010E8Z86I/ref=cm_sw_r_fa_dp_cuzJvb1H2P9FQ

https://www.createspace.com/5578333

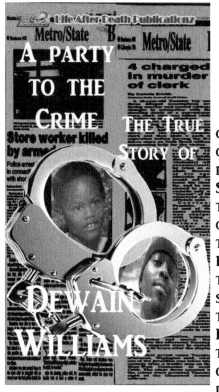

A PARTY TO THE CRIME:
THE TRUE STORY OF
DEWAIN WILLIAMS

FOLLOW THE TRUE STORY OF AN INTELLIGENT YOUNG MAN GROWING UP IN A WORLD OF DRUGS, ALCOHOL AND CRIME. SHARE IN HIS BATTLE AS HE TRIES TO DO THE RIGHT THING AND BE A GOOD ROLE MODEL BUT FALLS INTO TROUBLE AT EVERY TURN. JOIN DEWAIN AS HIS FAMILY GOES THROUGH CHANGES AND FIGHTS TO SURVIVE AND STAY TOGETHER IN A TIME OF HARDSHIPS AND TRIALS. HIS JOURNEY WILL TAKE YOU THROUGH THE JOYS OF HIS ROUGH CHILDHOOD AND INTO AN EVEN ROUGHER ADULT LIFE. WHAT IS IN STORE FOR DEWAIN NEXT?

http://www.amazon.com/dp/B012DWBZZ6/ref=cm_sw_r_fa_dp_yUvSvb0C2NMRV
https://www.createspace.com/5633915

Tears of Evidence
By Jonas Brinkley

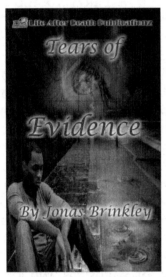

Caught up in the fog of a dream that feels too much like reality, Troy's awakening will be one of calmness, followed by disappointment. Misunderstood as a young man growing up, it seems that even trouble and hardship cannot cripple Troy's determination to triumph over the chilling grip of misfortunes that have followed him from adolescence to adulthood. His never ending flights to escape one situation after another only take him into the grips of yet another situation, each one with the same agenda. That agenda, as Troy sees it, is to interrupt and strip him of whatever happiness he finds. With so much pain and disappointment, it seems Troy should be a man embittered by the fact that he can't seem to escape from the troubles of his past, which seem destined to follow him into his future. Instead of feeding him hopelessness, those troubles, mishaps, maybes and misfortunes only make Troy dig deeper for the truth that will free him from the grips of ignorance and circumstances. As he searches for the truth, he dreams of living the life of the second chance he is granted. What will determine his dream? Truth will not be the reality that he dreams of living, it will be the actuality of his situation.

http://www.amazon.com/dp/B013IT8EAC/ref=cm_sw_r_f
a_dp_Cu8Wvb0CAXRB1
https://www.createspace.com/5656973

CPSIA information can be obtained
at www.ICGtesting.com
Printed in the USA
LVOW01s1808300916
506909LV00015B/742/P

9 781517 791438